PRAISE FOR

The Alex Lightwood Mystery Series

"I had a hard time putting it down last night and fell asleep with my iPhone in hand. I really enjoyed the twist at the end." (Glen Lemert, Mystery Author)

"Funny and cute. Relatable characters. Interesting photography aspects. Very real dialogue. I loved it!" (Tennille Gilreath, Cozy Author)

"Well-written"
"Loved the witty banter"
"I look forward to reading more from [Kari Ganske] in the future"
(Goodreads reviews)

Also by Kari Ganske

Alex Lightwood Series
Secrets in a Still Life
One Click in the Grave
Bait and Click
(a Halloween short story available Fall 2021)
Lenses Leather and Lies
(a FREE novella for subscribing to Kari's Cozy Newsletter)

ONE CLICK IN THE GRAVE

Alex Lightwood Mystery Book 2

Kari Ganske

Blue Heron Press

If you want more cozy mysteries, photography tips, and
Alex Lightwood adventures, join Kari's VIP Readers Club: https://dl.bookfunnel.com/ssn3i8nmeh

To my real-life second chance love
My love of a lifetime, Tim

CHAPTER 1

T HIS WAS SUPPOSED TO be a straightforward shoot. One to ease me into my new business adventure. The subjects were slow moving and therefore simple to capture in my sights. A couple of hours, tops, the client had promised and offered a generous fee for the few shots this would take. In and out. Easy, breezy. Payment upon completion.

What they forgot to take into account was my nana.

"Nana K? Do you need those glasses to see?" I asked her. She was wearing star-shaped, rainbow-colored glasses which were ridiculous in their own right, but the lenses were also causing a nasty glare in the camera.

"No, but they do enhance the outfit. I'm not losing them," she answered, sealing her thin lips into a pout.

Her "outfit" consisted of a formfitting rainbow unitard with interspersed sequins, a plethora of brightly colored plastic necklaces and bangles, and chunky, bedazzling wedges that added a few inches to her five-foot-nothing frame. She colored the tips of her spiky white hair to match the rainbow that threw up on the rest of her. For my mother's sake, I hoped it wasn't permanent.

"You can keep the glasses, but I'm popping the lenses out. They're causing a glare I'm not in the mood to edit out in post-processing," I said, snatching the glasses from her face before she could protest and popping the plastic lenses into my hand.

"You break 'em, you bought 'em," my loving nana said.

"They'll be fine." I handed her back the frames and put the lenses into my camera bag. "Now, what did you have in mind for the portrait?"

Normally, I would be the one directing the subject of a portrait shoot. Or gently nudging as I prefer to think of it. However, with my spirited eighty-going-on-eighteen-year-old nana, I knew she'd want to call the shots. Literally.

The other members of the Aged Pines Retirement Community had all chosen unassuming activities to engage in for the annual yearbook photo shoot. Beatrice Cornwallace showed me her knitting. Antonia Mayburn laid out a hand of bridge. Harold Breezy met me at the little fishing pond on the property. My nana, on the other hand, looked like she was about to strap on some roller skates and join a derby.

As I waited for her reply, I held my breath and thought about what led me to this exact place. If you had asked me a few months ago if I'd still be in Piney Ridge, the teeny-tiny town in teeny-tiny Maryland that I left right after graduation, I'd have laughed in your face. If not for a narcissistic ex-boyfriend, who ruined both my career and my personal life by blacklisting me from the photojournalist community, I'd still be living in New York. Or off on a shoot in an exotic locale. His lies and cheating prompted me to tuck tail and return to my childhood hometown to try to piece my life back together.

What I thought would only take a few weeks—surely the industry would realize they made a terrible mistake and beg me to return—had now turned into several months. And although I'd never admit it to my conniving ex or my past, ambitious eighteen-year-old self, I didn't mind being home as much as I thought I would.

This assignment—photographing the Aged Pines Retirement Community yearbook—was one of the first in my attempt at starting a photography business here in town. I'd started where my heart was with documentary-style shots during everyday activities. The retirement community director and I compromised on the portraits. He wanted traditional headshots; I wanted complete candids. We'd settled on environmental portraits where each staff member and resident could show their personalities a little more. I used the first-responder calendar I shot a few months ago as proof that environmental portraits were more genuine.

Of course, starting a business from scratch was more difficult than I anticipated. Websites, business accounts, tax forms, advertising, and client contracts all had to be developed and executed. Not to mention the current source of my anxiety—trying to think of a name. I was ready to simply choose Alex Lightwood Photography and call it a day. Not super inspired, but at least it was straight to the point.

"Where can we find a cigar?" Nana K asked, pulling my attention away from thinking about a name for my new photography business. Since the first-responder calendar shoot, residents had been tentatively asking when I was going into business so they could officially hire me for their events. Not a bad problem to have since my photojournalism income was now nil, and I had a needy beta fish to support.

"A cigar? You don't even smoke!" I said.

She shrugged a bony shoulder. "Yeah, but these old biddies don't know that. I like to give them a shock. Keeps them alive."

"Or you could give them a heart attack."

"When it's their time, it's their time." She noticed my gaping expression. "Oh, don't be such a prude, Alex. Death is a constant companion around here." She looked toward the residential buildings. "I bet Dennis has a cigar hidden in his room."

"Nana K, I'm kind of on a timeline here. Do you have a plan B?" I crossed my fingers behind my back. We were already behind schedule since rainstorms last week halted the outdoor portraits.

She pursed her lips like a disgruntled teenager. "Fine. I guess by the wishing well will do. I can pretend to climb in the bucket."

Faster than I would have thought possible for an octogenarian in three-inch wedges, she took off toward the front of the building. I grabbed my gear and scrambled after her, hoping I reached her before she fell down the well.

Just as she leaned headfirst into the wide opening, I grabbed the elastic belt around her waist and yanked her back to standing. When she said wishing well, I thought she meant one of those decorative lawn ornaments. Although this one did have the circular stone ledge surrounding the opening and the wooden archway top like the novelty versions, this was an actual well. Or at least it used to be. It looked pretty dry and unused now.

"Aww, I wanted to see if I could reach any change," Nana K whined.

"You know those are other people's wishes," I said.

Her smile broadened as she shrugged. "How would they know? No amount of pennies in a dinky old well will help most of those wishes come true. No twentysomething Clark Gable look-alike is going to come strutting through the lobby looking for a sugar mama." She turned to the grouping of apartments behind her and yelled, "You hear that, Doris! You're wasting your pennies!"

If I had a penny, I'd wish for Doris to be out of earshot.

"Hey, maybe you could pretend to be making a wish," I said, trying to get Nana K back on track for the portrait. Her allotted time was almost over, and I'd yet to take a single picture.

"Perfect," she agreed.

I gave a sigh of relief and stepped back to get the full scene in the frame. She stood to the side of the well, leaned a hand on the stone edge, and raised a leg like she was kissing a lover. She looked down in the well and made a little "o" with her mouth. I may be biased because she was my nana, but it was the cutest thing ever.

Until she turned, crossed her eyes, and stuck her tongue out.

"Nana K! You're worse than the preschoolers!" I scolded.

I'd photographed the end-of-the-year picnic for the preschool where my best friend, Colleen McMurphy, worked. Anytime one of the little rascals saw me pointing the camera their way, they made a face. That group made me work for the handful of candid shots I felt were salvageable. Very rarely did the "outtakes" folder contain more than the final edits, but it did that day.

"Get one of me doing that duck face. It'll make my cheekbones look fierce." Her duck face more resembled my beta fish, but I snapped away to make her happy. And made a mental note to check who she was following on social media.

"Okay, Nana. I think we got a keeper in that bunch." I wasn't going to tell her it was the first shot I took.

"Let me see 'em," she said, her deluge of plastic costume jewelry jangling as she tottered toward me. I held my camera out of her reach.

"Oh no. I have a strict policy. Clients do not peep at the back of my camera."

"I am not a client, Alexandretta Lightwood. I'm your grandmother! The matriarch of your family. The life blood of your lineage."

"All true. But today, you're also a client. So, hands off."

She crossed her arms like a petulant child again. I giggled, remembering my earlier comparison to the preschoolers. Life really was a cycle.

I swear I looked down for one second to pack up my gear in anticipation of meeting the next client in her room as we'd arranged—she was going to pose by her collection of porcelain cat figurines—only to glance back up and see Nana K with her head in the well again, both feet suspended in the air.

"Nana K!" I shouted.

She started, tipped precariously forward but managed, through some miracle of physics and luck, to right herself, thank goodness.

"What were you doing?" I admonished.

"I dropped my glasses down there," she said. "And I wanted to see if I could reach the pennies. We've got bridge tonight. It would teach those card sharks a lesson if I used their own wishes to bet against them. Half of them pretend to be senile just to get away with things."

"I'm sure you've never done that," I said sarcastically.

"Who, me?" She batted her eyelashes. Wait a minute, were they fake? I didn't even wear fake eyelashes.

"So, you gonna get my glasses or what? I paid two bucks for those suckers at the dollar store," Nana K said.

There was no way I'd be able to reach them either. I may have three and half inches on her in height, but my arms were equally as stubby. Still, it was easier to pretend to try than to argue with Nana K. I put my camera bag beside the well and peered into the darkness. It was deeper and darker than I thought. I leaned over the edge in a half-hearted effort to reach the bottom, which I couldn't see.

But Nana was hip to my pretend-to-look game. She pulled my feet up and pushed me forward until my entire upper body was down in the well.

"Pull me back up this instant!" I shouted, trying to push against the wall of the well with my hands. They kept slipping on the damp and mossy surface. The rancid smell of stagnant water and mud and who knew what else made my eyes water.

"I got you. Reach a little farther. I almost had them before."

"I'll buy you new ones. Just pull me up."

"See if you can grab some change while you're down there too," she suggested.

Completely at her mercy, I sighed and slowly reached down toward the dark abyss. My fingers felt nothing but air. As a passing cloud revealed a bit of sun, something shone from the side of the well opposite me.

"I think I actually see them on a little ledge. Can you push me a smidge forward without dropping me?" I asked. I suddenly flashed to the scene at the end of *Indiana Jones and the Last Crusade* when Indy was reaching for the cup of Christ in the ravine. Luckily, Indy's dad was able to pull him back to safety.

My nana, on the hand, dropped me.

CHAPTER 2

T HERE ARE NOT MANY times that being short has been to my advantage. In fact, I could probably count them on one hand: when playing hide-and-seek, I can squeeze into impossibly tight spots; when buying clothing, my size is always in stock; when flying on an airplane, I don't mind a middle seat; and when falling, my head is closer to the ground, so it doesn't hurt as much.

I could now add "when being pitched down a well" to the list. Like a cat, I somehow managed to curl myself into a ball, managing to avoid the rocky edges with my head and land mostly on my hands and knees. And if I screamed, it was totally in a sexy, screen-siren way and not at all like a banshee.

"*Kurwa!*" Nana K's voice echoed down the well. I don't know a lot of Polish, but I know I got my mouth washed out with soap for saying that one when I was younger. Grampa K thought it was hilarious to teach me. I thought he should've been the one eating Ivory.

"I'm okay," I said, when I got my breath back. Marginally okay anyway. It was darker than midnight in a jungle cave and smelled just as bad. At least I landed on soft dirt and not in a pool of stinky, old water. Only about an inch or so covered the bottom of the well. I could feel the years of coins digging into my knees and hands as I slowly sank into the muck.

"I'm calling security," Nana K said. "Hold on."

"Tell them to hurry. We might have a quicksand kind of situation happening here," I said, trying not to breathe too deeply. Seriously, the bottom of this well smelled worse than when I photographed the Baltimore football team's locker room after a game. And trust me, that was nose-hair-burning body odor and sweat and a little desperation.

I sat back on my heels, using the rocky sides of the well to help me sit up. I still felt a little dizzy from the fall—and the smell—and didn't trust myself to stand right away. How deep was I? Could I simply climb out? The fall didn't seem that long.

While I waited for the nausea to clear, I felt around for Nana's glasses. My eyes weren't adjusting to the pitch darkness, so I shoved a handful of the dirty coins in my pocket instead. Maybe that would get me an extra line in her will. Or at least an extra slice of cheesecake.

No luck on the glasses by feel alone.

"What's happening, Nana?" I called up the well.

"They're on their way. They gotta find a ladder that fits down there. They didn't think the bucket would hold you."

And now I was conjuring images from *Silence of the Lambs*. Great.

My nausea and dizziness had abated some, so I took the risk to stand. Reaching up as far as I could, I was still over a foot away from the top edge. Being stuck in the well was absolutely *not* on the plus side of being short.

I kept moving my feet around to make sure they didn't get sucked too far down into the muck. It was like when you stand in the sand at the beach and let the waves crash over you. Little by little the sand underneath is carried out to sea and more sand takes its place until your feet are buried. Sometimes you could even see little sand crabs rolling up and down with the ebb and flow of the waves.

Envisioning sand crabs made me wonder what critters could be lurking in the undisturbed depths of this void. I didn't want to think too much about it, but I had to know. Against my better judgment, I reached into the back pocket of my jeans for my phone.

The pocket was empty.

Well, poo. Had it fallen out? If it landed in this mess on the bottom, that probably meant I needed a new one. The smell alone would be hard to combat. I crouched down again and started feeling around in the dirt and along the sides of the well. I'd made it almost all the way around the edge, when my hand disappeared into an opening. I caught myself against the side of the well.

With my face.

Leave it to me to not get a scratch falling down, but instead, because of my clumsiness, I would have stone burns on my forehead. Maybe if I blamed those on the fall, Nana K would make me my own cheesecake out of guilt.

Trying to wipe the grime and slime from my cheek, I slowly felt along the wall for the opening again. There was a shaft or tunnel or something at the bottom. Probably originally to fill the well from the local reservoir when it was still functional. I reached in and felt something solid and cold blocking the way. Too soft to be a rock, too hard to be vegetation.

I pulled my hand back immediately, hoping I wasn't patting the backside of a Jurassic-sized spider.

I really hated spiders. I met my first neighbor in New York that way. There was a huge spider holding my only bathroom hostage. Seriously, he sat unmoving on the wall for ages, mocking me. It was one of those big, hairy, jumpy kind, so clearly, I couldn't walk by without the possibility of it landing on me. So, I did what any independent woman of the world would do. I banged on the neighbor's door to beg him to come kill it.

The neighbor turned out to be Rick, my ex-"what was I thinking" mistake. Meeting him in the context of spiders should have been red-flag number one that our relationship was doomed from the start. The fact that he teased me about my phobia for our entire relationship should have been red-flag number two.

"Nana! Turn on your phone flashlight and shine it down here." My voice sounded high pitched and thin.

"Okay, Peanut." A minute later the shaft was filled with a surprising amount of light. I located her stupid glasses right away and shoved them into the pocket with the coins. I glanced around once again for my phone with no luck. It had either been sucked up by the goop never to be seen again, or I'd left it in my camera bag. Please, let it be the latter.

"Did you find my glasses?" Nana K asked.

I rolled my eyes. "Yes, Nana. I have them."

"Oh goodie." She moved the light away from the well.

"Hey! I'd rather not be stuck in the dark down here!" The light reappeared.

Taking a few deep breaths, I worked up the courage to peer into the small opening at the base of the well.

Please, don't let it be a spider. Please, don't let it be a spider.

When I finally saw what it was, I would have gladly used all those ill-gotten coins in my pocket to wish it were a spider.

I recoiled immediately and swallowed a scream.

"Nana, call the cops," I screeched. If I thought my voice sounded scared before, this was full-on panic mode.

Still, my nana needed an explanation. "Why?" she asked. "Security can handle a ladder. If I called anyone else, it would be the fire department. If they can get cats out of trees, they can get a Peanut out of a well."

"No, Nana. Call the cops." I took a deep breath and pressed myself as far as I could away from the opening. "There is a dead woman down here."

CHAPTER 3

D ON'T PANIC. DO NOT panic. Breathe in through the nose and out through the mouth like that yogi taught me in Tibet when I was sure the shaman of the tribe I was photographing cursed me. Turned out I was having an allergic reaction to some bad goji berries. But the panic attack was real.

Comparatively, this was no big deal. I'd seen dead bodies before both in Piney Ridge and abroad. I hadn't *touched* a dead body before though. And with that lovely thought, the heebie-jeebies started again.

"What is taking so long?" I yelled up the well. "Seriously, let's try the bucket. I'm pretty small. Do they know how tall I'm not?"

"You want me to sing to keep you calm?" Nana K offered, ignoring all my questions.

"No!" I shouted, interrupting the opening bars of "Sweetly Sings the Donkey." "I want you to lower the daggone bucket."

"Oh, I hear the sirens now," Nana K said, her rainbow head, and the light from her cell phone, disappearing again.

A few moments later, a shadow crossed over the opening again, amping up my panic by blocking what little sunlight still illuminated the dark space.

"Nana, please turn on..." My voice trailed off as I looked up right into the smirking face of Lincoln Livestrong, my childhood best friend turned high school crush turned current bane of my existence for many reasons. The top one being I couldn't stop thinking about him at inopportune times.

"Of course, you're here," I said, crossing my arms.

"Well, well, well," he said. I rolled my eyes at his lame pun, but he wasn't done yet. "I guess wishes do come true."

"Ha ha. Why must you always be present for all of my embarrassing moments?" I asked, trying to look fierce despite being covered in gunk. I concentrated on his chin stubble instead of his amused, piercing blue eyes.

"Why must you always put yourself in embarrassing situations?" he countered.

"Can you just lower a ladder? The dead body and I are running out of small talk."

He leaned over the side of the well. "Give me your hands," he said, reaching toward me.

I put them on my hips instead. "Are you crazy? You can't dead lift me out of here. What if you drop me?"

"You've proven you can survive that. Give me your hands," he said again. "Then you can walk yourself up the side while I lift. It'll be faster than unhooking the ladder from the fire truck."

I rubbed a hand over my face. Bad idea since they were still covered in muck from when I fell. I did want out of this well like yesterday. I looked up into his stupid, handsome face.

"I swear if you drop me back in this muck, I'll tell everyone it was you who covered the school door handles with grease, sophomore year," I threatened in a stage whisper.

"You wouldn't."

"Don't drop me, and you won't have to worry about it." I reached up and grasped his wrists. His strong, capable fingers—yes, I was talking myself into those adjectives—easily wrapped around mine.

"Alex," he said, more seriously this time. I looked into his denim-colored eyes. "I got you."

And he did. In less than a minute, I was up and out of the well.

Linc steadied me as I stepped back onto solid ground. His thumb brushed my wrist, stayed there. "You okay? Your pulse is elevated."

He was in EMT mode. Not rugged hero saving the beautiful damsel in distress mode. "I'm fine. Thanks."

He dropped my hand. "You smell gross. Might want to take a shower. Or six."

I scowled at him. Guess it's hard to be a beautiful damsel when you smelled like a sewer and were covered in mud. A clank, clank, clanking from the adjacent parking lot pulled my attention away from Linc before I could form the perfect comeback. Chief Clive Duncan, Officer Andrea Martinez, and two Aged Pines security officers rambled toward us carrying a ladder.

"Now they get here," I mumbled under my breath.

"Heard you found another body," Andrea Martinez said as she approached.

"It's her fault," I said, hitching a thumb at my nana who was avoiding me. I wasn't sure whether that was because she was afraid of retaliation for dropping me or because of the smell. She gave Andrea a little wave.

"We'll need to get your statements, so don't go far."

I nodded. I knew the drill.

She led the ladder carriers to the well. Chief DunnoWhatI'mDoing... I mean, Duncan, waddled behind the group, pretending to be in charge. He and I had a love-hate relationship. As in, we loved to hate each other. I was still waiting for an apology for the last case he bungled. But not while holding my breath because I don't have a death wish.

I watched as Andrea disappeared down the ladder into the well. A hand on my arm made me jump.

"Alex," Linc said, his features still in EMT mode. "I have some rags in the fire truck. Let's get some of that gunk off you before I have to help bring the body up."

As we attempted to wipe as much of the now drying mud off my skin, Andrea jogged back and forth from the well to her police car and back again at least three times. Chief Duncan stood stationary by the stone edge of the well, looking down into it and making grumbly noises. Or maybe that was his rotund belly. Hard to tell.

I tried to concentrate on the conversation by the well instead of the way Linc's fingers felt on my skin as he helped me wipe off the gunk. An exercise in futility.

"I've removed most of the debris down there," Andrea said, patting a large paper evidence bag. She set it on the side of the well as she descended again.

"Geez, Martinez. You think any of this stuff is actually evidence? These old farts have probably thrown God knows what down here over the years." He turned to Nana K. "No offense, Ms. K."

"None taken. I call these geezers old farts all the time," Nana K explained. "Especially on baked beans night."

The crowd of onlookers grew as time passed. Workers, residents, and guests gathered around the well to see what the commotion was. Linc and I joined them. Why were humans so fascinated with trouble? Flashing lights often equaled large crowds wanting to know what happened. In our small town, that was mostly due to the main currency—gossip. The more you had, the higher your status. "I saw" carried a lot more weight than "I heard."

"Female," Andrea called up the well. "Looks to be in her thirties or so. She's wearing an Aged Pines polo shirt."

"Did she say a polo player was down there?" one resident asked.

Another answered, "No, Doris. Check your hearing aid. She said it was a female ape. Maybe the zoo is missing one?"

"No, no, no," a third onlooker chimed in. "She said it's dirty shirts. Boring. I'm going back to my room. *Wheel of Fortune* is on."

Nana K rolled her eyes. "You all are ridiculous. Female human. Wearing a work shirt."

"Work shirt? From here?" Doris asked. A collective murmuring spread through the crowd. It sounded like a swarm of bees buzzing around my head. Either that or I was concussed from my fall.

"Linc!" Andrea called. "I need your help."

He gave my arm a squeeze. His eyes were full of concern. I wished it were for me and not because he was the EMT. But since I smelled like a ferret threw up a dead opossum, that was unlikely.

He said, "Duty calls. You don't have to be here for this if you don't want to."

I glanced at Nana K, hands clasping and unclasping by her chest, weight shifting from one bedazzled wedge to the other, teeth gnawing on her cherry-colored bottom lip. She may put up a tough front, but since the deceased was wearing an Aged Pines shirt, chances were my Nana knew her.

"I'll stay." Linc followed my gaze and nodded. I stood sentinel by Nana K's side, taking her trembling fingers in mine. She smiled up at me tightly.

Chief Duncan was riffling through the paper sack Andrea had deposited on the well edge. Sans gloves. Did the man not watch a single episode of *Law and Order*? Even I know you should wear gloves while handling potential evidence. I swear I was going to make it my goal to have someone run against him in the coming election.

"Broken glass, tons of change, a playing card, a broken girly hair thingamajig, a candy wrapper." His head reemerged from the bag. "Martinez, this is a bunch of trash," he called down the well.

"Little busy right now, Chief. I'll look through it more closely when we get back to the station."

Nana K leaned over to whisper, "Did you get any change while you were down there?"

I patted my pocket. A slight jingle made her smile. "That's my girl," she said.

Through careful manipulation and care, Linc and Andrea managed to get the woman out of the well. When Andrea brushed the mud off her slacks and looked around at the crowd, she threw up her hands.

Giving Chief Duncan the side-eye, she shouted, "Okay, everyone. Let's give the woman some privacy and dignity. Back to your rooms or your jobs. Disperse." No one moved. "Immediately," she shouted, walking toward the crowd with upheld, super-dirty hands. That had them shuffling backward a little, at least. No one wanted that foul-smelling mud on them.

She looked at Chief Duncan. "A little help here?"

He puffed up his stomach and blinked at the bystanders as though seeing them for the first time. "Everyone out," he bellowed. I swear the crowd collectively rolled their eyes. He marched toward them, using the bowling ball technique—plowing into them with his girth—to get them to move.

All the while, Nana K was staring at the woman lying supine on the ground by the well. Linc was checking her vitals, although I don't know why since she was clearly dead.

"I know her," Nana K whispered, bringing a shaky hand to her mouth.

Linc looked up at her. "Are you sure?"

Nana K nodded. "That's Camilla Marjadi. She's one of the Nayas."

"What's a Naya?" I asked.

"That's what Aged Pines calls the nurses and other care staff. It's some woo-woo word meaning guide or wisdom or something. Supposed to make us feel less like we're being poked and prodded by medical staff." She snorted lightly, though not with her usual gusto. "A needle's a needle no matter if it's a nurse or a Naya or Fred Astaire sticking it in your arm."

"I'm sorry, Nana," I said, squeezing her hand. "Did you know her well?"

She nodded slightly. "She used to be assigned to my cluster but recently switched shifts. That was a month ago."

"Wait? Did you say Camilla Marjadi?" I asked, the name finally sinking in.

"Yes, why?"

"I took her portrait a few days ago. She seemed really distracted and disengaged," I explained.

Just then, a balding man in a brown suit and yellow tie came running down the hill toward the well, looking more 1970s cop with his handlebar mustache than Piney Ridge resident. He put on the brakes right before mowing down a group of lingering lookie-loos. Rubbing the bald spot on top of his head, he beelined for Chief Duncan.

Nana K told me, "That's William Remora, alleged director of Aged Pines."

"I recognize him from our initial meeting about shooting the yearbook. Why do you say 'alleged'?" I asked, raising an eyebrow.

"Everyone knows the resident council actually makes all the big decisions."

I smiled and nodded agreeably. "Of course they do."

"What's going on, Clive? Medical emergency? Why didn't anyone call me straight away?" William asked the chief. His expressions reminded me of those viewfinders I had as a kid. The one where you clicked through the slides while holding it directly toward the sun. Click—angry. Click—confused. Click—worried. Click—angry again.

"Time is of the essence in these matters, you know," Chief Duncan said, pulling on his belt buckle. "The important thing is you are here now."

He stepped aside to reveal Camilla's body. All the color drained from William's face. So much so, Linc stood to catch him as he swayed. William put up a hand.

"I'm fine," he lied. He didn't look fine. He looked like a baby calf trying to stand for the first time. An all-brown baby calf. "It's just a shock."

Andrea approached. "You know the victim?"

"Victim? You think she was," he gulped and whispered, "murdered?"

Chief Duncan interjected before Andrea could say anything else. "It's too early to tell. For all we know she fell down the well and broke her neck."

William nodded vigorously. "Yes. Yes. That makes sense. Just an accident. Tragic, tragic accident. We'll look into putting a cover on this old thing."

Linc caught my eye and gave a slight almost imperceptible shake of his head. His meaning was crystal clear.

This was no accident.

CHAPTER 4

N ANA K GRACIOUSLY OFFERED to let me shower at her bungalow, so I didn't transfer the bottom of the well into my car. Okay, bungalow was a little misleading. Like Naya, Aged Pines called these mini-apartments bungalows to make the residents feel more like they were on vacation than in a "home." Truthfully, it was nicer than my old apartment in New York. Each similarly designed space included a small dining area connected to a fully functional kitchen, a small sitting room, a bathroom, and a separated bedroom. Each was one story—no threat from falling down any stairs—and had a sliding glass door that opened onto a paved patio. The retirement community offered to furnish the bungalow for a nominal fee, or the resident could choose to furnish it themselves. I'll give you one guess what Nana K chose.

Instead of re-dressing in my ruined, smelly clothes—they could go right down the garbage shoot on my way as far as I was concerned—I borrowed a shirt and shorts from Nana K. Somehow, I managed to find something that wasn't rainbow or sequined or an old Davie Bowie concert print.

When I emerged, Nana K stood by the door, purse in hand, tapping her foot impatiently.

"Jeez, girl. I could have washed three times with the amount of time you took. Come on. We're going to dinner at your mother's." She didn't even wait for me to put my shoes on before she bustled out the door. After looking at the muddy boots, I opted to not put them on anyway. Driving while barefoot may be illegal in Maryland, but only if you got caught. Our police force, which consisted of Chief Duncan and Officer Andrea Martinez, was a bit preoccupied at the moment, what with the dead body and all, so the risk was minimal.

My father met us at the door wearing his signature sweater-vest over a button-down dress shirt despite the uncharacteristic autumnal heat and the fact he was retired. He had a newspaper tucked under one arm.

"George. We're here for food," Nana K said. He leaned down to brush a kiss against her cheek as she fluttered by him.

"Hi, Dad," I said, giving him a hug.

"Hey, princess. Heard you fell down a well," he said, returning my hug.

"Yeah. It was a real *Last Crusade* moment. I was Elsa, only instead of reaching for a priceless artifact, I was reaching for Nana K's dollar-store glasses."

"Did you get them?" he asked as we walked to join my mother and nana in the kitchen.

"I told you I was Elsa. Nana K dropped me. But unlike Elsa, I did find the glasses."

"About that," Nana K said. "I can't wear them any longer. They smell like when your Great-Aunt Prudence tries to make sauerkraut and cabbage. I'll never get the smell out of that cheap plastic. But I appreciate the effort you went to, Peanut."

I stared at her openmouthed as I sat in my usual spot at the already set table.

"Really? I could have died for those glasses, and you aren't even going to keep them?"

"But you didn't die. So, it's fine," my mother said. She stood at the stove in a leopard-print dress. I don't mean like the spots of a leopard. I mean like actual leopards in various states of jumping or climbing. Seriously, between the three of them sitting here—and my mom's sister, Aunt

Delores, whose wardrobe was equally as questionable—it was no wonder I wore mostly black and white.

"Rumor has it Nana's glasses aren't all you found," my mother said, putting homemade meatloaf in the center of the table.

I gaped at her. "How can you possibly already know?"

"I called her while you were in the shower," Nana K admitted.

"And then Sally from my botany club called because her mother, Mildred, who lives at Aged Pines, heard from Doris that you'd found another dead body," she said, spooning mashed potatoes on everyone's plate.

I pushed mine around the plate with my fork. Suddenly I wasn't that hungry. Which wasn't like me at all.

Nana K, whose appetite seemed just fine even though she actually knew Camilla, pointed her loaded fork at me and said, "See. It's a good thing you fell down that well. Otherwise, who knows if we ever would have found her."

"I didn't fall," I reminded her. "You dropped me."

"To-*may*-to. To-*mah*-to," she said, taking a bite.

"Can we please talk about anything else?" I asked. "You all are ruining my appetite."

"Sure, Peanut," Mom said. "Are you excited to host your first book club meeting next week?"

I bit my lip to keep from rolling my eyes. From one dreaded topic to the next. "I guess. I can't believe you voluntold me I was hosting. I don't know anything about hosting. Or how to run a book club meeting."

"Oh, it's easy. You provide the wine and the space. I'll bring the snacks. Everyone else will bring the conversation. That table Linc made you is perfect for a meeting."

I knew when I saw that table, I would be roped into at least one of Mom's millions of clubs. Shelf Indulgence, the book club, seemed the most innocuous—it didn't involve needles, motorcycles, or insecticides. The worst thing that could happen was a paper cut.

The best part? Since it was Linc's fault for making me that gorgeous wood table, I made him join the book club too. And then roped Colleen in as well.

The second-best part? Our book this month was the Jane Austen classic *Emma*. The look on his face when he read the book jacket was priceless.

"What are we supposed to be reading again?" Nana K asked. Her membership was sporadic at best. She claimed she didn't have enough time left on this Earth to read books she wasn't interested in. Therefore, she was choosy about which months she participated.

"*Emma*," I reminded her. "It's actually really good. Not *Pride and Prejudice* good, but still good."

"Have you finished yet?" Mom asked me. She fiddled with her napkin instead of looking at me.

I narrowed my eyes. "Why do you ask? And in that way?"

"What way? I'm not being any sort of way." She still avoided my gaze. "Just wondering if you got to the very satisfying ending yet."

"Not yet. I should finish in the next day or two depending on when I can get back to the retirement community to finish their photos."

She took a drink and nodded. "I can't wait to hear what you think. You and Linc. You'll both bring a youthful voice to our discussions."

"Me, Linc, and Colleen," I reminded her.

"Oh, of course. And Colleen," she said quickly. Was she hiding a smirk? I think she was hiding a smirk. I tried to catch my father's eye to give him our signature "What the heck is wrong with her now?" look, but he was suddenly very interested in his meatloaf.

I dropped my fork on my plate with a loud clatter. Everyone finally looked up at me. "What is going on?"

They all feigned innocence. "I don't have any idea what you mean, Peanut. Finish your meatloaf. I want to talk more about the incident today."

"Fine, be evasive," I mumbled around a bit of meat. "I don't even care."

"Willy Remora and Chief Duncan both think it's an accident," Nana K said, switching the subject back to the well.

"Was it?" Mom asked. "Could she have fallen down there and died?"

I shrugged. "I fell and didn't die."

"You were also already hanging halfway down in it," Nana K said. "And you're the size of a prepubescent boy."

"Thanks, Nana," I said. Just what every single woman wanted to be compared to. To my mother, I said, "Linc doesn't think it's an accident. He examined the body at the scene."

"The body has a name," Nana K reminded us. "Camilla Marjadi."

My mother crossed herself. "May she rest in peace."

Nana K pointed a fork at her. "That stays here, Constance Klafkeniewski Lightwood. No spreading that around until they can tell her poor family."

My mother tried to look offended. Really, she was mad she couldn't immediately pick up the phone. "I would never."

"It's probably not a secret anymore anyway. If Nana K recognized her, I'm sure other residents and workers at the scene did as well." My mother's eyes flicked to the phone.

"I guess we'll have to wait for Dr. Wells to confirm or deny," Dad said. "Until then, let's keep the speculation to a minimum."

I patted my mom's hand. "I'll see what I can find out when I go back to finish the yearbook pictures. Anything juicy, and I'll text you right away."

She smiled and covered my hand with hers. "I always knew you were my favorite daughter."

"I'm your only daughter," I reminded her.

Conversation halted as the ghost of my missing brother, Harrison, ever present, clogged the room. We were coming up on the anniversary of his disappearance. On the day he disappeared, the weather was unusually snowy for that time of December in Maryland. Harrison and I were excited for an unexpected snow day off from school. Mom was still working then, so she hired a local teen to babysit us. Harrison wore the poor girl down until she let him go to the reservoir to play with some friends. He never returned.

My mother cleared her throat. She got up to spoon some meatloaf into two takeout containers for me and my nana. "In any case, I'll try to hold my tongue. But I have access to the two people that were literally there when she was found. I can't help it if people call me for information."

On cue, the phone started ringing. She looked at my dad who had his brows furrowed and lips pinched, and, after hanging up, wisely took it off the receiver.

"Gossip can wait until after family dinner," she said, retaking her seat. Dad's expression softened. "Tell me about the yearbook portraits, Alex. Any interesting choices for the—what did you call them—environmental portraits?"

I grinned at my nana. "You want to take this one, Roller Derby Debbie?"

Nana K smiled innocently as she kicked my shin under the table. "I don't know what you mean?"

"If your hair is any indication, I'm gonna have to take my blood pressure medicine before opening that book," Mom grumbled.

"Surprises are good for longevity," Nana K said. "I'll be the most interesting one in there."

"So far. I still have a few more to do this week, so we'll see if anyone gives you a run for your money," I said.

"The only time that happens is at bridge. But I'm catching up with those old biddies," Nana K said. "And with my magic pennies, I definitely have an edge."

My mother shook her head. "I don't even want to know."

CHAPTER 5

T HE NEXT DAY, I once again stood in the common area of the Aged Pines Retirement Community trying to figure out the labyrinthine maze of hallways and walkways to get to my next appointment. I swear every time I visited Nana, they'd added a new wing or more rooms or updated something. Even now there was a huge hole in the ground at the side of the building near the basketball court with a large pile of dirt beside it. I kept forgetting to ask Nana K what they were adding this time. From the size of the hole, my guess would be a swimming pool. Aged Pines either had some amazing benefactors, or they seriously overpriced their baked goods at the Saturday farmers' market in town.

The fact that I'd stopped at Solomon's for some fried chicken on the way here and therefore came in a different way exacerbated my confusion over which direction to go.

Okay, that was a lie. Not the stopping at Solomon's part, the why I'd parked in the back part. It was totally to avoid walking past the well. I hadn't slept well last night since images of zombies and spiders and, shudder, Rick pervaded my unconscious thoughts. Even though it was the middle of the day and so bright I needed sunglasses, I didn't want to tempt my ability to hold it together by walking past the wishing well.

I checked the list on my phone for which resident I was to meet first. Dennis Martingale. Age seventy-five. Wants to be photographed in his room, Sunset Cove Building, D159.

Sunset Cove. Someone either watched too many romance movies or had a sick sense of humor when they named the buildings here. Sunset Cove was different than the bungalows where my nana lived. This building was designed for seniors who needed a bit more help. Or those who couldn't be trusted with a stove. The rooms on all three levels were laid out like a hotel —each with a bedroom, small common area, and a bathroom. These residents relied on the Aged Pines staff for their meals, and Nayas were ever present in case of a medical emergency.

Dennis was only seventy-five, rather young compared to most of the other residents in this particular building. Could mean he's lazy and didn't want to cook for himself. Or it could mean there was an underlying physical or mental condition I'd have to take into consideration as I was shooting. I made a mental note to add "any known ailments" to the request form for next year. Finally, I found the D hallway and ticked off doors until I saw 159. I rapped on the door with my knuckles, and after a short pause, a hunched, white-haired gentleman opened the door.

"Hi, Mr. Martingale. I'm Alex, Regina Klafkeniewski's granddaughter. I'm here to take your photo for the yearbook." I held up my camera as proof. It might be time to invest in some business cards, if I could ever decide on a name for my business.

He grunted and, leaning heavily on a cane, took a wobbly step to the side so I could enter. The room was dark, lamps off, and curtains drawn, with only the television providing a flickering light. I could make out the shadowy shapes of the furniture as I turned slowly around the space.

Most of my "clients" had a very clear idea about what they wanted in their portrait. The only indication Dennis even remembered we had this appointment was the fact he was wearing a dress shirt with a patterned tie and not his bathrobe.

I cleared my throat. "Did you have a particular place or pose in mind? Did you want to include any favorite items or hobbies?"

His upper lip lifted on one side as though he smelled something foul. I resisted the urge to take a whiff of my hair. I'd washed it again when I got home from my parents's house yesterday, but maybe some of the well yuckiness still remained. Oh well, *natch,* not much I could do about that now. I smiled brightly and waited for him to answer.

"Don't care. I'm expecting company, so if we could just hurry this up," he finally said.

"Great. Photographer's choice. I love it." I feigned excitement. "Do you mind if I open a curtain? The natural light is so much better."

He shrugged a shoulder. I took that as a yes. With the amount of dust that flew off into my face as I yanked the heavy curtain open, I couldn't imagine the last time they were open. I coughed into my elbow while Dennis scowled at me from his spot in front of the television instead of offering me a glass of water.

When I recovered, I said, "Mr. Martingale. Can you please stand with your right shoulder beside the window?"

Begrudgingly, he did as I requested. I annoyed him more by motioning him a little this way or that way and asking him to turn his head just so. His hunched back proved to be a little problematic, but I crouched down to get on his level and managed not to make him look too much like the grumpy old man from *Up.* The result was a beautifully side-lit portrait that bathed his features in soft light. A perfect Rembrandt triangle kissed his opposite cheek.

Reading his crossed arms and cross expression, I didn't bother asking for a smile. I snapped a couple of safety shots and then, on a whim, asked him to step farther away from the window. This divided his face into a light side-dark side dichotomy reminiscent of Cruella DeVille's hair. Coupled with his serious grumpy-grampa expression, it worked on an artistic level. If I were making his portrait for me, that was the only way I would have shot it. But I'd have to use the more evenly lit shots for the yearbook. These later ones I'd convert to black and white and add to my portfolio.

I did a quick check on the back of my camera to make sure his eyes weren't closed before asking, "Are you sure you don't want something special in the photo? Do you have any hobbies or interests?"

His eyes flicked to the small television table by the door where a deck of playing cards was set out as though he were in the middle of a hand with someone. A glimmer of a smile lifted the corners of his mouth, then was gone. I kicked myself for not having the camera ready. He ran his hands down his tie and shook his head.

"These people see me every day. I don't know why they need a picture of me too," he grumbled, moving away from the window.

"For posterity. Generations to come can remember the legacy you left here," I said. I picked up my camera bag from where I left it by the door. "Thanks for letting me take your portrait."

"I guess it wasn't too bad." He walked to the window to close the curtain while I turned the doorknob to step out.

Before I could pull it open, the door swooped in on me, knocking me backward into the small table. In all my grace and poise, I pulled the dang thing down on top of me while trying not to fall.

The door buster let out an expletive and hoisted the table off my torso. "Are you okay, miss? I'm so sorry."

"No problem," I groaned from the floor. "A few more bruises won't matter."

I squeaked an eye open to see a man about my age leaning over me with his hand out. His dark hair was slicked back from his prominent forehead, and his dark eyes were... well, dark. Especially in this dim light. They looked like shark eyes. He had a small scar on his protruding chin and curly, black chest hair that crept out of his half-unbuttoned shirt and up his neck.

I took his hand, and he easily lifted me to my feet. He was fairly tall and muscled. Although his muscles all looked fabricated at the gym and not from actual labor like Linc's.

Not that I was thinking about Linc's muscles. Because I wasn't. Not at all.

I looked down at our still clasped hands. He followed my gaze and shook my hand to make it less awkward. "I'm Rodney Martingale. Sorry to scare you." To Dennis, he said, "Gramps, you've been holding out on me. I didn't know you entertained such beautiful women."

I removed my hand from his. Something about Rodney's slickness, the dim light, and the elder Mr. Martingale's grimace gave me some serious *Godfather* vibes. Rodney's slight New York/New Jersey accent added to the effect.

I said, "I'm Alex Lightwood. I'm taking Mr. Martingale's picture for the yearbook. I don't actually work here."

"A photographer. Beautiful and talented." His smile widened. Much like my ability to walk without bruising some part of my body, taking compliments was not my forte. I busied myself by cleaning up the mess from the table. Playing cards, a notebook, and a paper plate were strewn about the floor. A half-eaten apple had rolled toward the front door.

"I'm sorry, Mr. Martingale," I said, picking up the now hairy fruit by its stem and tossing it in the trash. "I can get you another apple from the commissary if you'd like."

"Leave it," he said, snatching the notebook out of my hands. "Leave it all. Rod will help me clean. He's good at it."

I looked from one smiling Martingale to the other scowling one. "Okay. Don't clean out my nana too much at bridge." I gestured to the playing cards.

Rod clapped his grandfather on the shoulder. "He wouldn't think of it, would you, Gramps?" He escorted me to the door. The door that was literally like two steps away.

"Alex, I'm so glad I ran into you today. Maybe we'll see each other again as we're visiting our grandparents."

"Maybe," I said evasively. Something about him rubbed me the wrong way. Probably because he reminded me of my ex-mistake, Rick. I could feel his eyes on my back the entire way down the hallway. Luckily my next appointment was in a completely different building.

Ms. Gladys Wickerson. Aged seventy-seven. She lived in the bungalow next to Nana K. Hopefully she would be less of a sourpuss.

CHAPTER 6

M S. GLADYS WICKERSON WAS, in fact, even more of a sourpuss than Dennis. But at least she had a very clear vision of what she wanted for her portrait. A vision that did not include rainbows or porcelain animals but did include a rather persnickety cat.

When I knocked on the door, a crisp voice called, "If you're the photographer, come in. Otherwise, I'm very busy."

I opened the door a crack and peeked in. "I'm the photographer. Alex Lightwood. Regina Kla—"

"Yes, yes. I know who you are and who you're related to. I make it my business to know who is entering my personal space. Now, hurry and close the door before you let Duchess out." She waved me in from her perch on a chaise lounge in front of the sliding glass door. She wore an elegantly embroidered silk robe over a 1920s-style, floor-length gown. A huge, layered string of pearls adorned her neck. I half expected her to pick up a long cigarette and call me "Dah-ling."

She stroked the back of an impressively large and beautiful Maine Coon cat who I assumed was Duchess. She looked as elegant and unimpressed as her owner. The rest of the room screamed old Hollywood. Touches of gold mixed with an abundance of red accents and soft lines. In addition to the chaise lounge, the main sitting room held two humongous armchairs. The woodwork framing was even more intricate than my purple velvet couch I had yet to replace. A huge mirror adorned one wall. An equally large portrait of a younger Gladys adorned the other.

The whole place smelled like someone tried to spritz cheap perfume over menthol and Ben-gay.

Still, everything looked pristine and precise, and I was kind of afraid to move in case I bumped into something and broke it. I mean, I couldn't even find a stray cat hair anywhere but on Duchess herself.

"Don't just stand there catching flies, girl. I *am* busy," Gladys said. She ran a hand delicately over her perfectly coiffed white hair.

I moved farther into the room. "Sorry. I'm assessing the light. Seems about perfect where you are right now actually."

"Of course, it is. I was a model in my youth." She gestured grandly at the portrait. "I know my good side and what lighting flatters my face. Hopefully with my expertise, you won't be able to mess it up too much." She didn't make eye contact with me as she spoke. Which was probably a good thing since I'm sure I had daggers in my eyes. I swallowed my retort and my pride and lined up my shot. To my dismay, she was annoyingly photogenic. And she knew it. I moved to get a different angle, and before I could ask her to adjust her chin, she'd already done it. She'd left the large patio door covered in an almost opaque white sheer which softened the light perfectly to decrease the effect of her wrinkles. In camera, she looked ten years younger.

The cat, like its owner, barely acknowledged my presence, sitting calmly on Gladys's lap, slowly swishing her tail, eyes half closed in contentment.

"I'll need to approve those before you submit any to the yearbook. Provide me with copies. One four-by-six print of every shot you edit and a zip drive of all the electronic files," she said when I stood to leave.

"Oh, I don't usually..." I started, but I trailed off when I saw her sharp expression. Cheese and crackers, she could put out a fire with that gaze. I felt like I was getting scolded by some sort of icy amalgamation of my mother, my third-grade teacher, and my Catholic guilt.

"I'll get right on that," I said quietly. Her tight lips softened slightly into a smug smirk as she unfolded herself from where she lay on the chaise to a sitting position. The cat meowed in protest and jumped down to stalk, tail up, past me into the kitchen.

"Beautiful cat," I commented. "I didn't think residents were allowed to have pets." I swear that was in the lease agreement we signed when Nana K moved in.

"Are you always this intrusive and rude? It's none of your business, really, is it?" I shook my head in the negative. "Now, fetch me that water glass. Sitting so long in the sun makes me dehydrated," she commanded. She pointed with a gnarled bony finger to a glass on the kitchen counter. I took a deep breath and tried to remember that she was my elder, and throwing the water in her face wasn't an appropriate reaction. But if I "accidentally" tripped on the carpet as I carried it to her, and it "accidentally" slipped out of my hand, I couldn't be blamed for that. Right?

"Are you hard of hearing, girl?" she said when I didn't move fast enough for her. "You're as bad as that Naya that died."

My ears pricked at the mention of Camilla. "You knew her?" I asked, handing her the water without incident. I gave myself a mental high five for my restraint.

"Knew her? Of course. Live here long enough, and you get to know everyone. She was assigned to this group of bungalows, but I heard she got demoted to a less-demanding position because of incompetence."

Less demanding clientèle, I thought, but kept it to myself. Still, if Camilla was having trouble at work, that could support suicide. Or Chief Duncan's whisper-thin theory of an accident. If she were leaning over the well to make a wish for better working conditions...

"Was there anything else?" Gladys's nasally voice interrupted my musing.

I forced a smile and a thank-you and slammed the door a little harder than necessary behind me. She shouted something through the door, but I couldn't make it out. Probably for the best.

I stopped by Nana K's bungalow before leaving.

"You smell much better today," she said, giving me a hug when I entered. Unlike Gladys's overly rich-toned interior, Nana's bungalow was an explosion of color. She'd left the walls white but covered them in pop art, record covers, my photographs, and live plants. Her furniture was a mishmash of her favorite items from her old house, the one she lived in with my grandfather and the one I remembered visiting when I was younger. A round wicker papasan chair with a bright-orange cushion and mushroom-patterned pillows took up one corner of the room. Two navy-blue love seats faced each other in the middle of the room. A coffee table made from an old wooden wire spool sat between them. Her almost sheer curtains had a repetitive peacock pattern on them and even when closed, they still allowed the room to be bathed in light. The whole place was kitsch and happy and perfectly Nana K.

But even the quirky interior wasn't enough to drag me out of my sour mood. "Thanks, Nana," I said flatly in response to her comment.

At my tone, she held me at arm's length to give me a once-over. "What's wrong with you? You look like someone ate your precious fish, Lash."

"Nothing that extreme. I had a few tough cookies to photograph today."

"Let me guess. One of them was Gladys Wickerson." We moved into the sitting room to plop down on one of the love seats. She turned down the reality show she was watching.

"Yup. She was the last one. Was she famous in a former life? She told me to 'fetch,'" I said. "Like I'm a dog or some sort of trained hamster."

Nana K laughed sardonically. "If you ask her, she was famous. One small modeling campaign in an off-season Sears catalog when she was in her twenties doesn't equal famous in my eyes."

"For not caring, you sure know a lot about her," I teased.

"I don't want to, but she tells everyone and their guests all about it. Doris and I have a theory that she has low self-esteem and is making up for it. Either that, or she's a delusional narcissist."

"How does she get to have a cat? Did your lease say no pets?" I asked.

"It's Gladys. She seems to get her way on everything. I don't know if she's blackmailing the director or throwing money at him, but he practically eats out of her hand. Another reason Doris and I try to avoid her. The less we see her, the less she has to complain about us."

"Must be hard to do since she lives a few doors down," I said.

She shrugged a small shoulder. "I manage okay. Until bridge night. That brings out all the crazies. You'd think we were playing for millions instead of pennies. People are ruthless!" She held up a bandaged finger. "I even got a paper cut last night!"

I shook my head. "You could always not go," I suggested.

She scoffed and waved the comment away with her hand. "Absolutely not. Doris and I are this close"—she held her thumb and pointer finger an inch apart—"from beating the smug grins off Gladys and her partner. We're both at the top of the leaderboard. The winner this week gets a gift certificate to Solomon's. No way I'm letting that greasy goodness slip through my fingers."

"You have Solomon's all the time," I said.

"But free Solomon's tastes so much better than paid-for Solomon's. Trust me, Peanut."

"Hey, speaking of bridge. Mr. Martingale sends his regards." I rolled my eyes.

Her eyes widened and mouth gaped. Then she laughed like a hyena. Like the slapping her knee, wheezing kind of laugh that quickly turned into coughing. I fetched her a glass of water too. "Take a breath, Nana. I don't want to perform CPR on you."

She gulped the water and calmed down. "Woohoo. You said a few tough cookies. Understatement of the year. Dennis and Gladys are the resident king and queen of salty sourpusses. If they don't think you can do anything for them, they have no need for you. They mainly stick together because no one else wants to hang out with them."

"Note for next year: do not schedule them on the same day."

CHAPTER 7

THE NEXT DAY, AFTER feeding my fish and my visiting chicken friend, Nugget, I treated myself to ice cream at Scoops, There It Is, our local homemade ice cream shop. I've been all over the world, and I've never had ice cream quite like this. The trick was to find the perfect combination of flavors. In the fall, I loved one scoop of apple pie and one scoop of cinnamon. So, freakin' good.

Mary Huffman, the owner of Scoops and currently the only one in possession of the secret family recipe, stood sentinel behind the counter, taking orders from the residents of Piney Ridge. She smiled at me when I walked in and took my place in line. She'd been behind this counter for as long as I could remember—first as a teenager working nights and weekends under the father's tutelage, then as a young adult working during college breaks, and now as an adult herself having inherited the business when her parents retired. She barely looked at the labels on the ice cream counter, knowing intuitively where each flavor was housed and feeling by muscle memory the perfect-sized scoop for each cone. Today she had her ebony hair pulled up into a tight knot on the top of her head and a Scoops apron tied around her waist.

"Good morning, Alex," Mary greeted me when it was my turn. I used to call her Ms. Huffman when I was younger, but since returning to Piney

Ridge earlier this year, she'd insisted it was silly for a grown woman to call another "miss." She insisted on Mary. It still felt a little weird in my mouth.

"Morning! I didn't expect the ice cream side to be this busy this early," I commented. Scoops had an ice cream counter and a full deli connected by a short, narrow hallway. The deli side offered breakfast sandwiches, lunch items, the best homemade soup, and hot dinners. Residents could also pick up bags of chips, candy, bread, milk, and boxed goods if they didn't want to make a full trip to the grocery store in town.

"You'd be surprised how many people enjoy a morning milkshake." She laughed lightly, taking a sip of her own.

"I guess it isn't that different from a smoothie." And if she still looked my age despite being at least a decade older, then maybe ice cream in the morning was the secret fountain of youth. At least that was what I was going to continue to tell myself to justify all these trips to Scoops.

"Want to try one? Or are you opting for your usual?" she asked.

"The usual," I said, unsure how I felt about having a usual at an ice cream shop. I might need to switch up where I cull photos in the future for fear of not fitting into my clothing soon.

"Cup or cake cone?" she asked, holding the ice cream scoop aloft.

"Cup," I said. Since I was culling the retirement community yearbook photos with my laptop and external hard drive on the table, a cup seemed the safer choice. While I always hope to be as graceful and fluid as a dancer, I'm also no fool. Trying to hold a double-dip cone without dripping it all over my electronics was tempting my clumsy karma. Best to use a spoon like a toddler. And cheaper than fixing my laptop in the long run.

"Coming right up," she said, flitting around behind the counter easily.

I exchanged the exact amount for my cup when she handed it to me. She smiled as she glanced at it.

"Tell your mother hello for me," she said, opening the register to record the sale. "I'll see her at the Fall Fest planning committee meeting later this week."

"Will do." I grabbed a plastic spoon from the dispenser on the counter and headed to my favorite table by the front window to set up my culling station.

Curiosity had me looking at Camilla's pictures first. I quickly clicked through the candids and staff portraits to keyword the ones in which she appeared. I sorted by that keyword and had a handful of shots I could use in a memorial page. I'd ask relatives and residents if they had any others they might want to add.

My earlier instinct that she seemed distracted came through in the portraits as well. It was a nice shot of a beautiful woman. Long, glossy black hair held back with a few barrettes. Only a light brush of makeup on her dark olive skin. Her hands were crossed by her chest revealing manicured nails. But her deep-brown eyes were flat. Her big, toothy smile didn't reach the rest of her face. I would have to lighten the dark bags under her eyes. She was definitely worried about something. Or at least distracted. Could it have been suicide after all? Nothing about her demeanor suggested that extreme when I interacted with her, but that was only for a few minutes on a busy day.

Because of her insistence to proof her portraits, I switched to Gladys next. Even in the candid shots, she always managed to find the best angle. She was always overdressed for the activity in something lacy or beaded or floor length. The lady definitely had a committed style. And like Nana said, even in the group activity shots, she was either seated a little away from the main group or with Dennis. In one shot, they had their heads leaned toward one another with identical scowls as they watched a group of residents paint ceramics. I might include that one in the yearbook out of spite. I could caption it, "The Statler and Waldorf of Aged Pines"—a reference to the two old-guy Muppets that heckle everyone in the theater. Only once did I capture Gladys actually participating in an activity—making beaded jewelry.

I was contemplating Gladys's pictures—annoyingly, they were all pretty good in terms of lighting and posture, but I didn't want to edit and print all of them—when the bell above the shop door jingled.

Instinctively, I looked up to see who had come in. Danny Tidwell. I hadn't seen him in months. He caught my eye and scowled at my smile, which caused mine to falter. I thought we had a fairly nice conversation the last time I talked to him. He had given me some pointers on how to photograph the first-responders calendar. Not that I took any of his suggestions, but in my recollection, we'd ended on a fairly positive note.

He ordered his ice cream and sauntered over to my table still looking a bit cross.

"Hi, Danny," I said brightly, ignoring his ire. "How are you?"

"I would be better if someone would stop encroaching on my business," he said, giving me a pointed look. Danny was a few years younger than me and had recently been through a divorce. His ex-wife volunteered at the fire station with Linc.

"I'm sorry. I'm not sure what you mean," I said. I felt my face start to flush. I didn't really enjoy confrontation. I was much better an hour after any confrontation when I finally figured out the perfect thing to say. You know, after obsessively replaying the conversation over and over in my mind for eternity.

He flicked his cone at my laptop screen. A small drop of ice cream landed on Gladys's face. I wiped it off with a napkin.

"Who do you think did the yearbook shoot for Aged Pines in the past, hmmm?" he asked.

"I didn't really think about it," I said lamely. "They asked, and I said yes."

"Of course you didn't think about it. You big-city types are uber ready to come back here and snatch away the honest living of everyone in your path. First the calendar and now this." He actually snarled.

"I'm sorry, Danny. I didn't go seek them out. They came to me," I explained.

He ignored me. "And now I hear the Cavannaghs have hired you for their Christmas card shoot." He gave a derisive laugh. "Actually, that one

I'm not sad to see go. Good luck with those little hellions they call children. Last year I had to bribe them with quarters to get them to sit still and not make faces."

"Thanks for the heads-up," I said.

He refocused his scowl on me. "It wasn't a favor." He pointed his ice cream cone at me. It dripped onto the table. I discreetly shut my laptop to save it from any more flying debris. He continued, "If you continue to take business away from me, you'll be sorry."

"Danny, I'm pretty sure there are enough families in Piney Ridge for us both to be lucrative. We could even help each other out by being each other's second shooter at the bigger events," I suggested. We had very different photography styles that would appeal to different clients. Danny leaned more toward posed portraits with studio lighting and external flash whereas I fell back on my photojournalism background with a natural light, documentary-style approach.

"Ha!" he shouted, drawing the attention of the few other patrons around us. "I will never be your second shooter. I'm the better photographer. Just ask anyone. No one liked your unconventional first-responder calendar. Linc will be begging me to come back next year since I'm sure their sales were dismal. In the meantime, stay out of my lane."

He stormed out the door. I shrugged my shoulder at Mack, the owner of the hardware store in town, who was sitting at the table next to mine and probably heard the whole thing.

"For what it's worth, he's wrong," Mack said, his gruff voice carrying loudly across the small space. He wore his signature overalls over a flannel shirt, and even though I couldn't see his feet, I knew he wore tan work boots.

"How do you mean?" I asked.

"We all love the new style of calendar." He gestured with one thick hand to the one hanging on the wall behind the ice cream calendar. Joy, who worked the front desk at the police station, laughed as she plucked a curious kitten from her keyboard. When I looked back at Mack, he was smiling too.

"You can't help but smile at that moment," he said. "And I'm not saying that to make you feel better. That kid wouldn't know a good photograph if it was labeled with a big neon sign. His calendars were always so stiff and impersonal."

"Thanks, Mack," I said. "I appreciate that."

"A lot of us Piney Ridgers followed your career. You have an amazing portfolio. You should consider selling some of those prints," he suggested, taking a bite of his breakfast sandwich. "I'd be happy to set up a display in the hardware store."

"Thank you so much! I appreciate everyone's support." I smiled and didn't tell him I already sold pictures online. The ones I retained the rights to, the ones *Nature* magazine didn't use in their spreads, were all on a stock-photography site. It wasn't much, but it helped supplement Lash's spending habit. That fish was high maintenance.

My good mood soured a little, though, as I considered Danny's words. A few months ago, I had practically accused him of murder even though he was a little too daft to catch on. And now I was allegedly taking away his business. I was honest when I said I hadn't considered who had done the Aged Pines yearbook in the past. Should I focus more on Mapleton, the next closest town? Of course, that would mean I'd be in competition with any photographers already established there.

I shook myself a little. This was ridiculous. McDonald's didn't have a hissy fit and close up shop when a new fast-food restaurant came to town. Having a variety and a choice was part of our economy. Danny Tidwell was going to have to up his game if he wanted to keep his clients. Or *he* could go nosing around in Mapleton. I had just as much right as anyone else to open a photography business here in Piney Ridge.

If only I could decide on a name. And focus on actually editing instead of looking for a murderer.

CHAPTER 8

I FOCUSED ON CLICKING through the rest of the yearbook photos I still had to edit. Thankfully, I'd been doing the editing a little at a time as I went through the shoot. The candids were easy. All they needed was a quick fix for white balance, because of the terrible florescent indoor lighting, and a bump in contrast for better print quality.

The portraits were a bit trickier. How much skin softening should I do on the residents? Their skin was like a badge of honor, every wrinkle and pore and blemish and freckle helped tell the story of their lives, and each one was beautiful. Still, I knew people were a bit more critical of their own portraits. Often, we saw ourselves as much younger versions. Until we looked in the mirror. And wasn't that a shock. Especially in the morning after being awoken by a rude rooster.

No? Just me.

The bell above the door jingled again, causing me to look away from the screen and toward the entrance. A smile lit my face as Colleen McMurphy, my best friend since we were in diapers, approached my table.

"Figured I'd find you here," she said as she sat and plopped her oversized purse on the floor. "Once you finish a shoot, you're looking through them here or at the picnic tables by your loft."

"You don't know me," I teased. Besides my parents, she knew me best. Well, her and Linc.

She closed her green eyes and hovered a hand over my ice cream cup. "Our connection is telling me that this is apple pie and cinnamon."

"Okay, you know me a little," I said. "What brings you here?"

"I needed a break from the littles at work. I told my supervisor I had a doctor's appointment and took a half day."

"You rebel!" I said, impressed.

She swooshed her red hair off her shoulders theatrically. "I'm a new me. A 'put me first' kind of me. A 'get ice cream in the morning if you dang well please' kind of me."

I laughed. "Let me know how I can help. Especially with the last one."

"I'm going to help myself right now." She grabbed her purse—seriously, how did she not have back problems from the sheer size and weight of the mammoth thing?—and headed to the counter.

The bell jingled above the door again. All eyes, including mine, whipped that way like a human version of Pavlov's dogs. Rodney Martingale sauntered through the door. I ducked behind my laptop, so he didn't see me. Coward? Maybe. But avoidance was the name of my game when it came to awkward social interactions. Or really any social interactions, if I'm honest.

He leaned a hip and an elbow against the ice cream case and threw a toothy smile at Colleen. She blushed as red as her hair and batted her eyelashes as they talked. Please, don't invite him over here. Please, don't invite him over here.

She pointed to our table. I poked my head up from behind the computer and gave a little wave. She totally invited him over here.

When he saw me, his smile intensified. He pushed off the counter to take the seat across from me. And by take the seat, I mean he turned it around and straddled it backward, leaning on the back rest with his large, hairy forearms. One of them had a tattoo of a snake wrapping around an ace of spades. I wondered if he played bridge too. Then hid my snicker by taking a bite of ice cream.

"I didn't think I'd have the pleasure of seeing you again so soon," he said. His voice sounded like he watched one too many James Bond movies. I half expected him to say, "I'm Rod. Rod the Bod" with one eye raised and a martini glass filled with ginger ale in his hands. Ginger ale or a light beer. He didn't seem the type to drink martinis—shaken or stirred.

"Here I am," I said. I refocused on my computer, hoping Colleen would come back soon to distract him.

"What are you working on?" he asked.

"The pictures from the retirement community shoot," I answered. His chair screeched in the quiet shop as he dragged it around to sit beside me. I cringed and shifted my computer.

"I'd love to see the ones of my gramps," he said. I had a quick hallucination that his curly chest hair, prominent yet again since his shirt was unbuttoned to below his chest line, was going to reach out and tangle me up. I'd be a prisoner on his chest, forced to eat the crumbs that fell from his mouth. I shuddered.

"You okay?" he asked. "You look a little pale."

"I'm fine. The pictures aren't edited yet," I added, in response to his earlier request.

"I don't care," he said, trying to peer around my body block.

"I do. I don't like to show people my unedited files," I explained. Why did people always insist on looking at the unedited pictures even after I told them no? Would they go into a kitchen at a restaurant and demand to look at their uncooked food?

Thankfully, he sat back in his chair. The correct way. "I like my women a little mysterious."

I blinked at him. Did this guy not understand social cues?

"I guess we'll have to get together once you edit them. I'll take you to dinner. Here's my card." He flicked a business card onto the keyboard of my laptop.

Rodney Martingale, Esquire

Entrepreneur, Promoter, Influencer, Enforcer
410-555-6735

That was a lot of "ers" and not a lot of actual employment. What exactly did he promote? Based on the gold, gem-studded rings embellishing almost every finger and thick gold chains hanging on his neck, I didn't want to know. Although, in all fairness, knowing my family's ability to dress themselves, who am I to judge other people's fashion, but he wasn't someone I would choose to influence me.

On the other hand, Colleen, with her flushed face, fluttering eyelashes, and girly giggles, would absolutely like the chance for him to influence her. I slipped her the card across the table when she sat down.

"I'm really busy. You can see the portraits in the yearbook when your grandfather gets a copy," I said as politely as I could.

He laughed lightly. "Sure, Mystery Woman." He turned his attention to Colleen, a much more willing subject. "Feel free to use that business card she gave you, Red. I'd love to get to know both of you better."

She giggled again and pressed the card to her chest. "Sure thing, Rod."

He pushed back from his chair, winked at us, and walked back to the counter, making a big show of sliding his hands into his back pockets. I chuckled as his rings got caught on one side, and he had to try a few times. Instead of looking enticing, it kind of looked like he was itching his backside.

Colleen sighed, pulling my attention away from Rod.

"You can't be serious," I said to her.

"What?" she said, peeling her eyeballs away from the spectacle by the counter and back to me. "He's cute. And new. And did you see his car?"

"His car?"

She pointed out the window. A shiny, silver convertible Mazda Miata straddled two parking spaces toward the back of the parking lot.

"What about it?"

"It's a sports car! People in Piney Ridge don't drive cars like that. Not even those that live on The Hill. He's gotta be rich, right?" she asked.

I tilted my head at her and pursed my lips. "Since when do you care about the size of a guy's wallet?"

"I don't really. What I care about is that I didn't throw sand at him in elementary school. Seriously, the number of new single men in Piney Ridge is slim to none. The fact that he's rich is an added bonus."

"Rich and hairy," I mumbled.

I went back to culling my pictures. Linc was single. And admittedly handsome. But he wasn't new. And something about suggesting him to Colleen sat weird in my chest.

"You could travel? Go to Baltimore? Join a dating app?" I suggested.

"Tried it. Tried it. Tried it. But now that you're home, and single-ish, we can go out together!"

"What do you mean single-ish?" I asked, but Rod chose that moment to come back to the table.

He took a long lick of his cone as he held eye contact with Colleen. She sighed like a teen at a Beatles concert.

"Gotta run but use that card. I have friends that would love to party with two hot chicks like you ladies," he said with a wink.

Unabashedly, Colleen watched Rod walk out the door to his car.

"Need a napkin for your drool? You can have my empty ice cream cup." I nudged it across the table toward her.

She rolled her eyes at me. "It's been slim pickings here lately. Working in a preschool doesn't allow me to meet single guys." She paused to eat her ice cream. "Let's change the subject to something a little less depressing than my nonexistent love life. Any new information about your... discovery?"

I blinked at her. "You mean Camilla? Um, not that I know of."

"Everyone in town is saying it was a tragic accident. That she fell down the well."

I snorted. "That's what the director of Aged Pines and lazy Duncan want it to be. Less of a PR problem and less work for the police."

"You don't agree?"

I lowered my voice. "I found her tucked back in a small opening in the well. I'm pretty sure someone who died upon impact couldn't crawl into that space."

"Fair point."

"Although, looking through her pictures from Aged Pines, she does seem out of sorts," I conceded. "Who knows if whatever was on her mind led to her murder or to her suicide."

"Uh-oh. I know that look. You're going to get involved," Colleen said with a knowing smile.

"I'm already involved. I found the body," I reminded her.

"Didn't you learn your lesson last time? Don't go borrowing trouble. If the cops say it's an accident, it is probably an accident."

"Linc agrees with me that it probably wasn't. I trust him over Chief Duncan."

She smiled at me. "Of course he agrees with you. If you said apples were purple, he'd agree with you."

"He would not."

She lifted an eyebrow. "That boy has it bad. How can you not see that?"

I shook my head. "No way. Maybe a month ago when I was new to town. Not now after he's been privy to *all* of my embarrassing moments. Nothing says 'run away as fast as you can' like falling down a well. You didn't smell me afterward. Trust me, that ship has sailed."

She laughed. "If you say so." She held up her ice cream cone. "Cheers to all the single ladies trying to find The One in a small town full of relatives or been-there-dated-thats."

I tapped her cone with my spoon. "Don't feel bad. I spent years in New York City and traveling the world, and I'm still single too."

CHAPTER 9

A FEW DAYS LATER I was ready to deliver the digital proofs of the yearbook portraits to William Remora, director of the Aged Pines Retirement Community. I did not ask Gladys Wickerson's permission before including her portrait in the proofs. No one bullies a Lightwood!

Okay, in all honesty, I didn't want to see her again.

Director Remora's office door stood slightly ajar, and when I knocked, it swung open all the way to reveal a small, cluttered office. And by cluttered, I mean it looked like a band of toddlers were left unsupervised in there for a few hours. Stacks and stacks of files and folders and papers and boxes dotted the floor, desk, and what I thought was once a couch. One box was full of unopened playing cards. Another contained boxes of medication samples. Yet another looked like it was full of linens. Most concerning was a dust-covered one labeled "Chips." I certainly hoped they checked the expiration date before giving them to residents. An old apple core rotted beside an overturned plastic soda-fountain cup on the bookcase. A tall lamp leaned lazily on a dusty file cabinet. In fact, everything seemed to be covered in a thin layer of dust. It gave the entire room a musty, brown, fuzzy quality.

In short, yuck.

"Mr. Remora?" I called, taking another tentative step into the room. I made myself as small as possible so I didn't accidentally hit one of the many stacks of things and cause a domino effect of paperwork. I cleared my throat and tried again. "Mr. Remora? Are you here?"

No answer. I gladly escaped back to the hallway to wait in a space that didn't remind me of the inside of an ant hill. How was Aged Pines still functional if that was what his filing system was like? Nana K may be right: the resident council did run this place, and William Remora was merely a figurehead.

I didn't have to wait long before William came rushing down the hallway. He wore a very similar brown suit to the one I saw him in the day I fell in the well. I tilted my head. Or was it the same brown suit? In any case, it matched his office. And his personality.

"Ms. Lightwood," he said, slowing to a stop and pumping my hand up and down in greeting. "So sorry to keep you waiting. You, uh, found my old office, I see. We use that more for storage than anything else lately." He reached around me to shut and lock the door. "No one is supposed to be in there. Follow me to a more comfortable space."

We ended up in a bigger and, thankfully, cleaner office space in a newly renovated part of the main building. The open-concept design and minimalist décor style reminded me of high-tech thriller movies in high-rises, not a retirement community. It certainly contradicted the style of William Remora, Mr. Brown Suit, Brown Tie, Brown Shoes.

"Hold my calls," he said to his administrative assistant as we passed. I saw her eye roll in my periphery as she lazily flipped a page in her magazine. I hadn't heard a phone ring since I'd been here.

He ushered me into his office, not quite as cluttered as the other but getting there quick. Only a few boxes were stacked in here. The one on the visitor's chair was marked "Camilla." William moved it to the side so I could sit down.

"We cleaned out her locker. I'm waiting for her husband to come pick it up," he explained, then shuffled a stack of files around on his desk so he could peer at me through them.

My eyes flicked to the file cabinets in the corner of the room before I could control them. He laughed when he saw my gaze.

"I'm not the best at file keeping. But I prefer to handle that all myself. We take patient confidentiality very seriously around here." He sat behind his desk and gestured for me to take the seat across from him. I perched on the edge and removed the zip drive from my pocket.

"I brought the proofs of the portraits section of the yearbook. Can you take a look and approve the layout?" I handed him the zip drive across the desk. A file folder had opened slightly when he moved them a moment ago. I saw Camilla's name on a list of other employees. The top said, "Promotion Candi—" before disappearing under the flap of the folder. He quickly put his arm on the folder and moved another folder on top of it.

Was Camilla up for a promotion? Her name was on the top of the list. Couldn't be alphabetical since her last name started with an M. If someone else knew she was the front runner, that could easily be a motive for murdering her.

While the yearbook file loaded on his computer, he said, "You know, we are unveiling a brand-new shuffleboard and tennis court next week. Are you available to photograph the ceremony for the yearbook?"

"Sure. Email me the date and time. I can add it into the activities section of the book," I said. If he kept adding things, it would be time for next year's shoot before this book went to print.

"Thanks. We're dedicating the tennis courts to Camilla. Lincoln Livestrong is making a special wooden plaque and everything."

I smiled. "That's a nice tribute. Linc does amazing work. Is that the big pile of dirt outside?"

"Yup. Should be state of the art," he bragged.

"I didn't realize you had to dig so deep for a tennis court," I mused.

"Oh yeah." He rubbed the bald spot on the back of his head. "We had to be sure the irrigation wasn't affected. The construction company is running new lines."

"I see," I lied. I had no idea what he was talking about. "Did Camilla like tennis?"

He shrugged. "How should I know? The courts are the next new thing going in, so we chose them."

I nodded. "Had she worked here long?"

He clicked around on the computer for a moment, then said stiffly, "A few years. She was a valued member of our staff."

Colleen's warning not to borrow trouble popped in my mind, but the Lightwood women's penchant for gossip quashed it before it got any real traction. I asked, "Gladys Wickerson wasn't a fan. She told me Camilla had to be transferred recently because of poor job performance."

William absently ran his fingers over his handlebar mustache, smoothing it down over and over again. A bead of sweat trickled down his forehead. "Ms. Wickerson isn't really a fan of anything except Ms. Wickerson," he spat. Then, taking a deep breath, adjusted his tone. "Sometimes the personalities of staff and residents don't mesh well. As an administrator, it's my duty to keep my employees and my clients happy."

"I see," I said. What I saw was a wannabe politician spouting the party line. Despite my better judgment, I poked the bear some more. "With all the new renovations and added amenities, it seems like you are keeping your donors happy too. I can't remember the last time I didn't notice some sort of improvement."

His Adam's apple bobbed up and down as he gulped. Avoiding my eye contact, he leaned forward toward the computer screen to examine something. Finally, he said, "Yes. Yes, they have. I've been diligent in my efforts to fundraise. All part of the job description."

"Does everything look okay with the proofs?" I asked, changing gears.

"The proofs?" He played with his necktie. Something about his large tie tack seemed familiar. It may have been the same one I saw him wearing at the crime scene.

I pointed at the computer screen. "The yearbook. Please make sure all the names are spelled correctly." I pulled a release-for-print form from my bag and slid it across the desk toward him. "Sign this when you've reviewed everything. If there are any changes, indicate them on the bottom of the form."

"Okay. I'll have my assistant check the names. From what I see, this is the best yearbook we've had in ages. Last year's lacked life, if you know what I mean."

I nodded. If Danny Tidwell's last calendar was any indication, then the yearbook was full of fake smiles against the same backdrop in even light. Like the boring photos from high school yearbooks of the past.

"Thank you. I try to capture people's emotions and personalities along with how they look at any particular age."

"You've done just that from the ones I've seen. I hope you'll come back next year as well." He stood, so I did too. I was being dismissed.

"I'd be happy to. I'm glad you decided on the environmental portraits. They paint a much more vivid picture of the residents. I'll pencil you in for the same week a year from now." I held out my hand for him to shake. He gripped mine firmly, then immediately dropped it when I said, "Sorry again for your loss of Camilla. It must be hard to lose a valued employee so suddenly."

"Yes, yes. Tragic accident. I'll see you again next week for the unveiling. Thanks for bringing this by." He ushered—well, really pushed—me toward the door.

My momentum was stopped by Ms. Wickerson's frail frame filling the doorway. Today she wore a lace dress that hit her calves, white gloves, and a cream sweater. Cream from age or dye, I wasn't sure. She leaned heavily on a cane.

"Willy, what time are we meeting to..." Her voice trailed off when she noticed me in the room. "What are you doing here?"

"Hi, Ms. Wickerson. Good to see you again so soon. I just dropped off the yearbook proofs." I stepped to the side so she could enter.

William stepped forward to grip her elbow. "Let me help you to a chair, Gladys. Alex was just leaving."

She threw her cane at me to hold while William helped lower her into the chair I'd just vacated. The cane had seen better days. The top had an ornamental metal bird head as a grip. One side was dented in. And the wooden handle was scuffed and dirty. I was surprised she didn't insist someone get her a new one or at least clean this one.

I handed it back to her when she was seated. She snatched it from my hands and said, "I told you I wanted to approve my portrait before you included it the yearbook."

"You weren't the one who hired me. If Mr. Remora wants to show you the one I chose, that's his choice."

She scowled at me. "How rude. And for a simple request. Although knowing you're Regina's granddaughter, I don't know why I'm surprised at your brazen disrespect."

I lifted my eyebrows, popped a hip. Who did this woman think she was? "What are you implying?"

William stepped between us. "Now, now, ladies. No need to get upset. Gladys, I'd be happy to show you your portrait. It's gorgeous. Although it doesn't hold a candle to the real thing. Alex, thank you so much again for your hard work. I'll be in touch."

Gladys and I glared at each other over his shoulder. I figured getting into a fistfight with an old lady wouldn't be a good start for my family photography business, so I let it go. I didn't like her insulting my nana, but I was pretty sure Nana K could handle her own.

As I was leaving, I heard her say, "Isn't there something you can do about her and her crazy nana? They are ruining the image of Aged Pines. I want them gone."

William gave me an "I'm sorry" glance as he shut the door between us.

CHAPTER 10

O N A WHIM, I stopped by William Remora's assistant's desk instead of leaving like I planned. I swear my feet propelled me there with very little forethought on my part. I guess the old saying, "You can take the girl out of Piney Ridge but not the Piney Ridge out of the girl" was true. Add in a healthy dose of my mother's gravitational pull toward gossip, it was no wonder my "stick my nose where it doesn't belong" DNA was back with a vengeance.

The woman seated behind the desk didn't glance up until I cleared my throat and dropped my bag onto her desk with a *thunk*.

"Can I help you?" she asked, smacking her gum and absently twirling a box-blonde curl around her finger. Maybe "woman" was a little generous; she looked like she just graduated high school.

"Yes"—I leaned forward to look at her name tag—"Tiffany Dawn. Thank you," I said in my most honey-laden voice despite my simmering anger over Gladys's rude comments about Nana K. "I'm the photographer for the Aged Pines yearbook."

"I remember you. I hope you edited out my acne. I had a terrible breakout that day," she said with an eyebrow raised. Her teal and blue eyeshadow reminded me of Nana K. If Nana wore the same style as a teenager, did that mean she was hipper than I was?

Oh, who was I kidding? Lash, my fish, was hipper than I was.

"Of course," I lied. I didn't do much retouching. In photojournalism we weren't really supposed to, so I'd never gotten into the habit. Also, on my list of fun Friday night activities, cloning out other people's individual zits was right up there with cleaning the bathroom. And if I wasn't taking the time to edit each resident's wrinkles, I wasn't going to do that for staff as well. There were way too many people at this facility, and individually removing blemishes would take until next year's photo shoot.

I smiled broadly at her without an ounce of regret for my decision.

"Great. What can I help you with?" She seemed much more eager to help me now.

"I overheard the director and Gladys talking about an upcoming activity. I wanted to get some more information about it. You know, for the yearbook."

Tiffany Dawn frowned at me. "Besides the usual stuff and the new memorial shuffleboard and tennis courts, I don't recall anything else coming up." She punched a few buttons on her computer. "Nope. Nothing that they seem to be planning together. Gladys isn't really a joiner, if you know what I mean. She comes to the events to people watch and judge, if you ask me."

"Don't we all?" I mumbled. In that way, Gladys and I were like peanut butter and marshmallows. People watching was literally my life for the last decade and a half. But I only judged a little. Hence the peanut butter and marshmallows, not jelly.

I sighed and picked up my purse. "Thanks for checking. I must have misheard."

She gave a little wave and went back to her magazine.

Before I could walk away, raised voices from William's office had us both leaning in to hear a little better. They were muffled, but I got the gist of it.

"I don't think you appreciate what I've done for you, Willy," Gladys shouted, her usually feeble voice carrying some bite.

"Keep your voice down, Gladys," William responded. "We don't know if Alex is still out there."

"I don't care who hears. I'm entitled to that money. I put more into this little venture than anyone else, and I deserve to be compensated," she said.

Tiffany Dawn and I shared a look. "The new tennis courts?" I asked.

She shrugged. "Who knows. That woman is in here every day screaming about what she's entitled to. I almost feel bad for Mr. Remora, but he doesn't do much to shut her down. Honestly, I think she's lonely. She doesn't get many visitors."

"That's kind of sad," I said.

I felt a little sorry for her until I heard her scream, "If I don't get my money by the end of the week, you'll be sorry, Willy. I didn't get this far in life by allowing people to railroad me."

"Be careful who you're threatening, Gladys. You'll get the cut you were promised and nothing more, like always."

I heard a bang, like Gladys hit her cane on the floor, hard. Her shadow lengthened.

"Shoot. They're coming," I said. "Thanks for your help." I gave Tiffany Dawn a little wave and scootched out of sight.

I hid around the corner to see if Gladys and William exited. I'd give it ten minutes, then I was leaving. Mainly because I had to use the bathroom.

In under eight, they both came out of his office and walked slowly down the hallway, their earlier fight seemingly forgotten. Maybe I'd left the reception area too soon? I should have stayed to eavesdrop some more. Too late now.

If he was escorting her all the way to the bungalows, that gave me ample time to snoop around his office. Yes, I was embracing my nosiness. For justice for Camilla, of course.

When the duo was out of sight, I made a show of searching through my purse as I reapproached the desk.

"Forget something?" Tiffany Dawn asked blandly.

"Actually, yes. I can't find my car keys. They may have fallen out of my purse in the office. Mind if I take a quick look?"

She barely lifted her head before waving a limp wrist at the open office door. "Be my guest. I'd say don't mess anything up, but, well, you've seen the place."

I laughed politely and tried not to run through the door in my anticipation. I pushed the door closed slightly behind me. Enough so anyone passing by couldn't see in, but not enough that I couldn't hear if someone was about to enter.

Primary target—the desk. Sure enough, the list in the folder contained the names of other Nayas up for a promotion. The C-wing needed a new head Naya. It came with a substantial pay raise and prestige. Another perk would be not dealing with Gladys or Dennis. At least in my opinion. But then again, I chose a profession where I didn't really have to talk to anyone, so take that with a shaker of salt.

Camilla was at the top of the list with the highest rating despite a column indicating some complaints. Mostly recent. Most from Gladys Wickerson. No surprise there. In fact, looking down the list, several Nayas had complaints from Gladys. None as much as Camilla, but Gladys's penchant for dissatisfaction was evident even here.

At least I no longer had to take her rebuffs of me personally. Gladys found displeasure in pretty much everything.

A woman named Maura Reilly was second to Camilla on the list. A close second. I tried to remember Maura from the portrait shoot. A robust woman, a few years older and about half a foot taller than me, came to mind. I shot her helping to feed a resident in the nursing-home wing of the retirement center. That wing was more like hospice care for those needing help with even basic daily activities like dressing and eating and showering. I could see how being a Naya assigned to that wing could be both rewarding and taxing on the psyche. She had to encounter a lot more death than in other wards.

Was that enough to desensitize her to it? Was she willing to kill to get off that ward?

A shiver ran down my spine as another question crossed my mind. What if Maura was next? If the murderer was someone further down the list, then I'd potentially stumbled upon a kill list. Especially if the candidates had already been told the outcome. I snapped a quick picture of the names with my cell phone and tucked it back under the folder. Thank goodness Director Remora was equivalent to a thirteen-year-old girl in terms of housekeeping. He'd never realize if anything was moved slightly.

I turned my attention to the box marked with Camilla's name. Not a large box by any means. Apparently Nayas didn't keep a lot of personal items at work. Did William mention a locker? I couldn't remember.

I carefully shifted through the items in the box. Deodorant, partially used. Extra shirt and shorts in a plastic ziplock. A few pictures of her and a handsome young man I assumed was her husband. A handful of hair ties. Feminine hygiene supplies. Typical, boring, locker stuff.

Until I saw a small notebook that had fallen to the bottom of the box. A diary? Notes for a tell-all book about the retirement home? Doodles? I snatched it up and opened it.

None of the above. Page after page of what looked like checkbook entries. Columns with dates and dollar amounts filled about half the book. Some dollar amounts had plus signs, most had minus signs. If this was an alternative checkbook ledger, the Marjadis were in some financial trouble.

And by some trouble, I meant a lot of trouble. The majority of these amounts had commas in them. My banking records were a list of piddly gas station runs and Scoops visits. We're talking two figures at most. I couldn't imagine what, besides monthly bills, ordinary Piney Ridge residents would be spending thousands of dollars on a few times a week. Which made me realize there were no notes beside the entries. No mention of what the amounts were for. Not even shorthand.

And why would she keep it at work?

Weird. I set the notebook on the desk to take some pictures. I was three pages in when William Remora's voice from the hallway snapped my head toward the door. With Tiffany Dawn's amazing conversational skills, I only had a matter of seconds. Mother of pearl, I was going to get caught.

After a moment of flapping my hands like Nugget, my adopted chicken, in a complete panic, I shoved the notebook into my purse and threw my car keys and myself under the desk, ignoring the pain in my knee as it slammed into the side of the desk. There was nothing I could do about Camilla's box being open except to say a prayer William didn't notice.

Just as William opened the door, I said, "Oh, there they are!"

"Is someone in here?" he asked.

I popped my head up from behind the desk, keys in hand. "I dropped my car keys earlier. Your assistant was kind enough to let me look."

"Okay," he said slowly. "I don't usually like to have people in my office without me here."

"So sorry. I'll be on my way. See you next week for the unveiling of the memorial." I sidestepped around him and shut the door behind me before he could ask more questions.

"Found them," I said to Tiffany Dawn.

She slowly blinked her eyes at me and gave a half smile. "Great."

"Hey. I need to follow up with Maura Reilly for the yearbook. Do you know where I can find her?"

Tiffany Dawn sighed loudly and unlocked her computer screen. She clicked through a few screens and said, "She's still on shift. Hospice Ward. You know where that is?"

"I can find it. Thanks for all your help," I said. Jeez, my voice sounded like a cheesy telemarketer trying to sell a cruise, all high pitched and crazy fake happy. Before I could add a "Have a super day now, you hear?" I turned on my heel and headed for where I thought the Hospice Wing was located.

"Sure," Tiffany Dawn said to my retreating back.

CHAPTER 11

OR ONCE THE COSMIC universe was on my side as I hobbled my way in the correct direction toward the Hospice Wing. Although my poor knee was absolutely going to bruise from where I'd smacked it during my desk dive, I found Maura Reilly right as she was ending her shift. As we passed in the hallway, I caught a glimpse of her name tag to confirm and stopped her.

"Maura?" I asked.

She stopped and turned with a fake smile, probably assuming I was a lost guest in need of directions. When she focused on my face, her smile broadened, making her small eyes slit to the point that I couldn't even tell what color they were.

"You're the photographer, right?" she asked. Then her smile fell, and her hand fluttered to her neck. "You're the one who found Camilla."

"That's right. Alex Lightwood. Such a tragedy about Camilla. Did you know her well?" I asked. I'd planned on easing into talking about Camilla, but Maura had opened the door, and I was walking through it invitation or not.

"We worked together. I saw her mostly in passing. It's a big place," Maura said evasively.

"Of course. You know, I was actually coming to find you," I said.

"Me?"

"Yeah. Director Remora mentioned you were being considered for a promotion. I thought that might be an interesting angle for a page in the yearbook. Do you have a minute to talk?"

"I'm going off shift," she started.

"This will only take a minute. I can follow you to the break room," I suggested before she could finish her protest.

She hesitated another moment, so I channeled my inner telemarketer again and smiled like I had Vaseline on my teeth.

"I guess that would be okay," she said. I followed her down the hallway.

"So, tell me about the promotion," I prompted as we walked. She reiterated what I already knew from the form in William's office.

"Was there a lot of competition for that spot?" I asked.

She shrugged. "I think there were a few of us that put in for it. No more than usual when a transfer opportunity arises."

"Director Remora hasn't made the final decision yet?" We turned into the empty break room. Maura shut the door behind us.

"Not yet. And before you ask, yes, Camilla was on the list of candidates. Tiffany Dawn let it slip that she and I were at the top of the list."

"I guess now you are the only one still up there," I said, looking around the room to hopefully keep the tone conversational and not accusatory.

"I guess. Although with all the recent complaints against Camilla, I'm sure I was edging her out anyway. She may have had more seniority, but I have better bedside manner. And I know for a fact, William didn't especially like her," she said, moving toward her locker.

"Really? Why is that?"

She shrugged. "I heard from a few other Nayas that they had a small but angry altercation the other day. Everyone believes the fight had to do with Camilla's fall out with Gladys Wickerson. William is never happy when he has to deal with conflict. He'd rather everything be painted in sunshine and rainbows."

"Rainbows? Not brown?" I asked with a smile. Maura snickered as she reached into her locker for her coat.

A few doors down from hers was a locker covered in letters and pictures and Post-its. I gravitated toward it and read the kind words Camilla's coworkers had left for her. Instinctively, I pulled my camera out and snapped a few pictures—full length and close-ups. This would be perfect for the memorial page.

When I finished, Maura was leaning against her own locker watching me. She'd put her coat on, unzippered, over her fall-themed scrubs. I'd noticed some of the Nayas wore scrubs, while others wore the work-issued Aged Pines polo shirts. I would imagine working in the Hospice Ward meant more chances of getting messy. Nana K did say Aged Pines wanted to give the impression the Nayas weren't nurses whenever possible. Could not wearing scrubs be another selling point to getting the promotion?

"Amazing how many friends you have after death," Maura commented.

I cocked my head at her. "Meaning?"

She pushed off the lockers and flicked a card taped to Camilla's. "Half these people didn't even know her. Camilla mostly kept to herself. She was a bit standoffish and quiet. You know, did her job and went home. She wasn't here to be bosom buddies with anyone."

"And that's a problem?" I asked. Sounded pretty perfect to me.

"Not especially. But everyone usually has one person at work they commiserate with, you know? Especially dealing with some of the personalities we have here. Camilla didn't seem interested." She opened and closed another card on the locker. "Most of these people simply want to insert themselves into the narrative in some small way."

I nodded. "What do *you* think happened to her?"

"Who knows? William is pushing the accident angle pretty hard. Most likely for PR reasons than anything else. He doesn't want an elderly riot or a mass exodus of employees on his hands."

"I don't know if I buy that." I paused a moment, pretending I'd just thought of something. "If people know about the promotion, you and everyone else on the list could be a suspect."

"Me?" She looked genuinely surprised. "Why me?"

"People have killed over job security before," I pointed out.

She scoffed. "Not here. The turnover rate among Nayas is really high. Camilla had seniority over most of us, and she'd only been here for two years. If I didn't get this promotion, another one would come along soon enough. Mainly I just want off Hospice Ward. Even if Camilla somehow got the promotion despite the complaints against her, I could have taken her spot."

"But without the raise," I pointed out. I wasn't sure what the pay scale was at Aged Pines, but promotion usually implied a raise where a lateral move did not.

"The raise was minimal. In case you don't know, retirement community staff aren't rolling in the dough, no matter how many promotions you get. Most of us request transfers for a change of scenery or if we clash with the residents. Kind of like Camilla and Gladys."

"How did you know about the complaints between them?" I asked. "Aren't staff files confidential?"

She gave a rueful laugh. "The files, yes. But the rumor mill never shuts off. Gladys Wickerson has no filter when it comes to her displeasure. I'm not even assigned to her bungalow group, but I knew all about the bad blood between her and Camilla."

"What happened between them?" I asked, genuinely curious.

She leaned in conspiratorially. "It started with the cat. Apparently, Camilla was allergic and refused to brush it or whatever. She allegedly called it a stupid hairball with a brain the size of a pea."

"To Gladys's face? That's brazen," I said.

"Right? I mean residents aren't even supposed to have pets. Camilla knew this and wanted the blasted thing gone. She was royally pissed that Gladys got her way and demanded to be moved to a different ward. Now, keep in mind, this is all what I've heard from other Nayas and residents." She sighed and slung her purse over her shoulder. "Honestly, I don't know how much I believe, since, like I said, Camilla always seemed a little like a rat in a rainstorm to me." Maura shrugged again. "But then again, I didn't know her that well. And Gladys doesn't really engender tenderness."

"Very true. Was that why Camilla was transferred? Because of Gladys's complaints?"

"According to Gladys, yes. William let Gladys believe Camilla had been demoted, but it was more of a lateral move. To keep the peace."

That tracked with what William had told me earlier.

"Makes sense."

"Listen, I gotta get going. My kid is waiting for me at daycare. Was there anything else you needed to know for the yearbook?" she asked, hitching a thumb toward the door.

"Is there anyone else on the list of candidates that really needed the job? Anyone else that would be frustrated by the competition?"

To Maura's credit, she did consider it for a minute before answering. "Not that I can think of. Like I said, another job would come along sooner rather than later. I haven't heard anyone desperate enough to kill for it."

"If I were you, I'd keep someone you trust on your six," I said. "You never know."

She laughed lightly. "You just said I could be a suspect. Now you're saying I could be the next victim?"

"Again, people have killed for less. I heard about a guy who killed his sister because she wouldn't give him the WiFi password. For all we know that promotion list is a kill list."

She shuddered. "Well, on that happy thought, I'm going to go hug my kids extra tight tonight."

I winced. "Sorry. Thank you so much for your time. Sorry again for your loss," I said, following her to the door.

"Like I said, I didn't know her that well. I'm not sure anyone really did."

We went our separate ways in the hallway. Well, there went one theory. The promotion wasn't the cutthroat contest I'd envisioned. If Maura was telling the truth, that is. Her body language read relaxed and honest though.

I didn't discount the kill-list theory completely, but it went to the bottom of the list.

If I hadn't seen Gladys hobbling around with her cane the last few days, she'd be at the top of my suspect list. But I couldn't really imagine a feeble, old lady overtaking a spry, young woman like Camilla. I needed to talk to someone who knew these people better, who knew if they could be lying or not. My obvious choices were Linc and Colleen. They'd lived in Piney Ridge all their lives and knew the people and their personalities better than anyone. I hoped Maura also lived in Piney Ridge and didn't commute here from Mapleton or one of the other surrounding equally small towns. That would be the only way to see if Linc or Colleen knew her and whether she could be trusted.

CHAPTER 12

I TAPPED MY SPOON on the linoleum tabletop at Plum Crazy diner while I waited for Linc to end his shift at the fire station. Colleen was busy, although she wouldn't tell us with what, so she couldn't round out our usual trio, but I promised her I'd fill her in. I checked my phone again. What was taking him so long? The more I thought about Camilla's death, the more I was convinced it wasn't an accident. I really needed to bounce my ideas off someone else.

My phone vibrated with an incoming text. It better not be Linc backing out too, otherwise I might break down and make Peggy Sue, the long-time Plum Crazy waitress, listen to my theories. I breathed a sigh of relief when I saw it was Colleen:

Colleen: Have fun on your date!

Me: Not a date. A business meeting.

Colleen: Totally a date. Make him pay for your milkshake

Me: Goodbye

Colleen: You better kiss and tell

Me: Not. A. Date.

Linc sure had plenty of opportunities to officially ask me on a date or to kiss me since I'd been back. Not counting that time in my kitchen after he gave me the table, he hadn't acted on any of them. My novelty had worn off. I was now old news. No one wants to date a clumsy, unemployed head case.

Not that I even wanted to date right now. After my crash and burn with Rick, I was totally enjoying some independent, single lady time. I turned the interrogation to Colleen. Why wouldn't she tell us where she was?

Me: Where are you anyway?

Colleen: Tell you later

Me: Why are you being so evasive?

Colleen: Goodbye

I let it go when Linc slid into the booth across from me, his signature half smile on his tanned face. He leaned his elbows on the table, which accentuated his ripped biceps. I always thought of myself as more of an abs gal, but Linc was quickly making me a convert. I took a long sip of my milkshake to calm the heat rising up my neck and reminded myself about the single lady time.

"What's up? You sounded breathless on the phone," he said.

"You don't think Camilla Marjadi's death was an accident any more than I do, right?" I asked.

He shook his head. "I suppose it's possible but highly unlikely."

"I'm glad you agree. I have a theory, but I need more proof. Tell me about her wounds."

He pursed his lips. "You aren't about to get involved in this, are you?"

"I'm already involved! I found her, in case you forgot."

"I didn't forget. At least not the way you smelled after coming out of that well," he teased.

"You went down the well too," I reminded him.

"Don't remind me. I had to throw those shoes away. Not even worth trying to get that stench and debris off."

Peggy Sue wandered over to take Linc's order. "You want the usual?" she asked, snapping her gum. She was only person my mother's age that I knew who still chewed gum. She also wore her long salt-and-pepper hair in a high ponytail and occasionally donned some purple eyeshadow to match the apron she wore as part of her uniform. She'd been taking our orders in this same booth since we were in middle school. Linc, ever reliable, rarely ordered anything different than "his usual."

Linc said, "You know it. Add a second order of seasoned fries."

"Feeling hungry tonight?" Peggy Sue asked.

He looked and me and smiled. "Nope. I know Alex is going to steal most of the ones off my plate."

I scoffed. "You don't know that."

Peggy Sue laughed. "Honey, even *I* know that. I'll throw a couple extra on there for you." She patted Linc's arm.

When she left, I asked, "The wounds?"

He sighed. "The only reason I'm telling you is because I know you'll figure out some other way to find out anyway."

I shifted in the booth, lifting my thighs one at a time off the sticky plastic seats to lean forward. "You betcha."

"Okay. Obviously, we have to wait for the official autopsy results and tox screen. We also don't know that much about Camilla or her background —"

"Get to the point, Linc. I know all that stuff."

He chuckled. "You're like a dog with a bone."

"Woof. Woof. Give me the details before I bite you," I said. Then cringed inside. Comparing myself to a dog probably wasn't moving the needle toward "date me."

He sighed and shook his head. "Besides the typical wounds you'd expect —a few scrapes and scratches, some insect activity—she also had a contusion on the back of her head."

I tried not to look too excited. It was awful, sure, but it definitely leaned the investigation away from accidental death and toward murder by person or persons unknown.

I asked, "Any guesses what caused it?"

He shook his head. "Wasn't shaped like anything I'd ever seen before. Then again, I haven't seen that many head wounds. Not fatal ones anyway."

"Okay, don't poo-poo my theories until you've heard me all the way through," I said. I pushed my milkshake aside, so I didn't knock it over with my flailing hands. It had happened before. More than once. Okay, almost every time we came here. But I'm learning my lesson.

Peggy Sue brought our plates then. She set the extra plate of fries and a huge stack of napkins in the middle, with a wink for Linc. I was determined not to take any just to show him. The mozzarella sticks I ordered were plenty.

"You were saying," he prompted when Peggy Sue walked away to check on another table.

"I swear most of this information I came across organically by being in the right place at the right time," I said. "With only minimal snooping."

"Define minimal," he said, trying to hide his smile. I threw one of his extra fries at him. Annoyingly, he caught it easily and put it in his mouth.

"I have a few theories of who could have killed her, but I need a Piney Ridger's take on the people and motives," I explained.

He dressed his burger with extra ketchup and mustard from the table and added a few of the seasoned fries on top. Seriously, how did he stay so fit eating like that? Simply looking at the dang thing added inches to my thighs. He lifted the burger, but before taking a bite, said, "How long before you realize you are a Piney Ridger yourself?"

I shrugged and dipped a mozzarella stick into the marinara sauce. That was the million-dollar question. Even with a potential photography business, I wasn't sure how long I would stay before wanderlust took over.

"That's not what I meant. I meant someone who's been here awhile and knows all the players. I've been away too long and don't know who could potentially be lying."

"And that's where I come in," he said after swallowing his bite. I nodded. "Well, hit me with your list of suspects."

"Okay, but don't get your panties in a twist if someone you know really well is on the list. This is all speculation."

He frowned at me. "First of all, men don't wear panties. Second of all, no promises. But I'll try to keep an open mind."

"Thanks. First on the very short list is Maura Reilly. I spoke with her today at Aged Pines actually," I said. I filled him in on our conversation and the promotions list.

He munched a fry and considered. "I don't know Maura that well. Colleen might actually be better to ask since Maura's kids recently went to preschool where she works. But from what I know, she's never been violent in her life. You can probably believe what she says. I know for a fact that the turnover rate among Nayas there is pretty high. We sometimes get applications from people who want out."

"Rats," I said. "But lines up with my take on her too. She seemed sincere when I spoke with her." One suspect down. I opened the picture of the promotions list on my phone and shoved it across the table to Linc.

"Anyone else on the list jump out at you as a possible murderer?" I asked.

Before even looking at the list, he said, "Most people who become nurses are caring and nurturing and gentle. They take an oath to help people, not hurt them."

"I know. But then you have a few Angel of Death types in the mix," I reminded him.

"True, but don't they usually go after patients and not fellow nurses?"

I tapped the phone screen so it didn't go black. "Just look at the list, please."

He did then shook his head. "Some of these names I don't recognize, but the ones I do don't seem capable of murder. And the further down the list you go, the more unlikely it is. If number twelve wanted to be seriously considered for a promotion, that's a lot of bodies she'd have to explain."

I sighed. "I guess you're right."

"Who's next on your list?" he asked. I appreciated he was taking this seriously and not telling me to butt out like he usually did.

"Director William Remora," I said. "He's low on the list but still there. Maura said she overheard them having a fight the other day. And he goes out of his way to protect Gladys Wickerson, with whom Camilla also had issues."

He pointed to the promotions list. "Why would William Remora consider Camilla for a promotion if he didn't like her to the point of killing her?"

I scrunched up my nose. "Fair point. But he was delaying making a decision about the promotion. Maybe Camilla's aggression toward Gladys and their fight was giving him second thoughts about awarding it to her."

"And he killed her because of it?" he asked, skeptical.

"I don't know. People have killed for less, right?" I said. "It's a working theory not a call for his arrest. I'll put a pin in that one and come back to it."

"Good idea. Anyone else? Aren't you forgetting the most likely person?"

"Her husband," we said in unison.

"Aww, you do listen when Colleen and I ramble on about true crime," I patted his hand across the table and pretended the physical contact didn't send a zing through my system.

"Hard not to since it somehow manages to come up in every conversation," he teased.

I ignored him. "Shane Marjadi. I don't know very much about him at all. Although it is curious that he didn't report her missing. You said there was insect activity?"

He nodded. "I would guess she'd been down there a day or two before you found her, but I'm no expert."

"So why didn't he report her missing?"

"Why would he kill her at Aged Pines?" Linc countered. "Seems an unlikely place since he had no ties there beyond her."

"The wishing well is very close to the main parking lot, though," I pointed out. "Maybe he was going to pick her up and they got in a fight."

"I guess it's possible."

"I need to find out more about him. I'll bet someone at the book club will know. We'll have to somehow bring it up in conversation tomorrow night," I said. I pointed a finger at him. "You are still coming to the book club, right?"

He sighed and pushed a fry around in his ketchup. "I guess so."

"Did you actually read the book?"

"Did you?"

We held eye contact, then laughed. "I skimmed it," I admitted. "And watched one of the movie versions."

"Same." We smiled at each other a moment. It was almost like when we were little and were conspirators in any number of naughty childhood misadventures. Although now a small undercurrent of tension seemed to lace all our interactions. That could be completely one sided on my part though. In fact, I was pretty sure it was. I never saw Linc's Hollywood handsome face blush the color of a tomato when we touched.

He cleared his throat and broke eye contact. "Anyone else on the suspect list?"

"Okay, hear me out before you nix this one. It's a little out there. One of the residents at Aged Pines, a Gladys Wickerson, has means, motive, and opportunity."

Linc leaned back in his seat. "Oh, this I gotta hear."

In between bites of my gooey mozzarella sticks—totally worth the extra calories, in my opinion—I told him more about the contention between Gladys and Camilla, Gladys's "my way or the highway" personality, and how she seemed to have William Remora wrapped around her finger.

When I finished, and he didn't immediately respond, I asked, "Well? What do you think?"

He looked at the table, then back up at me, swallowing his last bite of burger before speaking. "I think... you ate all my extra fries."

"I did no—" I started, then looked at the plate. Sure enough, only crumbs remained. I snapped my eyes back to his which were full of amusement. "It's your fault for leaving the plate in front of me."

"Sure. We'll go with that."

"Never mind about the fries. What about my theory?" I asked again.

He sipped his soda, mainly to annoy me. "How old is Gladys again?"

"In her seventies."

"And she uses a cane to get around?" he asked.

"Yup." I gauged his expression. He wasn't buying my theory. "You don't believe me."

"It isn't a matter of believing you. Your theory is plausible. Only, it's hard to picture an elderly, cane-using, fragile woman overtaking a healthy, able-bodied thirtysomething. And how would Gladys get her body to the well? Much less stuff it into the crevice?"

My righteous balloon deflated a little. "I didn't think of that last part. But, if Nana K could get me over the well, then I'm sure Gladys could as well. Maybe she lured Camilla there, surprised her by hitting her over the head, and then let the body fall down there."

"The crevice?" he reminded me.

I tapped my lip with my straw. "Let me think. Let me think. Oh! What if she had help?"

"Help from whom? Who is in on this little conspiracy theory you have going on in your head?"

I went to throw another fry at him, but remembered they were gone. I settled on sticking out my tongue. In a totally mature kind of way. Not at all like a toddler. "I don't know. Maybe Maura Reilly. They were in it together so Maura could get the promotion after all. The old 'You scratch my back, and I'll scratch yours' routine. They both benefit from having Camilla out of the way."

"I'd buy Maura, someone much closer to Camilla's age, being the culprit much more than a resident. However, you just told me Maura seemed sincere when she told you the promotion wasn't that big of a deal," Linc reminded me.

I frowned. Wreck-it Rick aside, I usually was a fairly good judge of character. Or at least emotion. After photographing raw human emotions for most of my life, I'd come to recognize when people were faking it. Usually. Maura could be a really good liar.

"Okay, what about William Remora? He seemed pretty keen to jump on the 'It's only an accident' theory. Maybe he helped Gladys to keep everything all hush hush. Apparently, he has a lot of new donors helping fund the retirement community updates. Something like a murder could cause donors to pull their funding."

Linc sighed heavily. "Let me get this straight. Your theory is that a seventy-year-old woman who can't even walk without a cane killed a healthy, young nurse, shoved her down a well, and then convinced the director to help her cover it up. He, what... got a ladder, climbed down into the well in his brown suit, pushed the body out of sight, with no one else seeing either of them?"

"Stranger things have happened," I mumbled. When he put it like that, it did sound sort of far-fetched. Sort of.

"Alex, I know Piney Ridge isn't as exciting as New York, but you don't have to invent problems where there aren't any."

"Even you said it wasn't an accident!" I reminded him.

"Maybe so. But I'm not going around seeing murder in old ladies' eyes. Trust the police to do their job. We managed fine before you crashed back into town."

I gaped at him. "First of all, the police didn't do such a bang-up job last time, if you recall. And second, I guess I see where I stand. Maybe it would be better if I went back to New York since, clearly, I don't have what it takes to be a Piney Ridger after all."

"No, Alex. That isn't what I meant." He tried to grab my wrist as I stood, but I yanked it away. He stood and blocked my path to the door which wasn't hard to do with his six-foot-frame compared to my five-foot-three-and-a-half (the half was important). "Stop."

I glared up at him. "No. It's fine. Apparently Piney Ridge is better off without me meddling in the affairs of others."

He brushed a piece of hair out of my face. "Alex, I'm sorry. I—"

He was cut off by someone clearing their throat loudly behind him. I peeked around him as he turned. Rodney Martingale stood there, hands on hips, and a scowl on his face.

"This guy bothering you, Alex?" he said gruffly, not taking his eyes off Linc. Linc had him beat by a few inches, but what Rod lacked in height, he made up for in roughness.

"No," I said. "Just a misunderstanding."

Linc looked back at me. "You know this guy?"

"Rodney Martingale meet Lincoln Livestrong. Rod is the grandson of Dennis Martingale from the retirement community. We met the other day when I was making Dennis's portrait for the yearbook. Linc is the town fire captain, EMT, and perpetual pain in my butt," I explained.

"I could make him not be, if you'd like," Rod offered, still staring daggers at Linc. The word "enforcer" from Rod's business card jumped to mind. Was he a bodyguard or bouncer or something?

"I can handle him," I said. Linc raised his eyebrow at me. "Thanks, though, Rod."

Rod finally looked at me, and his face softened into a smile. "You let me know. Not a hesitation for you, sweetheart." Before I could react, he took my hand and pulled me around Linc to his side. "You know, I could afford to take you to a much nicer joint than this. We could ride in my Miata. Top down, music up."

I pushed on his chest and took a step back. "I chose this restaurant actually. I rather like it here," I explained. "But I'm actually on my way out."

Linc put a protective hand on my shoulder. "I'll walk you out." He gave me a gentle shove to start me moving. I felt like a Ping Pong ball being shoved between the two alpha-male egos.

"Call me, sweetheart," Rod called to our retreating backs.

Linc didn't say a word until we reached the parking lot. "I don't like that guy."

"You don't have to," I said. His eyes were dark again, the amusement from earlier gone.

"You can do so much better than him," he said, running a hand through his hair.

"Who says I'm interested?" I asked. "Besides, like Colleen pointed out, there aren't a ton of options if I wanted to date. The number of single guys who we didn't share a lunchroom with in middle school is rather thin."

"What's wrong with someone you went to middle school with?"

I shrugged and opened my car door. "I guess the same thing that's wrong with someone who crashes back into everyone's business. Neither of which will be a problem when I move back to New York."

I shut the door before he could respond. His comment hurt me. Of anyone, I'd hoped that Linc would believe my theory. Or at least agree that it was possible. Instead, he basically told me I was a nutcase with no value in this town. Fine. I'd do it on my own.

In the meantime, I had to push thoughts of frustrating firefighters and unexplained death aside to make room for more important matters. Namely how to host a book club.

CHAPTER 13

"**P**EANUT, PUT THE CHIPS and dip in the middle and the hot dishes on the counter," my mother instructed. "People like to nibble on the finger snacks while we discuss the book."

Mom had been "helping" me get ready for the Shelf Indulgence book club meeting since three o'clock that afternoon. It was now six. Luckily, the other members should be arriving shortly. She fiddled with this and moved that and rearranged those. I mainly sat at the beautiful hand-carved table that was the centerpiece of my studio space. Even though it had been months since Linc surprised me with it, I still got little goose bumps when I looked at it. He'd made this. For me. I ran my fingers along the textured, unfinished edges, traced the lines of the wood on top. The day he gave this to me we almost kissed. I was sure of it. I'd replayed that moment in my mind so many times since that day. If only Colleen hadn't interrupted us. When I told her about it later, she gushed apologies and assured me he would absolutely try again.

She was wrong. We were back to Linc and Alex—friends who tolerated each other because they live in a small town and have a weird history. Okay, that didn't have quite an easy ring to it, but it was true. In fact, we were fighting right now. At least it felt like a fight.

My mind kept wandering back to the conversation with Linc at the diner. Were we in a fight? Was I overreacting to his comment?

If I had to ask, the answer was yes. Clearly, I was overthinking everything with Linc lately. If he showed today, which was a big if, considering our parting words last night, I'd have to apologize.

I sighed and watched my mother move a casserole dish a fraction of an inch on the counter. "Wouldn't it have been easier to host at your place?" I asked. My mother brought practically her entire kitchen and pantry over. It took us three trips to get everything from the car up to my loft.

She waved her hand in dismissal. "Of course not. This gorgeous table is screaming for company. Wait until LuAnne gets a peek at it. She'll turn green with envy."

I put yet another basket of chips in the center of the table. Mom put small decorative bowls of different dips around it. I moved the queso dip closer to my seat.

One by one, the book club members started to arrive. Mom fussed over them, taking coats and purses and throwing them unceremoniously on my bed. She gave everyone a brief tour, explaining how Linc had helped the Bachmans renovate the space. The tour always ended with the coup de grâce: the table. I hovered in the kitchen, handing out plates, taking compliments, and cursing Linc for being late. He'd better not wimp out on me.

Colleen sauntered through the door with a plate of brownies. She looked around at the gaggle of ladies hovering around the hot dishes.

"Where's Linc?" she asked, handing me the plate.

"Your guess is as good as mine. But if he bails, he's in big trouble," I said.

"He won't bail on you," she said.

"I wouldn't be so sure. We kind of had a fight the last time we talked," I admitted.

"I leave you two alone for one night and you fight? That wasn't the plan," she mumbled.

"What plan?" I asked, narrowing my eyes as we moved shoulder to shoulder to an empty end of the counter, hopefully out of earshot of the gossiping older women.

"Did I say plan? I meant that I had a ton to do," she backpedaled. I was having none of it.

I gripped her arm. "You said plan. You get none of LuAnne's famous meatballs until you spill."

She sighed. "Fine. I wasn't really busy, but I thought if you two had some actual time alone, Linc would finally ask you out."

"Well, he didn't. Instead, he told me to butt out of Piney Ridge business and that everyone was better off without me." I grabbed a plate and heaped some meatballs on it.

"He did not," she said. "I'm sure you misunderstood."

"Not likely. But that's why he's totally going to bail tonight."

She took me by the shoulders. "Trust me. I'm so confident he'll be here, let's bet. I bet you a dollar he'll walk through that door right on time."

I held out my hand. "Deal. One dollar and bragging rights."

With a minute to spare, and everyone else already seated with their plates full, Linc finally made his entrance. All eyes swiveled to him as he walked down the narrow hallway of the loft toward the kitchen. Colleen held out her hand. I slapped a dollar into it. LuAnne literally broke into applause.

"Lincoln Livestrong," she said, rising from her chair to give his arm a squeeze. "You really outdid yourself with this table. Can I order one? Alex here won't sell me this one."

He smiled and patted her hand. "This might be a one-of-a-kind custom piece. It's hard to find rough wood like this."

A little pang hit me in the chest. He'd gone to more trouble to make this for me than I originally thought. He flicked his eyes to me in a question. I gave him a small smile which he returned. One small step toward forgiveness.

"Fiddlesticks," LuAnne said. "It reminds me of those fancy house designs you see on HGTV. If you ever do make another one, I get first dibs."

"I'll make a note of it," Linc said.

"Grab some food first before these vultures eat it all," I said.

His polite smile morphed into a teasing smirk. "I'm sure your bottomless pit had nothing to do with the depleting chips and dip."

I shoved another queso-laden tortilla into my mouth and shook my head. "Not at all," I mumbled.

He filled a plate and sat beside me. I swear he purposely pressed his thigh against mine. Since the table was so crowded, I had no choice but to leave mine pressed against his. That was my truth, and I was sticking to it.

"Alex, I'm so sorry for what I said at the diner," he said, looking at me from under his unnervingly long lashes. "I didn't mean it the way it came out. We all missed you during your time away. I missed you."

Another little flutter in my chest. "I'm sorry too. I may have overreacted a little."

He smiled and bumped his leg against mine. "So, we're okay?"

"Of course. As long as you don't try to take any of my queso," I teased.

When most of us had finished eating, my mother pulled out her copy of *Emma*, signaling a switch to book talk. She said, "What did we think of Emma? The character, not the entire book."

Victoria Munhouse, who I remembered from the one Ladies Auxiliary luncheon I went to, said, "I rather liked her. She was punchy and genuinely wanted to help her friends find love."

"Really? I thought she was kind of a meddling busybody," Nana K said. "No one asked for her help, and half the time she got it wrong."

"But her heart was in the right place," LuAnne said. She placed a hand on her chest. "She was a hopeless romantic."

"Except when it came to herself. She couldn't even see what was right in front of her face," Mom said. "Did you notice that, Alex?"

I lowered the chip that was on its way to my mouth. "You mean the whole Frank Churchill and Jane Fairfax engagement? I guess sometimes it's easier to look from the outside in."

Mom, about as subtle as a toddler screaming for a cookie, looked pointedly between me and Linc. I blinked at her. Linc cleared his throat.

"I meant her and Mr. Knightly. They'd been friends forever and clearly a great match right from the start. They were blinded to the possibility because of friendship," she added. "Linc, what's your male perspective?"

He choked on a cookie. He avoided answering for a moment by taking a long sip of his drink. "I think Mr. Knightly was equally as guilty of avoiding the inevitable as Emma. He criticized her so often because the alternative was to flirt or at least acknowledge his growing feelings."

"Yes, yes. That's exactly right," Victoria said. "Like when little boys pull the hair of little girls on the playground."

Linc nodded and nudged my leg under the table. "Or throw them into the neighbor's backyard fishpond."

I pursed my lips and narrowed my eyes at him. He'd done that exact same thing to me when we were younger.

To the group, I said, "Clearly, Mr. Knightly wanted Emma to be her best self. He had this image of perfection and scolded her when she didn't meet it. He only realized he loved her when he accepted her for who she was."

"Why do we do that as humans? Fail to embrace what we know to be true in our hearts?" Mom asked. Then she laughed, "I guess some people need an extra nudge in the right direction."

"Like Emma's friend Harriet," I said, looking across the table at Colleen.

"I think some people need time to find their one true love on their own," Betty Turngood commented. "Genuine connections are often better than forced encounters."

"Amen to that," I said, thinking of Rick. We'd basically gravitated toward each other because of forced proximity. We worked together on location a lot, were about the same age, had similar interests. It was a no-brainer. At first.

"Stop thinking of Rick," Colleen scolded. "We aren't mentioning him anymore, right? He's like a blackout blip in your dating timeline."

"Oh, I need to hear this story," Betty said, leaning forward on the table with her elbows.

"Another time," Mom said. "We're supposed to be talking about *Emma*."

LuAnne, rising to refill her beverage, said, "I'd rather talk about Camilla Marjadi. What can you tell us, Alex?"

I shrugged. "I didn't know her. My only connection was finding her."

"Do you think it was an accident?" Betty asked.

Before I could answer, Mom said, "If it wasn't an accident, I'd put my money on Shane, her husband."

"Her husband?" I asked. "Why him?"

All the ladies began talking at once. Mom shushed them with a flap of her hand. "Let Betty tell it. She works at the bank."

We all looked at Betty. She cleared her throat as though about to give a grand speech. "Well, from what I could tell, they were in a bit of a pickle with their finances. Money troubles is the one thing that can really bring down a relationship fast."

"What sort of money trouble?" I asked.

"Now, I can't say too much what with banker-bankee privilege—" Betty started.

"That's not an actual thing," I said.

"But from what I could tell, they were spread a little thin," she finished. "Camilla had several loans in her name, and the couple had taken out a second mortgage recently."

I remembered the little notebook I'd... borrowed from Camilla's personal effects. The lack of positive entries coincided with this revelation of their financial troubles. The husband was usually the prime suspect. Although, generally, it was because of infidelity, not money.

"What could they be spending so much money on?" I asked.

Theories abounded from the table.

"High-end shoes."

"Fancy jewelry and mink coats."

"Drugs?"

"Real estate ventures gone wrong."

"Maybe she got caught up in a Nigerian-prince scheme over email," Nana K suggested. "That happened to Velma at Aged Pines. She gave away most of her life savings before realizing she wasn't getting any of it back."

The ladies nodded. "Absolutely. Those scammers are getting worse every day," Victoria confirmed. "I blocked so many numbers from people offering to renew my auto warranty. Our car isn't even in my name!"

"Why do we assume she is the issue?" I asked. "Couldn't Shane have been the one overspending?"

"Very true. He does have a lot of car parts lying around his garage," Colleen said. "We could have a case of hobbies gone wrong."

Linc cleared his throat again. "Listen, ladies. This may be an unpopular opinion, but I don't think a little financial hiccup equates immediately to murder. This is still Piney Ridge we're talking about."

More nods from the table. Mom got up to grab the pitcher of water to refill everyone's drinks.

"I always thought Shane married a little below his station," Victoria said. "I know that sounds snobby, but Shane's family comes from a long line of self-made Piney Ridgers. What do we really know about Camilla? He brought her home from college."

"You're getting too caught up in the class system from *Emma*," Betty said. "My mother, Mildred, who lives at Aged Pines, really liked Camilla. Mom said she was quiet but always very nice and accommodating."

"All I'm saying is that sometimes when people without money get a little taste of it, they can take it too far," Victoria clarified.

"Do we know Camilla didn't come from money?" Linc asked.

Everyone was quiet. Mom broke the silence. "Who invited you, Linc?" She laughed. "Here we like to speculate wildly. There's no room for logic at this table."

Everyone laughed.

"Let's get back to talking about *Emma.* I was so pleased with the ending. Jane Austen definitely writes a good slow burn," Colleen said, looking at me. "The back-and-forth between Emma and Mr. Knightly was perfectly done."

I tried to kick her under the table, but she was too far away. Clearly, my mother had chosen this book to try to nudge Linc and I together.

"Absolutely. The important part is that they finally got their heads out of their dupas long enough to give each other a chance," Nana K said.

Linc and I reached for a chip at the same time. Our fingers brushed in the bowl. I snatched my hand away like it was on fire. I didn't need another chip anyway.

"Sorry," he mumbled. "Didn't mean to cut in on your path to chip domination."

"It's fine. I'm done anyway."

He pushed the chips in front of me. "Don't lie. You still have queso left in that bowl."

He wasn't wrong. Leaving queso dip was a party foul and unacceptable. I had a civic duty to finish the bowl. To leave no scoop of melty salsa cheese uneaten.

"That's what I thought," he said when I scooped another chip into my mouth.

I shrugged. "It is my loft."

He looked around the space he helped build. "Who would have thought that I'd be creating this for you?"

"Small world."

"Some might call it fate," he said, holding my gaze.

Slowly, I became aware that the entire table was silent and hanging on our every word. I wrenched my eyes away from Linc's to scan the ladies. They had glazed smiles on their faces and hearts in their eyes.

I pushed back from the table. "Well, it's getting late. I have to get my fish to bed. Do we decide what to read next now? Or is there a vote or something?"

Mom blinked a few times as little cartoon hearts popped. "Usually the host picks the next book. Do you have one in mind, Peanut?"

"Anything by Steven King. How about *Misery*?" I suggested. Anything without a romance subplot sounded good to me.

"I'm all in on Mr. King," Nana K said, rubbing her hands together. "Something with a little pizazz."

"We'll talk about it," Mom said. "We'll help you clean up, Alex, then be out of your hair."

CHAPTER 14

I N A COMPLETE AND utter coincidence that had nothing at all to do
with what Betty told us about the Marjadis, I had to go to the bank the
day after the book club meeting. With a few photography clients under my
belt, I needed to set up an official business account. The fact that I hadn't
yet decided on a name wasn't a deterrent. It would come to me.

I hoped. I also hoped I might finagle some information about the
Marjadis out of the manager.

When I arrived at the old stone building in the middle of Main Street, the
teller instructed me to take a seat in the waiting area since the accounts
manager was in a meeting. This old brick building had housed the bank for
as long as I could remember. In elementary school, we'd taken a field trip
here to open our first accounts, a few dollars provided by our parents
sealed in carefully labeled sandwich baggies. Through our young eyes, the
bank looked so official and impressive and domineering. Even the pens
were chained to the counters. We could barely reach the tellers behind their
high counter to hand over our pennies. Most of us were on our very best
behavior since Johnny Atwell, whose mother worked at the bank, told us in
hushed tones that unruly bank customers were thrown into the vault never
to be heard from again. None of us really believed him until we got there
for the tour and all saw the big sign indicating where the vault was located.

Only two little boys had the audacity to even attempt naughtiness. I have a distinctive memory of a young Linc and his friend Donovan shoving the free lollipops into their pockets when the chaperones weren't looking. Of course, the rest of us didn't rat them out, since we hoped to cash in on their haul on the bus ride back to school.

I'd kept that same account open all this time, depositing a few hundred dollars or so into it from each assignment. And thank goodness, or I'd have been in even more dire straits when my photojournalist reputation took a dumpster dive earlier this year. When I moved back to Piney Ridge, after coming to terms with the fact that *Nature* magazine wasn't going to realize their error and beg me to return, I moved all my accounts here.

I settled into one of the hard wooden lobby chairs for a few rounds of my current favorite phone game while I waited for my turn, but raised voices from behind a closed office door arrested my attention. Sounded like whoever was in there wasn't happy with their current service.

It wasn't until I heard Gladys's name being thrown around that I completed abandoned my feckless attempt to play my game and gave in to eavesdropping. I couldn't tell much because the office door was closed, but it was a man and a woman. The man's voice was agitated, rising and falling with emotion. The woman sounded more placating and level.

Suddenly the door burst open, and a man about my age came storming out, ripping up a paper and saying words that I won't repeat. I recognized Shane Marjadi from the photo in Camilla's box of personal items.

"This is crap!" he shouted, littering the floor with the ripped pieces of paper. "There is no way Camilla would agree to give that witch anything. Not after she almost got her fired."

"Sir," the agitated bank manager called after him, "I can assure you I did the paperwork myself."

Shane ignored the woman scurrying after him and exited the bank. I grabbed my purse and followed to make sure he was okay. It was the neighborly thing to do. People shouldn't drive when they're that upset. If I gave myself a mental high five for running into Shane today, no one else needed to know. My plan consisted of asking a few questions about their financial troubles, but speaking to the grieving widow directly was even better.

I caught up to him in the parking lot where he was leaning against the roof of his car, shaking a little from the encounter in the bank.

"Mr. Marjadi?" I said quietly.

He lifted his head quickly, squinting at me from behind his sunglasses. "What now?"

"I'm Alex Lightwood. I photographed Camilla at Aged Pines. I wanted to offer my condolences."

His expression tightened, then softened. "Thank you. It's been quite a shock."

"I can only imagine. Would you like copies of the photographs I took? I can email them to you," I offered.

He nodded his head, dark brown hair falling over his eyes and ears. He looked like he hadn't shaved in a few days. "Yes. Yes, that'd be nice."

"I couldn't help overhearing the end of your conversation in the bank. I've met Gladys Wickerson, so I can fully commiserate with your frustration." I crossed my fingers behind my back. This could trigger him into shutting down completely. Or, hopefully, if he was still in his feels about it, he'd want a sympathetic ear to vent to.

He nodded. "That woman is a nightmare. She made Camilla's working conditions terrible. Camilla requested the transfer to get some peace from Gladys. Now these idiots"—he flung his hand toward the bank building —"are you trying to tell me Camilla took out a loan payable to Gladys. Like some sort of backward grandmother internet scam."

I thought back to Nana K's Nigerian prince theory. Was Gladys a con artist? "Could she have been blackmailing Camilla?" I asked.

He played with the metal accent on his car roof. "I don't know. I just don't know. Camilla said she transferred to get away from Gladys's cat and her ridiculous demands, but maybe there was something more going on. I wish she would have told me what was bothering her. We could have worked through it together."

"You know, when I was photographing one of the other Nayas, she mentioned that Camilla did seem a bit distracted at work lately."

He pushed his sunglasses up on his head and blinked at me. The bags under his red eyes revealing his lack of sleep. "Really? Because a day before she died, Camilla said she had something to talk to me about. It sounded serious. We never got around to talking about it."

"And you have no idea what it could have been about?" Drugs? Internet scams? An out-of-control Smurf collection?

He glanced back toward the bank. "I'm beginning to think it has something to do with our finances. They're a mess, and I have no idea why. Camilla handled all the money stuff."

"I'm so sorry you have to deal with this on top of her passing," I said, meaning it. I put a hand on his arm.

He focused on me, really focused on me, for the first time. "Wait. You said your name was Alex Lightwood?"

"That's me."

"You're the one who found her," he said, realization dawning.

"Also me." I braced myself for his reaction.

He pulled me into a hug. "Thank you. Who knows how long she would've been down there if you hadn't fallen into the well that day. At least she isn't missing."

"I was dropped," I mumbled against his chest. "But you're welcome." When he released me, I asked, "Why didn't anyone report her missing?"

"We work separate shifts. Camilla during the day, and me on night shift at the Baltimore airport. By the time I drove home from my shift, she would be at work. We were lucky to see each other at all during the week," he explained. "I have no idea why no one missed her at work that day. That might be a good question for William Remora when I go talk to him later."

"He has a box of Camilla's personal items in his office. Be sure to ask about that," I offered.

"I will. That and all about Gladys Wickerson. I'm not leaving until I have answers. He can't hide the old hag forever. I have a right to know what was going on between her and my dead wife." His voice choked on the last phrase.

I placed my hand on his arm again. "Good luck. From my experience, Mr. Remora becomes very political when anything resembling a threat to his position comes up in conversation."

"No kidding. He's sticking to his story that it was an accident. Or"—his voice dropped—"suicide. Can you imagine? There is no way Camilla did this to herself."

"I'm no expert, but I don't think it was an accident either," I said, shifting my weight from one foot to the other.

"If the police and her employer aren't going to help, I'll find answers on my own. Gladys Wickerson can't hide behind Remora and her age forever. I need answers, and she's the one to give them to me," he said, his emotions swinging back toward anger.

"Be careful. She's a force," I said.

"I think I can handle her." He put his sunglasses back on his face. "Thanks again for your part in bringing Camilla home."

"No problem. I'll get you those pictures once they're edited."

We parted ways. I was so excited about what I found out, I completely forgot about going back into the bank to set up my account. Probably a good thing in the long run since I still didn't have any clue what to call my business.

I know Colleen and I tease about the husband being the person responsible when something happens to their wife, but I wasn't so sure in this case. He seemed genuinely devastated by Camilla's death. Although I supposed that could also be guilt.

The loan in Gladys's name was curious. She must have been blackmailing Camilla for some reason. Why else would Camilla be giving her money?

Rule number two after "the husband did it" was "follow the money." The money pointed from Camilla to Gladys. Too late I remembered the ledger with all the transactional amounts. Would Shane Marjadi have been able to shed some light on those numbers? Or conversely, would those numbers have helped clear up any financial discrepancies for Shane? I'd have to consider making a copy for him when I gave him the portraits.

As I drove back to my loft, all the information I'd gleaned since finding poor Camilla swirled around my brain. Could Gladys be behind Camilla's death? I'd ruled her out because of her age and feebleness, but just because she's old doesn't mean she isn't capable of violence or meanness. Look at the Golden State Killer, for example. When they finally caught him, he was pretty spry for an old guy.

I sighed as I made the familiar turn onto Bachman Mill Road. Was I looking for trouble where it didn't belong? I didn't even know the Marjadis, and even the police couldn't agree if Camilla's death was anything more than a tragic accident.

I tapped my fingers on the steering wheel in time to the music from the radio as I contemplated. I get having other cases to work on, as Andrea Martinez indicated, but suspicious death wasn't the norm in Piney Ridge. And regardless of the final reason, being found dead at the bottom of the well at a retirement community definitely qualified as suspicious.

From what Shane revealed, Camilla was hiding financial troubles from him. She and Gladys shared some sort of financial tangle.

What else made sense? Did something more happen between Gladys and Camilla to cause her work transfer and the loan? I didn't have enough information about any of it.

Suddenly I was parking in my designated spot by my loft. I'd autopiloted the entire way home with very little recollection of the trip. Another indication I was starting to feel more at home here. A few weeks ago, I was still unconsciously making the turns to my childhood home instead of this loft. Creating the business account at the bank and registering my personal photography business would be one more step in solidifying my stay here in Piney Ridge.

My breath caught as a smallish wave of anxiety rolled through me from my gut to my throat. Permanence had never really been my MO. Even in New York, my apartment was more of a holding space for my stuff while I jumped from assignment to assignment and country to country.

Taking a deep breath as I exited my car, I closed my eyes and embraced all the smells that came with living on the Bachmans' Farmers' Market and Orchard property. Freshly baked pies, cut grass, wood chips, and yes, even the underlying smell of the working farm. These smells reminded me of Piney Ridge even when I was in faraway lands.

I shook my head and walked up the steps to my loft. I had some time still before I absolutely had to decide on my level of permanence. The photography jobs weren't so out of control that the IRS would be on me if I didn't officially register my business yet. At least I hoped so. Like Shane, I didn't know all that much about finances beyond running my card through the register at Scoops.

Thoughts of Shane returned my attention to the pressing mystery at hand. Like Shane, I felt that the director was hiding something or protecting someone. The more and more I thought I about it, the more and more all roads pointed directly back to Gladys. Even if she wasn't the one who put Camilla in the well, she knew more than she was saying.

I needed to run my theories by someone else. Right now, I was a jumble of what-ifs and maybe that's. Colleen and Linc were always top of the list of coconspirators. Since the fire station was directly attached to the police station, Linc might also have extra insight into the investigation. If there even was one.

And maybe I could convince one of them to bring me dinner on their way over.

CHAPTER 15

A N HOUR LATER, LINC, Colleen, and I were seated in my loft at the kitchen table. Solomon's chicken, western fries, and frosted homemade raisin bread were spread between us. I even pulled out my actual plates instead of using the leftover paper plates from the book club yesterday.

"Okay," Linc said, distracting me by licking his fingers, "run it down for us."

"Are you going to keep an open mind?" I asked, unable to stop looking at his mouth. "No eye rolls until I finish completely."

"No promises," Colleen said. "But we'll try. Right, Linc?"

He nodded and leaned back in his chair. He ran his hands through his hair and left them clasped behind his neck, making his biceps bulge under his tight Piney Ridge Fire and Rescue T-shirt. The navy blue of the shirt emphasized the darker blue hues of his eyes. He was cute in high school, but age and maturity looked good on him.

"Earth to Alexandretta," Colleen said, waving a hand in front of my face. She leaned over and whispered, "Need a bowl to catch your drool?"

I cleared my throat and looked down at the table. "Sorry. I, uh, I really think Gladys Wickerson is behind this somehow. I know it sounds crazy, given her age, but every time I try to consider a different possibility, everything comes back to her."

I laid out my case for them.

First, Gladys and Camilla had a contentious relationship. Something dramatic enough happened between them that caused Camilla's transfer. A transfer that was very mysterious. According to Gladys, she'd gotten Camilla demoted, almost fired. According to Camilla's husband, she'd requested the transfer to get away from Gladys. William Remora refused to confirm or deny any theory.

Second, Gladys was mean and demanding. I could easily see her going to extreme lengths if she thought she was disrespected. If Camilla did get the promotion, then everyone would know that Gladys's complaints had nothing to do with the transfer. Her word wouldn't carry as much weight. Not to mention she carried a weapon around with her—the broken cane I saw her with in William's office.

Third, Camilla was in financial trouble. The ledger pointed to that, and Shane confirmed it at the bank. Gladys was a part of this, too, somehow. Camilla owed her money. Camilla had something she wanted to discuss with Shane, which he thought had to do with their messy finances.

When I finished, I looked from one friend to the other. They sat quietly contemplating the obvious evidence I'd laid out in front of them.

Linc cleared his throat. I braced myself for his derision. He surprised me by saying, "You may actually have a point. The motive is definitely there."

"Thank you!" I said, grabbing the last western fry from the Styrofoam take-out container and drenching it in ketchup.

"But what is the motive? What could be the reason Gladys was blackmailing Camilla?" Colleen asked.

I chewed while I contemplated. One of the theories from the book club took hold and I smiled. "What's one thing that there is an abundance of at retirement communities?"

Colleen asked, "Denture cream?"

"Hard candy," Linc suggested.

"Handkerchiefs?" Colleen guessed.

"All true. But what's one thing that could cause this much drama and cover-up and, potentially, murder?" I asked.

"Can you just tell us already? You clearly have something in mind," Linc said, raising his eyebrow.

"Meds. Pills, tablets, syringes. You name it, someone in Aged Pines has access to it. What if Camilla was stealing or selling drugs?" The more I thought about it, the more I liked the theory.

"And Gladys found out!" Colleen said, taking my theory and running with it. "She caught Camilla stealing, but instead of turning her in, she blackmailed her. Or wanted a cut."

"Or maybe Camilla was stealing from her. She was assigned to Gladys's group of bungalows before being transferred," I reminded them. "Maybe she requests to switch assignments every few months, so the residents don't get suspicious when their meds go missing."

"It would be easy to trick old people into thinking they are imagining things." Colleen changed her voice to one of mock sincerity. "Oh no, Ms. Wrinkles, you only had three pills left yesterday. You must have forgotten. Almost time to order more."

"Very true. They are a vulnerable and easily targeted group," I agreed.

Linc leaned forward on the table. "I don't mean to be a naysayer," he started.

"Yes, you do," Colleen and I said in unison.

He gave us a pointed look but continued. "I didn't realize this table would engender so much wild speculation," he said, remembering my mother's words from the book club. "And that's what this is—speculation. Besides, I've met Camilla before," Linc said. "She didn't strike me as someone who was doing drugs."

"She didn't have to be sampling her merchandise. She could be the supplier," I said.

Linc leaned forward on his elbows. "I'm trying to stay with you, Lexy, but the deeper you get into these conspiracy theories, the more I'm having a hard time."

"You say conspiracy. I say probability," I said with a half smile. "Those ledger notes could coincide with an underground drug ring. Instead of being line entries for her debts and income, like I originally suspected, they could indicate her customers. You know, like, who owes her money or who has paid already." Linc still looked skeptical. "Come on, that makes sense."

Colleen nodded her head in agreement.

Linc sighed. "All right. I concede that it is possible. Although I still can't really picture Camilla involved in any sort of drugs, I really didn't know her that well, so we can't rule it out completely."

I clapped my hands together. "Now I need to prove it and convince the police. They still classify it as an accident."

"It still could be an accident, Alex," Linc pointed out. "All this is speculation at this point. Even though some of these theories are possibilities, we still don't have any proof."

"I know." I pouted. "But with the way I found her body someone had to put her in that spot."

"And you think that someone is cane-using, seventy-something Gladys Wickerson?" Linc asked, eyebrow raised again.

"Gladys could have had help," I said. "She's super close with Dennis Martingale."

"Martingale?" Colleen's interest perked up. "Like Rod Martingale?"

I rolled my eyes at her. What was her obsession with that guy? "Yes, Dennis is Rod's grandfather. Even if Dennis and Gladys aren't agile enough to put Camilla in the well, Rod would be."

"He's the weirdo who accosted me at Plum Crazy?" Linc asked.

"He what?" Colleen asked. Linc filled her in on the encounter.

Colleen pouted. "No wonder he didn't call me back when I texted him the other day. He's interested in you, Alex."

"First, I think he's throwing out lines to see who will bite. His interest has nothing to do with me personally. Second, you actually texted him?" I asked.

She shrugged a shoulder. "So? We didn't think he was involved in a murder at that point. And I'm fishing too. He's the only new fish in the small pond."

She looked so defeated that her possible new flame might be involved in a murder, so I said, "He may be a bit intense, but I don't really think he's involved in the murder. I'm getting away from myself again." I surprised myself by actually believing it. Rod was new to town. Why would he get involved in a murder plot?

"Maybe you should consider a private investigator business instead of photography," Linc suggested. "You seem to have a passion for sticking your nose in other people's business."

"I can't help it if people talk to me," I said, taking a sip of my drink. People liked to have someone listen to them. Being behind a camera often afforded me that opportunity. That and the fact I was terrible at small talk so usually didn't volunteer any information. People liked to fill the silence by talking about themselves.

"I'm going to suggest it one more time for my own peace of mind: Why don't you leave this one alone, Alex? It seems like Shane Marjadi has more of a motivation to get to the bottom of his wife's death. I'm sure he'll be hounding the police," Linc said.

"But he has too much anger and passion. It'll cloud his judgment and cause him to overlook things. Besides, people might be less likely to want to talk to him since he is so close to the investigation," I reasoned.

"That's what I thought you'd say."

"I could help him. We could help him," I said, pointing between the three of us. "The police aren't being any help yet. More than likely, Shane isn't going to get anywhere by talking to William Remora."

"What do you have planned? Escorting Shane to Gladys's room so they can duke it out mano-a-mano?" Colleen asked, a laugh bubbling up in her throat. "I mean, can you imagine? Gladys in her lace sheath dress brandishing a cane while Shane yells at her."

"Add in the pretentious cat, and I'd pay to see that confrontation," I said with a smile.

"You two are too much," Linc said. His phone rang, and he excused himself to take the call.

I popped a piece of bread into my mouth, making sure to get the piece with the maximum frosting on top. The raisins could go, in my opinion. The bread was really a conduit for the frosting. Colleen forewent the bread completely and peeled a piece of frosting off the top.

This was why we were best friends.

"Why do we invite Linc to these brainstorming sessions?" I asked. "He always rains on my parade."

"Because we need a voice of reason, or we'd wind up stalking some innocent person in a car." She winked at me.

"That was fun, though, right? Besides the fact I was on crutches."

"Definitely fun. Who can we spy on this time? In a totally uncreepy, evidence-gathering kind of way, of course."

"William Remora?" I suggested.

She wrinkled her nose. "Ew. Why? You don't think he has anything to do with Camilla's death, do you?"

"Not particularly. I'm curious whether he has more than one brown suit or if he wears the same one all the time."

She shook her head at me. "You're terrible."

"What? It's a valid question. Everything about that man is brown," I said.

Linc came back to the table and sat. We looked at him expectantly, waiting for him to explain the phone call.

"It was Andrea," he said without further explanation. I felt a small pang of something akin to jealousy. Akin, not actually. Because that would be ridiculous. I meant what I said at the diner—I was enjoying being single.

"You know," he said to fill our questioning silence. "You should take your speculations to her. It might help them reconsider their stance that Camilla's death was only an accident."

I blinked at him. "Now you think my theories are credible enough to go to the police?"

"I think if you are serious about your accusations, you should put your money where your mouth is. Take your 'evidence' to the police. Let them sort it out."

Colleen and I exchanged a glance. He was right, but his method wasn't fun. I pouted. Colleen and I would have a much better time sleuthing it out ourselves. She pursed her lips.

"How do girls do that?" he asked. "I feel like you two just had a complete conversation without saying a word."

We laughed. "We did, actually," Colleen said.

I sighed dramatically. "Fine. I'll go tell the police. And by police, I mean Andrea Martinez because I don't trust Chief Duncan as far as I can throw him."

CHAPTER 16

THE NEXT DAY, I rethought my agreement to go to the police. Despite my efforts to ignore him, Linc had planted little fungus seeds of doubt in my mind about my theories. He did say they were plausible, but he also raised his eyebrow. A lot.

Andrea Martinez did have a level head. She would listen and at least consider my side of things. If anything, it couldn't hurt to tell her. That didn't mean Colleen and I couldn't still do some sleuthing on our own. And perhaps she'd offer some insight into what she knew about the case.

In the end, my desire to do right by Camilla Marjadi outweighed my insecurities about whether Andrea would think I was an idiot or not. I'd do my civic duty and, regardless of the police's involvement, still investigate on my own. Or at least keep my ears and eyes open.

I threw some birdseed on the stairs for Nugget, the buff-colored chicken that often visited me for breakfast, and drove to the police station. It wasn't until I was pulling into the lot that I realized I forgot Camilla's notebook with the dates and dollar amounts. I couldn't decide if that was due to a subconscious desire to hold something back or an actual legit oversight.

When I entered the station, I said, "I need to speak with Officer Martinez. Immediately," I said to Joy, the admin at the front desk. Really it was so I didn't chicken out, but it came out kind of demanding.

She raised her drawn-on eyebrows at my tone, and I knew my mother would get a call as soon as I was out of earshot. Like most people in Piney Ridge, I'd known Joy practically my entire life. She and my mother were on the Parent-Teacher Association at my elementary school. Despite their age difference—Joy had her son right out of high school whereas my mother was a "mature mom" by the time she had me—they expertly ran all the fundraisers and carnivals and play days and back-to-school assemblies. I think it was Joy who suggested Reptile Man come to our school to teach us about reptiles and amphibians. He brought a huge yellow boa constrictor named Butters that stretched across two of the folding cafeteria tables. We got to pet it on our way out of the assembly. I can barely remember the name of my second-grade teacher, but I'll never forget Butters.

I'll also never forget overhearing that a tarantula got loose while we were all so enthralled with Butters. One of Reptile Man's assistants whispered it to him as I was passing. They found it when it crawled over a kindergartner's toes an hour later. I've had tarantula nightmares ever since, and I wasn't even the kindergartner.

Joy, in a saccharine voice saved for unruly children and equally unruly criminals, said, "I think she's in her office. Let me see if she is available for visitors. Please take a seat, Alex."

I forced a smile on my face and plopped down in one of the uncomfortable visitor chairs. The last time I was here, Chief Duncan was interrogating me as a murder suspect. I shoved that pleasant memory down in the depths of my "embarrassing moments" lockbox in my brain. My feet stuck to the matted brown carpet as I crossed and uncrossed my legs in impatience. Why didn't they upgrade to tile floors when they moved the police station beside the fire station a few years ago? This was disgusting.

To avoid thinking about how many drunk-and-disorderlies either threw up or worse on this carpet, I looked at the plaques on the wall. Each chief got a portrait taken and hung along the border of one wall. The first one dated back to the late 1800s. From a photographer's perspective, the difference in each generation's portrait was interesting. I could trace the progression in photographic technology from one portrait to the next. Unfortunately, nothing else seemed to progress since they were all middle-aged, white males.

Which reminded me to talk to Andrea about running against Chief Duncan in the next election.

"Alex?" Joy called. I jumped to my feet. "Officer Martinez can see you." She pointed down the hallway.

"Thanks." I put my phone on silent as I walked so I wouldn't be interrupted when my mother undoubtedly called to scold me about being rude. But see, I'm not rude. I turned off my phone for an important conversation.

"Alex. What can I do for you?" Andrea Martinez greeted me when I entered. She was standing behind her desk organizing a pyramid of papers. Her office wasn't quite as bad as William Remora's, but it was getting there. Her long, ebony hair was pulled back into a tight bun at the nape of her neck. The uniform, bulky and boxy on some, fit her perfectly, accentuating her toned muscles and brown skin. I stood up straighter and lifted my chin, but I still felt short and dumpy next to her. I remembered how secretive Linc was about their call yesterday and tried not to let unbidden jealousy cloud my respect for her.

I cleared my throat and said, "I think I know who killed Camilla Marjadi."

She stilled in her stacking to look at me with deep-brown eyes. "We don't know that she was killed. Chief really thinks it was an accident."

I rolled my eyes. "I saw the way she was positioned. No way that was an accident."

She sighed and glanced through the open office door. Chief Duncan's booming voice echoed down the hallway. A phone rang in the distance.

She said, "Shut the door and have a seat."

I did so as she moved some of the stacks of folders aside to clear a space on her desk. She sat in her chair and pulled out an old-school yellow notebook and pen. Finally, someone was going to take me seriously.

"Tell me what you think happened," she prompted.

"Okay." I took a breath and told her about my Gladys Wickerson theory. I told her about Gladys's annoyance with Camilla, her "my way or the highway" snobby personality, the broken cane, and Camilla being transferred. I also mentioned my conversation with Shane about the loan to Gladys, their financial troubles, and Camilla's request for transfer, a fact backed up by Maura Reilly. While I talked, she, at times, nodded her head and pursed her lips and raised her eyebrows and cocked her head. I couldn't tell if she agreed with me or not. At the end, I threw in the idea of conspiring with either Dennis, Maura, or William Remora as well, so she knew I had thought it through. She jotted down a few notes while I spoke.

When I finished, she was quiet for a moment, contemplating. Finally, she said, "Listen, Alex. Between you, me, and this pile of paperwork, I don't think Camilla's death was an accident either. Linc clearly agrees. But an old lady who didn't like the service she was getting? Seems like quite the stretch." I opened my mouth to protest, but she held up a finger to halt me. "Still, it is more than we had before. And I suppose stranger things have happened."

"You haven't met Ms. Wickerson. I'm surprised I made it out of her room alive. She gives 'ice queen' a whole new meaning."

"I'll put her name on the list of persons of interest for when I do get to officially investigate. Until the autopsy results officially come back, my hands are tied. Chief Duncan insists that this is an accident, so I'm not authorized to do any questioning until I get the department go-ahead. Stupid bureaucracy," she muttered.

"Here. I'll text you the list of candidates for the promotion. I happened to snap a picture on my cell phone," I said.

"I don't want to know how you got this picture, right?" she asked.

"Consider it an anonymous source," I suggested. Her phone pinged with the incoming image. She didn't open it right away.

I sighed. This was going nowhere. "I hope nothing happens to anyone else while Chief Duncan is in denial."

"Alex, I don't disbelieve you. I really will follow up when I'm allowed. In the meantime, I'll keep my eyes and ears open as best I can. But as you can see"—she pointed to the stacks of papers—"we have other cases we're dealing with too. Real, open cases."

I pursed my lips. "What else is happening in Piney Ridge that is more important than a possible murder? Did Mr. Oliphant streak down Main Street again?"

She bristled, back going ramrod straight. She smacked the pen down on the pad. "Actually, we are working on a joint investigation with the Maryland State Police. It's very important and high profile and could help resolve a huge fraud scheme."

"Here? In Piney Ridge?" I asked. That was news to me.

"I've probably said too much already. But yes. Some sources indicate that the people involved have ties to Piney Ridge. So, I need to focus my efforts on that now. You aren't the only 'anonymous source' I've gathered information from. Although this tipster seems to be eluding us lately." She moved another stack of papers. "Look, as soon as the autopsy results come back listing Camilla's death as homicide, I'll take a closer look." Her face softened. "I promise, Alex. I want to see justice for her as well."

I smiled. "Thank you, Officer Martinez. That's all I'm asking."

"Please, call me Andrea." She reached out a hand for me to shake.

"Thanks for listening, Andrea. You should really consider running for chief next election. You do all the work anyway. You'd have my vote," I said, shaking and releasing her hand.

A blush crept up her neck as she rubbed the back of it. "I've actually been thinking about it. But I don't know how well Piney Ridge will receive a female person of color as chief of police."

"Oh, they definitely will. Let me know when you make it official. My mother and I will spread our support faster than you can say, 'Bye, Duncan.'"

She laughed. "Okay. I'll think about it some more. Clive still has a year left on his term, so I have time."

We said our farewells, and I managed to avoid running into Chief Duncan as I made my way back to my car. Not that I would admit it to Linc, but I did feel a little lighter having unburdened some of the responsibility to the authorities. Even if the authorities couldn't do anything about it yet.

According to Andrea, her hands were tied until Chief DoNothing gave her the go-ahead to investigate. Which meant I was on my own for the time being. If Linc and Andrea couldn't help me because of pride and procedure, then I'd have to rope in Colleen and do some digging ourselves. That way when the police finally did get the go-ahead, I'd have my case already laid out for them. I'd watched enough true crime documentaries to know that focusing on only one suspect was never a good idea. That made you fit the evidence to the suspect and not the other way around.

The first suspects in any murder case were those closest to the victim. In this case, the husband. I'd learned enough in my short time back here as an adult to know that Piney Ridge was not always full of family values. Shane couldn't be completely crossed off the list. Neither could Maura despite my belief that she was being truthful when she talked to me.

I turned into the parking lot of Bachman's Orchard and Farmers' Market, weaving around customers coming and going and parking in my designated spot. Nugget, my adopted chicken, greeted me at the bottom of the stairs leading to my converted loft above the barn.

"Hey, Nugs," I said. "Did you have a good breakfast? See me tomorrow morning for more treats."

She gave me a little chicken coo and pecked around at my feet. One of the side effects of living on a working farm—animal visitors. Nugget was cool though. So far, she hadn't invited any of her chicken friends which was a good thing because I didn't want my staircase covered in chicken poo.

I fed Lash, my beta fish, apologized for neglecting her, and slipped into my favorite He-Man shirt and sweatpants. I grabbed the worn copy of *Misery* I'd borrowed from the library—yes, Nana K and I had annoye... I mean, convinced the rest of the book club to read Stephen King—and went in search of something to eat for lunch. Unless Lash had somehow grown legs and opposable thumbs, I should have some Chinese left over from the other night. One of the many perks of living alone: leftovers stretched for several meals. I no longer had to label my food in the fridge so a certain ex-Mr. Yuckypants didn't eat it all.

A few moments later, the microwave dinged, indicating my chicken with broccoli was warmed. I brought it to the table and tried to concentrate on the book. When I'd read the same line three times, I finally gave up and focused on the next steps in the "Find Camilla's Killer" campaign. I was even more sure of my drug-connection angle after Andrea mentioned the money-laundering investigation. Don't drug dealers launder money? Did she actually say money laundering? Or was it fraud?

In any case, it had something to do with money. And so did Camilla's disappearance. I couldn't help but think they were connected somehow, however far-fetched that seemed. With the yearbook shoot finished, I needed another way to access the residents and hallowed halls of Aged Pines. Topping the list of ideas was gaining an invite to one of Nana K's infamous bridge games.

Watch out, Gladys Wickerson, Alex Lightwood is coming for you.

CHAPTER 17

HAVING SECURED AN INVITATION to the weekly bridge tournament at Aged Pines, mainly under the pretext of taking a few more photos to flesh out that part of the yearbook, I drove through town contemplating Piney Ridge and playing cards.

While our community was moving toward diversity, Piney Ridge, like many small country towns in America, was still predominantly white, second- or third-generation European immigrants. The East Coast Italians mainly stayed north in New Jersey and New York. The Irish congregated in Boston. Here we had a large Eastern European community to supplement the trickle of Irish and Italians seeking warmer climates.

The Irish had their car bombs and kale and potatoes. The Italians their sauce and their sass. We Polish had pierogies, St. Nick, and at least one deck of cards. Or maybe the cards were unique to my family.

Growing up, after every family meal, the plastic container of cards and dice would plop on the table, and an argument about which game to play—cribbage, help your neighbor, or rummy—would ensue. We usually had to devolve into rock/paper/scissors to settle the debate. Unless Cousin Pat was there and wanted to throw in fire or snakes (they beat everything, in case you're wondering). We tried to wait for Cousin Pat to be in the bathroom before deciding.

For as long as I could remember, card games were a part of my life. But never in that time did I ever learn how to play bridge. In fact, I know nothing about bridge except that it's a card game older women like to play. I tried to convince Colleen to come with me; apparently bridge needs partners, but she was once again busy and evasive about it. I assured her Linc wasn't coming, so there was no need to lie. She assured me that she did, in fact, have plans and she'd tell me about them later.

When I walked into the community room at Aged Pines, I was surprised by how many residents were already there. Apparently, everyone, regardless of where they fell on the gender spectrum, liked to play bridge. Anyone who was anyone at Aged Pines joined the dozens of tables in the community room. A huge chalkboard with past and present scores and standings stood sentinel along one wall. Merely looking at all the numbers and pairings made my head spin.

I leaned over to my nana, who I found practically skipping down the hallway dressed in a rather conservative fuzzy pink cardigan and brown corduroy pants, and asked, "You understand all those numbers?"

"Sure. We have a mini ongoing tournament. Mostly we play for pennies at our individual tables. But each week the top scoring partnerships can win bigger prizes."

I started to take a chair at the first empty table we passed. Nana K grabbed my arm and pulled me to my feet. "Ow," I said, rubbing where she gripped me.

"Don't sit there, Alex. Doris and I are at the top-tier tables near the refreshments," she said proudly.

"There are different tiers?"

"Do you have cotton in your ears? In order to decide the weekly winner, the best teams need to play the best teams. Of course, there are tiers."

I caught a Naya giving me a "who are you" look from across the room, so I unbagged my camera and played with the settings to accommodate the horrendous florescent lights of the room. Someone should suggest updated lighting to William Remora as the next renovation project.

I took a wide-angle picture of the room and said, "And you and Doris are among the top?"

"Duh," Nana K said. "We usually go head to head with Dennis and Gladys or Mildred and Antonia. Mildred has a head cold, so she's out this week." She rubbed her hands together. "Which means Dennis and Gladys are going down!"

She walked around a table closest to the refreshments a few times, then sat in each of the four chairs in turn, before settling on a choice. I watched in amusement at her little ritual.

"Happy with your choice?" I asked when she hung her fuzzy cardigan over the back of the seat, effectively claiming her space.

"Yup. Back to the wall so Harold doesn't breathe down my neck when his games undoubtedly finish early. Eye on the refreshments, so I can let staff know when the coffee is getting low. And at the perfect angle so the setting sun won't blind me as it comes through the windows." She patted her hands on the table. "It's all about strategy, baby."

"Sounds like you have it all figured out."

She leaned forward on her bony elbows and pointed her finger at me. "Anything helps when it comes to Gladys and Dennis. They're ruthless and petty, and even though I can't prove it, I'm pretty sure they're cheaters."

"Hiding cards up their sleeves along with their tissues?" I asked.

"You watch. Let me know what you think. Maybe you can catch them doing something since you won't be focused on beating their dupas," she said. She looked past me and waved. "Doris! Over here."

I moved aside so Doris could take the seat across from Nana K. Fascinated, I listened as they developed hand signals to communicate during the game. It reminded me of baseball signals between pitcher and catcher. Eventually, my eyes glazed over as they talked about bids and tricks and trumps and bonuses. Or maybe my head was fuzzy from the heady fragrances of overly applied makeup, medicinal creams, and bad coffee that permeated the space.

Around the two friends, other bridge games started. Exclamations of surprise, disappointment, and elation echoed around the community center. Each table's assigned staff member kept score and reported to the official board as games began and ended. Overall, quite the production. I captured a few more moments—Velma's hands thrown up in celebration when she won a round, two residents with foreheads bent together over the lemon bars, a Naya erasing and replacing the numbers on the board. I'd thought Nana K was exaggerating when she talked about the games being cutthroat, but looking around the room now, I was starting to believe her.

I was also starting to wonder where Dennis and Gladys were. My phone clock indicated they were already about ten minutes late. Nana K and Doris didn't seem to be worried however.

At quarter past the hour, I interrupted their strategizing to ask, "What happens if your rival team is a no-show?"

"No chance. They'll be here. They like to make an entrance," Doris said, nodding her tight gray curls and adjusting her own pink cardigan. I realized then that Nana K and Doris had matched their clothing.

As if on cue, the double doors to the community center burst open with a small bang. All eyes turned to the entryway. Gladys stood there in a full-length, chiffon ball gown complete with an ornate sash tied around the waist and a tiara. Dennis stood a step behind in a suit jacket and bow tie. I did a double take. Gladys's sash pattern matched Dennis's tie. They'd coordinated as well, right down to the canes they were leaning on. I snapped a picture of them in the doorway.

"Are they for real?" I asked, picking my jaw off the ground.

Nana K waved a hand to brush them off. "Theatrics. Trying to distract us with their ridiculous outfits. Won't work, will it, Doris?"

I smiled at my nana, the queen of ridiculous outfits.

"I'm blind to their tricks," Doris said, putting on a pair of sunglasses. "Let the bridge speak for itself."

With canes tap, tap, tapping a simultaneous pattern on the linoleum floor, Dennis slowly escorted Gladys to our table, one hand hovering slightly above the small of her back but not quite touching. I didn't blame him. She might actually be toxic. I had to move my chair to accommodate Gladys's dress.

She gave me a cursory glance, then slid her eyes away. She asked, "Come to learn from the masters?"

"Something like that," I said. I'd actually come to learn how someone gets away with murder. I took a page from Doris's book and concentrated less on their attire and more on how Gladys and Dennis interacted with each other.

Their partnership seemed more fluid and natural than the one between my nana and Doris. They didn't need time to talk about their strategy or hand signals or which seat to sit in. Gladys picked up the deck of cards and began to shuffle. Nana K plopped a coin purse on the table with a wink at me. Undoubtedly these were the coins I'd scooped from the well.

"Care to make this interesting. A little table betting to go along with the big prize?" she asked.

Dennis rolled his eyes. "Pennies and dimes? What would be the point?"

"The point, Dennis, is bragging rights. And the new vending machines. I heard they're gonna have those chewy Chips Ahoy in the red package. The ones that don't rattle your dentures," Nana K said.

"Oh, let her bet her pennies, Dennis. What difference does a few measly dollars make?" Gladys said. Dennis nodded and reached in his pocket for some change. Doris grabbed a cup from the refreshment table behind her to hold their wagers.

Their game started slower than I expected. Some of the other tables were already on their second or third hands already. Each of these four took their grand ole time deciding which card to play and using signals to alert their partners before carefully placing their suit in the middle.

From what I could gather, aces were high, and everyone had to play the same suit. Whoever put down the highest card in that round won the four cards. Then Doris put down a three of clubs after Dennis's Jack of hearts, the called suit for the round, and she won the hand with a whoop and a holler.

"What just happened?" I asked.

"Doris trumped Dennis," Nana K said with a smile and a high five for her partner.

"What does that mean?" But I was hushed by all four as Dennis dealt the next hand. Okay. Not time for learning bridge. I was here to people watch anyway, so I pushed my annoyance aside.

Dennis and Gladys exchanged quiet glances across the table. Occasionally, Gladys would touch the inside of her wrist or lightly run her fingers over her collarbone. Dennis smiled and played with his tie. And I swear when I got up to refill my drink I saw Gladys run her slippered foot up Dennis's leg under the table. I honestly wasn't sure if they were flirting or signaling each other for the game.

They also spoke in clipped sentences, seeming to know what the other was going to say before they even finished the thought. Reminded me a little of me and Colleen.

I asked Nana K about it between games as Dennis was refreshing Gladys's coffee. "Have they known each other long?"

"Who? Gladennis? I think they met here."

"Gladennis?" I asked.

"You know. Like Bennifer or Brangelina? It's their couple's name."

"So they *are* a couple?" I grabbed a lemon bar from the refreshment table.

Nana K laughed softly. "I highly doubt it. They take comfort in their equal misery and contempt for the rest of us. That, and no one else wants to hang out with them."

"They seem really in tune with each other."

We resumed our seats near the table. Doris was cleaning her glasses with the tablecloth. Gladennis were standing by the chalkboard pointing at the standings.

"That's what makes them good partners in bridge," Nana said quietly, resuming our conversation about the unlikely pair. "Cut from the same contentious cloth. Rumor has it Gladys was married to some hotshot Broadway somebody when she was younger. He ended up dead, and she got all the money."

Doris nodded. "Oh, I read all about it back in the day. His death was ruled suspicious at first. He fell from the balcony of their apartment building in New York City. Gladys was home at the time, and originally investigators tried to blame it on her."

I was riveted. Another suspicious death after a fall? Both involving Gladys? My theory was gaining legs.

"What happened? Did they arrest her?"

Doris shook her head. "Nope. It sort of faded from the headlines. But I remember them changing their theory to accidental death when they found out he was drunk when he fell."

"Interesting," I said, tapping a finger against my lips. I kept the rest of my questions to myself as the pair wound their way through the other games back to the table. Dennis held the chair for Gladys as she sat.

"All down to this round," Gladys said, folding her hands on the table. "Who will be victorious this week?"

"You're going down," Nana K said.

"We'll see about that." Dennis picked up the deck to shuffle. I couldn't be 100 percent sure, but I swear the bottom cards remained on the bottom as he shuffled each time. He was careful to always start with the same side of the deck.

The game resumed. About halfway through, the teams were tied. Or at least they each had an equal number of card stacks in front of them. Dennis kept rubbing his fingers along his chin, making a little scratch, scratch, scratch sound over his stubble. Nana K's leg jumped up and down under the table.

"Dennis, if you don't stop rubbing your face, I'm going to..." Gladys said, not looking up from her cards.

He immediately dropped his hand. "Sorry."

"You need to get those nervous habits under control," she warned.

He nodded. "I will. Especially before—"

"Yes," she interrupted. "Especially."

Nana K stopped jiggling her leg as well. Some of the other tables had finished their hands for the evening. Those residents gathered around our table to watch the final round of the "top tier" players. I could almost hear a quiet announcer commenting on the foursome's moves. Like a golf announcer or those at the poker tournaments in Vegas.

"Doris scratches her nose. A signal to her partner. Will she play the high card? Or will she defer to Regina? This could make or break this trick." I hid my laugh behind a cough but still got a stern look from Gladys.

The throng of spectators leaned in as Doris played a card. Their murmurs got louder as they judged her choice.

Gladys finally had enough. She banged her hands on the table, making the cup of pennies jump and rattle. "If you all cannot be quiet, please get out," she shouted. She glared daggers at the Nayas standing around.

One of them shuffled forward with a sigh. "All right everyone. If you're not in the bungalows, it's time for beddy-bye."

"But Dennis isn't in a bungalow," a gentleman whined.

"Dennis is still playing. Come on. We'll tell everyone how the game ended tomorrow." A few other Nayas gently took residents' hands or shoulders to guide them toward the door. The squeak of walkers and the tapping of canes resonated around the room as a large group left.

When I refocused on the game, Gladys had a smug smile on her face. Nana K looked ashen.

"Do you want to finish it or call it now?" Dennis asked.

"What happened?" I asked.

Nana K threw her cards on the table. "They won."

Doris pushed Nana's cards with her finger. "Let's finish with dignity. We'll get them next week."

They finished the round to a smattering of applause from the crowd. I half expected Gladys to take a little bow. Instead, she held out her hand for Dennis to help her out of her chair.

A woman I remembered as Antonia put a hand on my nana's shoulder. "You'll get them next time, Regina. This is the closest anyone has come to beating them."

Nana K's face relighted. "You know what? You're right." She leaned across the table and held up a hand to Doris. "Come on, Doris. High five! We had them sweating there at the end."

"Sure did, partner." Doris obliged the high five with a tiny smack of her hand.

I walked with them back to the bungalows. "Doris, you don't happen to have any of those old newspaper articles about Gladys's husband, do you?"

"Oh no. That was way back in the fifties. I'm sure you could Google it though. Everything is on the internet these days."

"Ready to join us for bridge next time?" Nana K asked.

"Me?" I pointed to my chest. "Heck no. I have no idea what just happened in there. I'll stick with Go Fish and 500 Rummy."

Nana K clucked her tongue. She said to Doris, "Her grandfather and I tried our darndest to teach her cribbage. No luck. She's not a numbers girl."

"Not when it comes to complicated card games. I'll stick with the numbers associated with photography," I said.

I farewelled the ladies when we got to the turn off for the parking lot. Even though I was no closer to understanding the rules of bridge, I did get some juicy tidbits to add to my Gladys Did It file. Next step, scour the web for information about young Gladys Wickerson. If she had killed once, she'd probably have no qualms about killing again.

CHAPTER 18

C OLLEEN CALLED WHEN I was at the point of throwing my computer across the room. She sounded as defeated as I did, so I suggested we meet to talk about our woes. We decided on The Barn, the local country-western bar and grill at the edge of town. I contemplated wearing cowgirl boots—yes, I owned a pair—but thought that might be a little too on the nose. I opted for my usual tank top and cargo pants, but I did throw on a light layer of makeup, mainly so Colleen wouldn't bug me about it.

When I entered the dimly lit space, karaoke was in full swing, and I winced at the woman currently butchering Sara Evan's classic "Suds in the Bucket." Maybe The Barn wasn't such a great idea after all. Colleen waved at me from the farthest end of the bar away from the stage.

"Sorry," she said, when I sat down and signaled to the bartender. "I forgot it was karaoke night when I agreed to meet here."

"No worries. The bar drowns out most of the screeching over here," I said. When the bartender came over, I ordered a hard cider and some mozzarella sticks.

"Some of them aren't so bad. There's a gentleman who sounds almost like Randy Travis," she said.

I rolled my eyes in disbelief. "Has anyone sung anything other than country?"

She laughed. "Of course not. I don't even know if they offer anything other than country."

When the bartender placed my bottle in front of me, I held it aloft to clink glasses with Colleen. "To our equally crappy evenings. It can only go up from here."

"Let's hope," she said, tapping her wineglass against my bottle.

"So, tell me why you're so bunched up in your feels," I said, taking a drink.

She scrunched up her nose. "I'll tell you, but you have to promise not to judge."

"I can't promise that. But I do promise to listen and do most of the judging in my head," I said with a wink.

"Fair enough." She took a deep breath. "I went out with Rodney tonight."

I coughed as I choked on the sip I'd just taken. "Rodney Martingale?"

"Yes, Rodney Martingale. Do we know any other Rodneys?" she asked.

I swallowed my drink and my sharp comments, trying to keep the sarcasm from my voice when I asked, "And it didn't go well?"

"It started out great. He picked me up in his Miata, and we zipped through town with the top down. It was a little chilly, but he had a blanket on the seat waiting for me. Wasn't that thoughtful?"

I nodded. Slick, Mr. Martingale, very slick.

She continued. "We ended up in Mapleton at Outback Steakhouse. He seemed really pleased that he took me there, so I played along and acted all impressed. I mean, it was nice to get out of Piney Ridge, but with the way he was talking when we set up the date, I was expecting to go to one of the fancier restaurants in Baltimore or Gettysburg."

"Fair assumption given his braggadocio the other day," I agreed.

"Right?" She took a sip of her wine. "But honestly, I was so excited to be on a date, that I didn't care where we went. And their blooming onions are totally worth it. Dinner was going fine. We talked. He asked a lot about our friendship." She paused and cocked her head. "Come to think of it, he asked a lot about you. You and Linc specifically. Then he talked about himself even more. Maybe the date wasn't going as well as I thought. The blooming onion lulled me into thinking it was amazing."

"I'm sure he was simply trying to make conversation. He doesn't seem to know anyone in town other than us and his grandfather," I said as another patron started a not-so-terrible version of an old Shania Twain song.

"Maybe. And honestly, I get that talking about preschoolers isn't super exciting if you don't have kids. Still, after dinner I suggested we go for a walk by the reservoir."

"Great idea!"

"I know, right? Holding hands under the stars with the slight breeze coming off the water. Maybe he'd see me shiver and offer me his jacket. Then pull the lapels in to kiss me gently. Nothing too much for our first kiss, but definitely enough to promise more," Colleen said, her eyes glazing wistfully at the fantasy.

"Thought about that a little bit, did you?" I asked.

She blinked back to reality. "Yeah, well, it didn't happen. Before I could even finish the suggestion, he'd already turned it down. He said he had an early morning, but we should totally do this again sometime."

"Don't tell me he patted you on the shoulder in parting," I said, my opinion of Rod diminishing by the minute.

"Not quite. I did get a quaint kiss on the cheek and a "See you round, Red.' He didn't even walk me to my door." She chuckled and shook her head. "How stupid am I?"

I squeezed her hand. "Not stupid at all. He's the one at fault here, not you."

"Can I ask you a favor?" Colleen played with the stem of her wineglass and avoided my gaze, a clear indication I wasn't going to like what was coming. She glanced at me sideways from under her eyelashes. I reluctantly nodded.

She asked, "Could you go out with him, too, to see how he acts with you? That way I'll know if he is like that with all his dates or if I'm the lucky recipient of his less than attentive... attention."

"I don't think that's a great idea," I said. "I'm not good on dates, so it would skew the data." I didn't add that I probably wouldn't be able to get through the date without excessive eye rolling.

She started to protest but involuntarily my head swiveled to the entrance as little goose pimples erupted on my arms. Linc walked in. He paused for a moment in the doorway to allow his eyes to adjust to the dim light, then surveyed the room. I smiled and gave a little wave when he spotted us at the end of the bar.

He walked over in a few short strides.

"What brings you ladies out tonight?" he asked, giving us both awkward side hugs since we were still seated.

"Mutual commiseration," I said.

"Which reminds me," Colleen said. "You haven't told me why you needed an adult beverage to ease your frustration tonight." She flicked her eyes to Linc in a silent question to me: *Is it him?* I gave a small shake of my head: *No.* She let out a breath, relieved she hadn't made a faux pas by mentioning it.

Linc took the stool next to me and ordered a beer for himself and another round for me and Colleen.

"Actually, I'm glad you're both here. My frustration has to do with Camilla's death," I said.

Linc rolled his eyes. "That again. I thought you handed everything over to the police?"

"I did. But they can't do anything until Chief Duncan gets his head out of his netherwhere long enough to realize her death should be investigated. So, I'm still looking into things." I took a sip of my new drink. "Actually, things keep falling into my lap."

"Is this a new frustration or a continuation of the same thing we discussed the other day?" Colleen asked.

"New. I found out some interesting things about Gladys, but my attempts to dig deeper into this information is what has me frustrated."

"Do explain," Linc said. "Maybe we can help."

I narrowed my eyes at him, looking for any deception or sarcasm or amusement, but he seemed genuinely interested.

"I accompanied Nana K to bridge earlier this evening, and she happened to be playing against Gladys Wickerson and Dennis Martingale. Gladys was her usual surly self, of course, and Dennis was no glass of sweet peach tea either. I asked if they were a couple, and Nana K and her friend Doris both said they doubted it highly. They think the only reason they hang out is because misery loves company."

"No one else can stand being around them, so they hang out with each other," Colleen translated.

"Bingo." I said, touching my nose. "They also told me that Gladys may have murdered her first husband."

Colleen's eyes went wide. Linc spit out his drink. "I'm sorry. Murdered?"

"Yes," I said, pleased with their reactions. "He was a Broadway star, and she was an up-and-coming model. Then one night a few months into their marriage, he 'fell' off the balcony of their New York high-rise apartment. Rumors at the time indicated he may have had some help over the edge, and the only person home was Gladys."

"She was never charged?" Colleen asked.

I shook my head. "It happened decades ago when police still thought a beautiful white woman couldn't be capable of such a horrendous crime. From what I can tell in the scant newspaper articles I mined online, police smelled alcohol on his breath and chalked it up to an accidental death due to intoxication."

"I guess she inherited all his money," Linc said.

"Yup. She never remarried either. Although her modeling career had a brief uptick after the mur... I mean death of her husband, it flatlined after the sensationalism wore off."

Colleen asked, "So what has you frustrated? Sounds like you have a lot of the story."

I sighed and pouted dramatically. "I wanted to know more about them before the accident. I wanted to read the gossip magazines to see if I could glean any bit of truth from their articles. But it seems like those are both modern trends when it comes to true crime. Besides a few mentions in articles about his latest Broadway debut, information about their marriage was minimal at best."

"Could you ask Gladys directly?" Linc suggested.

I rolled my eyes at him. "You don't really know her. She'd burn me out of the room with the flames from her death stare."

He shrugged and finished his beer. He was about to signal for another one, but his phone buzzed on the bar top. I saw the name Andrea before he snatched it up.

"I've got to take this," he said, answering and walking quickly outside.

I frowned at his back.

Colleen noticed my expression. "You could ask him out, you know."

I laughed. "Me? Ask out Linc? Why... why would I do that?"

"Because you two clearly like each other. And if he isn't going to get out of his own way and ask you first, you should do it. Get the ball rolling on the inevitable," she said.

"I don't know what you're talking about," I said, but the crimson blush creeping up my neck gave me away. "Besides, this is the second time he's stepped out to take a call from Andrea. They are a much more likely couple."

"Her calls are probably about police business. I've never seen him look at Andrea the way he looks at you," she said.

My witty retort remained unsaid as Linc came back into the bar, staring at his phone, his face ashen.

I stood when he approached. "What happened? Is everything okay?"

He looked up at me. "Either your theory about Gladys was just bolstered, or it ended before it got started."

"What do you mean?"

"That was Andrea Martinez calling from Aged Pines. Gladys Wickerson was found dead in her bungalow."

CHAPTER 19

L INC INSTRUCTED US TO stay at The Barn which was about as effective as telling a toddler not to eat the cookie on his plate first. Out of respect for his request, we did allow him to get to the retirement community first. Aren't we nice?

When we arrived, the patio area outside Gladys's bungalow was already crowded with people. They took on an otherworldly feeling in the glow of the blinking red and blue lights. For as late as it was, I was surprised so many residents were awake and out of their beds.

I grabbed my camera on the pretense of helping capture the scene. At the very least, it would give me an excuse to push past the spectators. We followed Linc, now in full-on EMT mode, to the front of the crowd. He put a hand in my face to hold me back from following him into the bungalow.

"I can help," I said, smacking his palm away. "I can take pictures. Preserve the scene."

"Andrea has her phone camera," he said.

"Phone camera? No way. Mine will be so much clearer. Especially in the darkness."

He sighed. "Let me clear it with Andrea first." He disappeared into Gladys's bungalow.

I waited patiently-ish outside, pacing back and forth and peering in the large glass patio door. How long did it take to tell Andrea I was coming in?

"Stand still," Colleen said eventually, placing a hand on my arm. "You're making me dizzy."

"Alex," Linc called. I scrambled over to the door. "You can come in to take some pictures. But do not say anything. Do not touch anything."

I mimed locking my lips with a key and throwing it over my shoulder. Linc didn't look convinced, but he let me in. I adjusted the settings on my camera to accommodate the indoor lighting. Dennis stood in the background, leaning on his cane near the kitchen counter, face gray and eyes even more saggy than normal. I wondered if he was the one who found her. I hoped not. Even if I didn't especially like Dennis, I wouldn't wish finding a friend deceased on anyone.

Through my viewfinder, I documented the scene. Gladys sat in a large ornate armchair in the middle of the room. If it weren't for the large knife sticking out of her chest, she could've been sleeping. The 1920s style, form-fitting, beaded gown she wore was now ruined by a large red stain spreading across her chest. A jeweled tiara sat on her perfectly coiffed head. The crocheted blanket draped across her lap showed only the tips of her slippered feet. Her white cat sat curled on top of the blanket, hissing as I got closer.

I stepped back, aware that claws in my face wasn't a happy experience and got a few shots of the entire scene. A small table beside the chair had been upended, sending playing cards and a glass of liquid sprawling across the oriental rug. The door to the hallway was open a crack, letting in a sliver of light. Shadows waving back and forth told me that there were spectators by that door as well.

Focused on capturing the details of the scene, I jumped when the patio door slid open with a creak behind me. The open door brought a breeze, ruffling the playing cards on the floor, and the distinct sound of a crowd tittering. I turned my head and, since I was still crouched, almost smashed my face into a large mass. I knew this gut had to belong to Chief Duncan before I even looked up into his red face.

He clapped his hands together, scowled at me, but didn't say anything, and zeroed in on Andrea and Linc.

"Another dead body at the same place," he said by way of greeting. Everyone turned at his louder-than-necessary voice.

"This one is a bit different—" Andrea started, wanting to explain the circumstances, but Chief Duncan wasn't listening.

"We could have a serial killer on our hands." Chief Duncan rubbed his hands together in excitement. He walked over to Gladys and pushed the knife with his fingers—his gloveless fingers. "No doubt this isn't an accident."

"Um, Chief?" Andrea said, rushing to his side. "Maybe we shouldn't touch the knife without gloves. There might be fingerprints on it."

"Well, obviously my fingerprints can be ruled out," he said, but he did tuck his large pudgy hands into his pockets.

I briefly wondered if they'd bring in Detective James Spaulding from the Maryland State Police again, now that this was officially a murder. He was a voice of reason during the last investigation. Not to mention intriguing with his sharp eyes and rugged scar along his chin. Since Linc wasn't interested in a relationship, maybe I'd take a page from Colleen's book and look for someone outside of Piney Ridge.

Not that I wanted a relationship. I was perfectly fine on my own.

A hand waving in my face refocused my attention on the scene around me and not conjuring Detective Spaulding's image in my head.

"Earth to Alex," Linc said. "Where'd you go?"

"I, uh..."

Chief Duncan registered my presence for the first time. "What are *you* doing here?"

I held up my camera. "I'm recording the scene. For evidentiary purposes."

He turned to address Andrea. "You're just letting anyone tramp through the crime scene now?"

I straightened. "I'm not tramping. And I'm not the one touching things." Before he could yell, I added, "But I'm almost finished here. A few more pictures of the adjoining rooms and I'll be on my way."

I pushed past him, careful not to bump into anything, to photograph the living room from the kitchen area. Take out the police presence and the upended table, and from behind, Gladys could have simply been sitting in the ornate armchair watching the world pass by out her patio window.

Dennis stood a little behind me. "Did she like to to look out the patio window in the evenings?" I asked him. When I'd been here last, the furniture was in a completely different configuration.

He lifted a shoulder slightly. "I guess. I didn't really know her that well. We only really spent time together at social gatherings. I'm not sure what she did in her private quarters."

"I'm sorry for your loss. You were excellent bridge partners," I said. I gave him a sympathetic smile and moved toward the sliding glass door to leave. As I passed Chief Duncan, he was still talking about the prospect of a serial killer.

"Does this mean I can treat Camilla Marjadi's death as a murder?" Andrea asked. I slowed my steps to eavesdrop.

"Let's not get ahead of ourselves," Chief Duncan said, unwilling to admit he may have been wrong at first.

"But if this is a serial killer, then her death must also be a murder. If you give me permission to investigate more thoroughly, I can either confirm your current theory or your past one," Andrea said. I smiled and gave her a thumbs-up behind Chief Duncan's back. Either way, he could still be right.

He mumbled something unintelligible, but I hoped he'd give in and allow the investigation. Camilla deserved at least that.

When I finally exited Gladys's bungalow, Nana K waved me over.

"What happened?" she stage-whispered. Everyone with a working hearing aid scooted closer to us to eavesdrop.

"Let me walk you back to your bungalow," I said, cocking my head at the audience.

"Good idea." She took off at practically a run. Her bungalow was only a few doors down, so we got there before others could follow. She shut the patio door behind us.

"Spill. Natural causes don't pull a crowd like that."

I told her what I thought she could handle. Or really, what I thought I could handle saying out loud. I was beginning to regret my choice of volunteering to photograph the scene.

"Knife to the chest. Could have been anyone," Nana K said. "No one besides Dennis could stand her."

"Could it be related to Camilla's death?" I asked. "There were playing cards at both scenes."

"Peanut, that's hardly evidence," my nana said, patting my hand. "Do you know how many cards are in this place? Playing cards, greeting cards, business cards, recipe cards, gift cards, credit cards, ID cards. The list goes on."

"I guess."

"There's even a rumor that the basement is built using old playing cards from bridge games of the past. The story goes that the original owners shellacked the crap out of the piles instead of trying to dump truck them out of there," she said.

"That's ridiculous," I said, but she'd succeeded in lightening the mood a little. At least until I had to look back through the pictures of the scene to cull and edit them. I pushed that lovely thought to the back of my brain to deal with later.

"Anyone specific you can think of that would want her dead so violently?" I asked.

Nana K moved to the kitchen to make some tea, the Klafkeniewski cure for anything that ails you. "If you'd have asked me last week, I'd have said Camilla Marjadi. But that's impossible."

My veins turned to ice. Impossible for Camilla, yes. But not impossible for her very alive and very angry husband, Shane. When I'd left him at the bank, he'd been heading to the retirement community to confront William Remora and Gladys. And now Gladys was dead. And, come to think of it, I hadn't seen William at the scene either.

"Has anyone checked on Mr. Remora?" I asked.

Nana K turned from the stove. "Why?"

"I didn't see him hovering around the scene. He may be in danger too. I'll be right back."

I exited Nana's bungalow in search of Andrea. She was still in Gladys's living room, trying to help Linc extract the cat from Gladys's lap.

"Alex, can you grab the cat carrier from the bedroom, please?" Linc asked when he saw me reenter the bungalow.

I did and also grabbed a bag of treats sitting on the dresser. I poured a few in my hand and a few in the cage. "Come here, Duchess," I cooed to the cat, shaking the treat bag. She stopped scratching at Linc to look at the treats. I held out a hand, and she nibbled one out of my palm. It was enough of a distraction to allow Linc to shove the furry beast into the carrier. I threw a few more treats in there for her.

"Poor thing," I cooed through the front bars. "You've had a traumatic day too."

"What about me? That thing almost took off my entire arm," Linc said.

"You gonna make it?" I asked. "Should we amputate?"

"Ha ha. This is why I'm more of a dog person," he muttered, turning his attention back to Gladys. With the cat out of the way, we could now see the entirety of her lap. Sitting dead center, as though someone placed it there, was a playing card—the queen of diamonds.

"Think it means anything?" I asked Linc.

He shrugged. "It probably fell there when the table got knocked over."

Probably. But the queen of diamonds seemed a little too appropriate for someone like Gladys who clearly liked to show off her money.

Andrea came out of the kitchen holding a towel around her scratched-up hand. "Thanks for the assist. I wasn't sure what we were going to do there."

"No problem. Hey, has anyone seen William Remora lately?" I asked.

"He was here a second ago," Andrea said. "Yelling about shutting the curtains so no one could peek in. I think he went back to his office."

A small rock on my chest eased a bit. At least we wouldn't have two dead bodies to deal with today.

"He didn't wait to deal with the cat?" I asked.

"Apparently, residents aren't supposed to have animals. Gladys was an exception. He said he didn't care what we did with it," Andrea said. She held the door as Linc brought in the gurney. "We'll probably take it to the Humane Society."

The poor thing let out a small, depressing howl from inside the cage. My heart broke a little. I knew what it was like to lose someone important. Praying Lash would forgive me, I said, "I'll take her to my house. I can't stomach the thought of her in a cage all night."

Linc blinked at me in surprise. "You sure? You've never had a cat."

"I'm sure." I grabbed the cage before I could change my mind. In all honesty, part of my motivation was selfish. Having a distraction from the images in the bungalow and having company as I edited those images was appealing. Even if that company was a spoiled, pretentious cat.

CHAPTER 20

T HE NEXT MORNING, I put the last Band-Aid from the box onto my arm. What the heck had I been thinking when I agreed to take Gladys's cat. No more moments of weakness for me. I didn't have enough blood or skin left to chance it.

The hissing monster was currently hiding under my bed, and she could stay there for all I cared at the moment. I grabbed Lash's bowl from my bedside table, my camera bag from the foyer, and slammed the front door without a second glance. If the fluffy terror wanted to live forever under the bed, so be it. I only had so much patience.

After getting some more Band-Aids at Rosie's, the local drug store, I made a quick stop at the fire station to check in with Linc. Only because I wanted to check on the investigation and see if he knew anyone who wanted a death wish... I mean, a cat.

When I pulled up, Linc was washing the ambulance. His Muppet of a dog, Fang, danced around him, trying to catch the spray in his jaws. Linc laughed and doused the dog in the spray. I watched man and dog for a moment, marveling at how easy Linc laughed and smiled. Forcing my own forehead to unwrinkle and my shoulders to ease, I turned off the car and got out. Linc turned off the water and waved me over.

Holding Lash's bowl under one arm, I forced a smile and a spring in my step. See, I could be upbeat and amused too. My forced good mood lasted until I approached the splash zone. Fang, dripping wet and no longer distracted by the running hose, chose the moment I stepped up to Linc to shake the water off his long mop-like fur. I held Lash's bowl over my head as dirty dog water drenched my shirt and pants.

"Fang, no!" Linc said, laughing. "Good thing you saved the fish. Wouldn't want Lash to get wet."

I lowered my arms and wiped my face with my free hand. "Good to see you too, Fang," I said.

"Come on, I'll get you a towel," Linc said. He let Fang into the apparatus bay to run around while we walked to the main office area.

He gestured to the fishbowl. "You and Lash running some errands?"

"I didn't trust Gladys's demon cat alone with her," I said, brushing by him on the way to the station. For self-preservation, I avoided looking at the damp T-shirt adhering to his chest muscles.

Mostly avoided.

"Kitty transition going well, then?" he asked sarcastically, holding the door open for me.

"Let's just say I bought out Rosie's Band-Aid stash." I put Lash's bowl on the desk, plopped down in the chair, and propped my feet on Linc's desk.

"Make yourself at home," he said, grabbing a towel for both of us from the adjacent connected bathroom and tossing it to me. I caught it and dried my face and arms.

"Do you know anyone who wants a cat, no questions answered?" I asked.

"Give it some time. Like you said, the poor thing has been through a lot. She lost the only person she knew," he reminded me.

I sighed. "You're right. I'll stop trying to make her love me. I'm more of a 'once you get to know her' kinda girl anyway."

"Put some food and treats out. She'll come out when she's hungry."

I held up my bandaged hands. "She's got a taste for blood now, so it could be a while before she's satiated with cat food."

"Oh my goodness, Alex!" Linc exclaimed, grabbing one of my hands. He pulled me out of the chair and over to his med kit on the table. "Did you put any ointment on these? Cat scratches get infected easily."

"No, Dad. But I did wash them," I said. He gently applied some ointment and rebandaged my cuts. When he finished, he looked into my face while still holding my hand in his. Our faces were inches apart. "Don't mess with the cat anymore, okay? Let her come to you."

"Sure," I croaked. "Thanks."

"Alex," he whispered, rubbing a thumb over my palm. I stopped breathing. Like literally all lung function came to a stop. As did any brain activity beyond the refrain of his name repeated in perpetuity. His eyes darkened.

"Excuse me?" A voice from the hallway had us jumping apart. Seriously, what did a girl have to do to get kissed in this town? I was about to slam the office door shut and pretend I didn't hear the voice, but an unfamiliar face appeared in the doorway before I could make my muscles move.

Linc smoothed a hand over his hair and wrapped the towel around his neck as he welcomed the young man in. "Can I help you?"

"I hope so," the guy said. He was a few years younger than us with a skater-boy haircut that he kept flicking out of his eyes with a shake of his head. He held out his hand for us to shake in turn. "I'm Brody Wickerson. Chief Duncan called me about my aunt?"

"I'm so sorry for your loss, Brody. I'm Lincoln Livestrong, fire captain. And this is Alex Lightwood. We can help you find the chief," Linc said, moving around the furniture to usher Brody out. The police station was connected to the fire station, so the walk over wasn't a long one.

"Do you know what happened to her?" Brody asked as we walked. "On the phone, Chief Duncan told me she had passed away unexpectedly, and I needed to come right away."

"I think we should wait for the chief," Linc said.

Joy smiled broadly at Linc when we entered. He had that effect on all women regardless of age and relationship status. It was the dimple.

She gave me a quick glance and nod of the head, clearly still holding a small grudge based on my brusqueness earlier this week, then turned her attention to the newcomer.

"Who do we have here?" she asked.

"Joy, this is Brody Wickerson, Gladys's nephew. Chief Duncan requested he come," Linc explained.

Before Joy could even pick up the intercom to call him, Chief Duncan's voice preceded him down the hallway. "Brody, my boy," he said, engulfing the young man's hands in his own. "Thank you for coming so quickly. Really quickly, actually. Where did you say you lived?"

"North Carolina," Brody said, extracting his hands from the chief's. "It sounded pretty urgent on the phone, so I came right away."

Chief Duncan narrowed his eyes. "Sure, sure. You're Gladys's emergency contact."

"That's right. I'm the closest relative. My dad, Gladys's younger brother, lives in Florida with my stepmom. They're on their way."

"That's a really good nephew. Most kids your age wouldn't care about leaving their frat parties and skateboard parks to run to the aid of an elderly aunt," Chief Duncan said. I shifted uncomfortably beside Linc. I'd been on the receiving end of Chief Duncan's weird interrogation questions before and didn't envy Brody now at all.

"I'm actually the IT manager at NC State," Brody started to explain.

Chief Duncan barreled right over him. "Are you also Gladys's beneficiary? Tell me, son, how much do you stand to inherit?"

Linc cleared his throat as Brody tried to pick his chin off the ground. "Uh, Chief? Brody here doesn't even know what happened to his aunt. He's looking for some information."

"So he says," the chief mumbled, giving Brody a severe side eye.

Linc took Chief Duncan's arm and pulled him to the side with an "Excuse us a moment," to me and Brody.

I gave Brody a sympathetic look. "Sorry about the chief. He's a little"—I struggled for nice way to say idiot—"overzealous. We don't get a lot of unexplained deaths in these parts."

"So, it wasn't natural causes?" Brody asked.

I shook my head. He was going to find out soon enough anyway. "Sorry."

"I didn't really think it was. If you'd known my aunt, you'd know that nothing short of a lightning strike from the heavens would take her out."

"I met her a few times, actually. I took her picture for the Aged Pines yearbook. She was definitely a firecracker," I confirmed.

"Firecracker." He chuckled. "I like that. Can you tell me what happened?"

I hesitated. I didn't want to mess up any police investigation, but I also didn't trust the chief to be honest with him. "Hold on," I said, turning toward the desk. "Hey, Joy, is Officer Martinez in her office?"

"She is," Joy said. "Do you want to take Mr. Wickerson back there to wait?"

"I think that would be best." I moved him down the hallway while Joy called to let Andrea know we were coming.

I introduced them and left Brody in her very capable hands. I passed Chief Duncan in the hallway. He smelled a little like beef jerky and sweat. Not a great combination, especially in a tight space. I pressed myself against the wall to let him pass. He paused when he reached me and pointed a stubby finger in my face.

"I find it very curious that you always show up whenever there's trouble," he said. He pointed two fingers at his eyes and then slowly back at me. I raised an eyebrow at him.

"Good to see you too, Chief," I said and scurried away.

Linc was leaning against the reception desk and talking to Joy while he waited for me to catch up.

"What was that all about?" I asked as we walked back to the fire station.

Linc shook his head. "The good news is that Chief Duncan seems to be off his 'serial killer in our midst' theory."

"The bad news?" I asked.

"He is now convinced that the nephew is the culprit. In his mind, there was no way Brody could have or would have made it here this fast. Therefore, he must have already been in town. Apparently, Gladys has quite a nice little nest egg to give to her next of kin."

"Wouldn't the next of kin be Brody's dad?" I asked.

Linc held the door for me as he always did. "That's exactly what I told Chief Duncan. Thanks for depositing Brody with Andrea. Hopefully, she'll be a voice of reason."

I nodded, swirling a finger absentmindedly in Lash's bowl.

"Uh-oh. I know that look. What's swimming around in that brain of yours now, Sexy Lexy?" Linc asked.

I squinched up my nose. "I can't believe I'm going to say this, but could he have a point? Brody seems to have motive and possibly opportunity. Gladys was sitting peacefully in her chair, and there was no sign of a break-in, so she probably knew her attacker."

Linc raised an eyebrow and scoffed. "You, Alex Lightwood, think Chief Duncan might be right? Well, isn't this a red-letter day."

"All I'm saying is at least he isn't laser focused on one idea."

"No, he's jumping between several crazy ones," Linc said. He grabbed our towels to hang them back in the bathroom.

"True. Still, money is a big motivator in murder. We were just talking about that in terms of Camilla as well. Maybe Brody and his father took advantage of one strange death to cover up another one."

Surprisingly, Linc didn't immediately tell me I was ridiculous. He sat behind his desk and swiveled in his chair with his fingers steepled on his broad chest. "You think the two deaths are connected?"

I shrugged. "I don't know. I mean, I don't necessarily think there is a serial killer. Different MOs, different victim profiles. But not being connected is really coincidental, right?"

He leaned forward on the desk. "Alex, I didn't really think about any of this stuff before you came back to town. I am the fire captain not the police chief."

I smiled and waggled my eyebrows. "But now you're curious, right? And you can admit that Chief Duncan is next to worthless?"

"I haven't been able to sleep because I've been thinking about you and all your crazy theories," he admitted.

"Great. Keep your ear to the ground, Livestrong." I pointed at him, then picked up Lash's bowl. "Brody is low on my suspect list, but he can't be completely removed yet."

"I'm going to regret asking this, but who is on the top of your list at the moment?"

"For Gladys, it's Camilla's husband, Shane. He was none too happy when he left the bank the day he found out about the loan between Gladys and Camilla," I explained, shifting Lash's bowl to the other arm.

Linc sat back in his chair. "Now, that is a theory that has some possibility. Do me a favor, Alex. Let sleeping cats lie. I mean that literally and figuratively. If Shane is the one behind this, don't put yourself in his crosshairs."

He looked so sincere, I swallowed my snarky comment. "I hear you, Linc. And I'll also let the fluffy demogorgon hold court under my bed."

CHAPTER 21

R AIN, RAIN, AND MORE rain. I thought getting drenched by Fang was a pain, but nothing really prepared Piney Ridge for the torrential downpour that hit us over the next week. Some sort of hurricane turned tropical storm from Florida knocked out the power and flooded the reservoir. I mainly stayed in my loft, ignoring the urge to coax the cat from under the bed.

I knew she'd been out since the cat food I left by my bedroom door was empty when I awoke in the morning. Good thing I'd had the foresight to lock Lash in the bathroom overnight. I didn't want her to end up as a kitty snack.

Not only did the rain keep Nugget away—who would have guessed I'd miss a chicken—but I also had to rearrange a family photo shoot due to the weather. Rain plus expensive camera gear did not mix well. Neither did me and flashes. I preferred to shoot in natural light. The dedication of the tennis courts and shuffleboard lanes at the retirement community was also on hold—both because of the weather and the ongoing police investigation, slow though it was.

By day four of rain and no sign of the cat, I was bored to the max. Colleen and Linc were both at work, so they couldn't entertain me. I could go to one of my mother's many clubs, but I wasn't in the mood for small talk with her friends. That left Nana K. Luckily, she was up for a visitor.

When I arrived, Nana K greeted me by her patio door with a pair of galoshes and a raincoat. She looked like one of those little white ducks in the yellow rubber rain jacket and hat. She had swim goggles covering her eyes.

"What are you doing?" I asked.

"Put these on. We're gonna play in the rain," she said, shoving the boots and coat in my hands.

"I was hoping for tea and cheesecake. Maybe a round of rummy or watching reruns of *The Bachelor*," I said.

"We can have tea when we get back," she said. "I've been cooped up in that bungalow for too long."

"You could break a hip if you slip," I cautioned, unable to hide my smile.

"That's why I waited for you. I'm not a complete idiot."

I looked down the row of bungalows to where wet police tape hung limply across what was once Gladys's bungalow. This time with my nana was fleeting. I put on the galoshes and coat.

"Come on," she said, grabbing my arm, the plastic of our coats squeaking as they rubbed against each other. "The best puddles are on the south lawn."

We splashed our way over there through the downpour. Luckily this storm was a soaking rain and not full of thunder and lightning. Although if lightning was attracted to the tallest thing, my nana and I were safe.

When Colleen and I were younger, she had a long-haired cat named Pangur after a famous Irish poem about a cat of the same name. One time Pangur got outside and was sprayed by a skunk. When we washed the poor thing, I hardly recognized it. All that fur made Pangur seem like a fat cat. But it turned out her girth was just that—all fur. With her fur pressed against her skin from the water, she looked more like a drowned rat than the fluffy cat she was.

That's kind of what I imagined I looked like by the time we reached the south lawn. My hair, although much thinner than Pangur's fur, was plastered to my head and face. My clothing stuck to my body despite the raincoat. All my eyelashes stuck together and dripped rain down my cheeks.

But seeing Nana K do a small little hop into a muddy puddle with a big giggle and even bigger smile made it all worth it. I wished I had my camera with me. Instead, I caught her smile with one of my own and jumped in a nearby puddle, sending a splash onto her calves.

"Oh, it's on like Donkey Kong," Nana K said, bending her knobby knees to jump into another puddle. I jumped out of the way before her splash hit my legs. We splashed around like little kids, trying to douse each other with water and mud. The piles of dirt from the recent renovations created lots of the latter.

Nana K put a hand to her chest, giving me a small heart attack thinking she was having one herself, and sat on a bench to catch her breath. She pushed the swim goggles onto her forehead.

"I'm fine, Peanut," she said when she noticed my face drained of all color. "I just need to catch my breath. I haven't jumped that much since Grampa Anton took me to crush grapes for wine."

"What made you want to do this today, Nana K?" I asked. Usually, I would find her curled up watching some trash TV show in an afghan.

She patted my soggy knee. "I figured we could both use the break. Rain always makes me feel a little blah. And what with Gladys and Camilla..." She sighed and looked at the rain dripping from the tree leaves around us. "I'm just feeling my age a little more these days."

"Hey, weren't you the one who told me 'Age ain't nothing but a number'?" I reminded her. I took her hand in mine, matching up our slightly curved middle fingers like I used to do when I was little. Along with being able to cross one eye, that crooked finger was a genetic trait on the Klafkeniewski side of the family.

"True, but death doesn't care about age. Your real age or the age you feel. Gladys was healthy and, for all intents and purposes, unstoppable. Until she wasn't. It made me realize that I need to carpe diem." She stood and pumped a fist in the air. She shouted, "YOLO!"

I laughed. "Do you even know what that means?"

"Of course. You only live once." She grabbed my hands and hauled me to my feet. "It's so good to hear you laugh. I haven't heard you do that very often since you've been back. If you won't let me help you find your joy again, let someone else. Maybe a handsome someone named after a very famous president."

I pursed my lips at her to keep from smiling. "Stop playing matchmaker. Linc knows where I am if he's interested. So far, he hasn't been."

"Sometimes men need a good kick in the butt. I asked your grampa out the first time, you know," she said.

"I didn't know that actually," I said, realizing I'd never asked about their romance. They'd always just been Nana and Grampa.

She nodded her head as we walked back toward the bungalows, her small hand tucked around my arm. "Oh yes. I knew he liked me, but he was too shy to act on it. Eventually I told him to ask me out already before I gave up on him and moved on to someone else."

I laughed. I could absolutely see a younger Nana K pointing her small finger at Grampa and telling him to get on with it already.

"Did he ask you?"

"No!" she shouted. "Can you believe it? He stood there stammering and 'uh-uh-uhing' until I threw my hands up and told him to pick me up at seven the next night for dinner."

"I guess he showed up," I said.

"With my favorite flowers. We were together ever since," she said wistfully. She squeezed my arm. "He brought me those same flowers on that same day every single year we were together."

"That's so sweet. That's what I want. Someone to remember the little things."

"Someone who will go above and beyond to make you happy. Like crafting a one-of-a-kind table from scratch. Or dropping everything to meet you at Plum Crazy. Or joining a book club full of fussy, old biddies because you asked him to," she said with a sparkle in her eye.

"You don't know what you're talking about," I said, hiding my smile by wiping rain off my face. When I looked back at her, she was holding a penny.

"Maybe, maybe not. How about we let the fates decide?" She steered me toward the wishing well.

"Whoa," I said, digging my heels in. "I'm not sure if I trust you and me near that well. It didn't work out so well the last time."

"Don't be a sissy. Make a wish, Peanut." She pressed the penny into my hand.

I stepped up to the well and looked behind me. "Stay back, Nana. I mean it."

She giggled and waved from a few feet away. I closed my eyes and made a wish, then flung the penny into the well. Except it didn't go in the well. It bounced off and landed somewhere in the muddy mess beside the stone exterior. If that was any indication about how a relationship with Linc would go, I counted myself lucky he hadn't asked me out. I wiped rainwater from my eyes and looked closer at the opening.

A wire frame now covered the well.

"I see they put up a cover," I called to Nana K who moved out from under the cover of a tree to join me beside the well.

"Yeah," Nana K said. "Someone found out I used wish coins at bridge the other night and made a stink."

"Or maybe they don't want anyone else falling down there," I suggested.

"Could be. At least they used wire so these old biddies can still make their silly wishes."

I started to walk away when a sound besides rainfall pricked my consciousness. It sounded like running water. I looked back down into the well. It was over halfway full.

"That's odd," I said. No way the falling rain alone would have filled it that much. Nana K looked down with me. "The well is almost full."

"When they built this thing, the goal was to have it be functional," Nana K said. "Someone had the quaint idea that we would like to relive our youth by pulling fresh water from a well." She rolled her eyes. "No, thank you. Give me indoor plumbing and Grub Hub any day."

"So it actually connects to an underground spring or something?" I asked.

"Probably the reservoir. It's so overfull because of all this rain, I wouldn't doubt it's filling all the forgotten tributaries and runoffs." She leaned over the opening and tried to reach through the wires. "Think the coins float?"

"No." I smacked her hands away. "Don't get your hands stuck in there."

I sighed and leaned against the edge of the stone surround. Nana K joined me.

"Pierogi for your thoughts?" she asked.

"I'm thinking that if the well fills up, then it reasons that it will also drain," I said. "More than likely through the opening where I discovered Camilla's body."

"Ah, I see," Nana K said. "The water could have dragged her body into the opening. It did rain a few weeks ago when she was killed."

"Exactly. Therefore, Camilla's death could have been an accident or a suicide after all."

CHAPTER 22

T HE NEXT DAY DAWNED sunny and clear. I awoke to the familiar sounds of the rooster crowing his head off. With the rain, I hadn't needed to wear my earplugs. Chickens didn't like to get wet apparently.

Today I didn't mind the early morning wake-up call since I had my first portrait-style family photo shoot scheduled. Even though I'd been making pictures since my mother first handed me a disposable camera at Aunt Delores's wedding, when I was a toddler, today's shoot made me nervous. Someone was paying me to take pictures of their family. I had a limited timeline to capture them, something I wasn't exactly used to. What if they didn't like them? What if they were somehow all out of focus? What if Danny's warning that the kids were little brats and refused to smile came true?

What if I had to make small talk? I shuddered. It was a very real possibility.

Since being hungry in the future was also a very real possibility, I pulled up my big-girl pants and resigned myself to my fate. Mama needs a paycheck.

I heard a light scratching at my door, and my grumpy mood lifted slightly. Grabbing the birdseed from the counter, I opened the door to find Nugget scratching around on the landing.

"Hey, Nugs!" I said, smiling like an idiot. "I missed you. You're much more personable than my newest live-in companion."

She clucked a little and cocked her head one way, then the other. I dropped some seed on the wood plank and watched her peck away. Never in my life would I guess that I'd be happy to see a chicken at my door. But here I was.

I gave her back a little pet, dropped the rest of the seed and, with the little black rain cloud over my head dissipating, went back inside to finish getting ready. Of course, the closer it came time to leave, the more my anxiety grew.

I rechecked my shots list, made sure I had extra batteries and SD cards, put some food out for the demon cat, and locked Lash in the bathroom. When I couldn't think of anything else to do to procrastinate—my rain dance didn't seem to be working—I packed up the car and headed to the Cavannagh's house. Mrs. Cavannagh wanted a head start on their family Christmas pictures. Like gossip, the holiday card exchange game could carry a family through the New Year. Who got theirs out first? Who had the best pictures? The best layout? Which was the funniest? Most poignant? Most sincere? Piney Ridge had an underground holiday card superlative contest every year. Apparently, I was now a part of it.

A little bit of extra added pressure. No biggie. Nothing I couldn't handle.

The Cavannagh driveway was full when I reached their house, so I parked on the curb with a frown. Ms. Cavannagh didn't say anything about extra people. I'd read about this in preparation for today. Some clients like to include their extended family—grandparents, aunts, uncles—at the last minute. I might have to add that as a clause in the contract. Once I had a contract. So far, I was banking on faith and small-town guilt to keep appointments and the agreed-upon rate.

Add contract creation to the list of things I needed to do for this new business. Being self-employed sounded glamorous, but it was turning out to be a lot of work.

I got out of my car as the front door opened. To my surprise, Rod Martingale stepped out behind Joe Cavannagh. They shook hands, reluctantly on Joe's part. Rod clapped Joe on the shoulder and leaned in to whisper something. Joe's face hardened as he nodded curtly.

As I walked up the driveway, Rod said, "I'll be in touch. Soon."

Both men noticed me when Rod stepped away from Joe. Rod's face opened into a bright smile. Joe's closed even more. Great, whatever had transpired between these two had put Joe in a foul mood. Trying to take his photograph was going to be even harder.

"Alex!" Rod exclaimed, rushing toward me to gather me in a hug. He, in direct opposition to my subject, was in a great mood.

"Ooof," I said, when I landed against his chest.

"We have to stop running into each other like two ships passing in the night. Let me take you out for a real dinner date. We'll go into Baltimore," he offered.

I pushed away from his embrace and adjusted my camera bag on my shoulder. "Maybe. I've been so busy lately. How's Dennis holding up?"

"Gramps? He's fine, why?"

"Well, one of his best friends passed away suddenly," I said. Rod still looked confused, so I added, "Gladys Wickerson was murdered a few days ago."

His face relaxed in recognition. "Oh, that. Yeah, Gramps is fine. It was a shock at first, but death at Aged Pines isn't an anomaly."

"But she was murdered," I repeated. "Surely that isn't common."

"No. I suppose not." He flipped another business card to me. "Here's my card again. Use it this time. I'll take you out proper."

I put it in my back pocket thankful he didn't ask for my number instead. Wasn't there a fake number you could give to people? I'd have to look that up. In the meantime, I'd keep holding on to his belief that any woman would be grateful to have the invitation to use his number. In his mind, there was no way I wasn't going to call him, so he didn't even think about asking for my number instead.

"What about Colleen?" I asked. He'd taken her out not that long ago.

"Colleen?" he asked, confused again. Man, this guy was a piece of work.

"Yeah, Colleen. Tall, preschool teacher, curly red hair. You two went out a few days ago," I reminded him.

"Oh right! Red!" he exclaimed. "She was fun." He leaned in a little closer and winked. The smell of his cologne was overpowering and, I'm sure, toxic. I held my breath as he said, "I'll bet you're even funner."

"Not a word," I mumbled. Stepping around him, I said, "Good to see you, Rod. I've got to get ready for the photo shoot."

"That's right," Rod said, loud enough for Joe, who was still standing in the doorway waiting for me, to hear. "Family is so important. Isn't that right, Joe?"

"Goodbye, Mr. Martingale," Joe said tightly. To me, he said, "Alyssa's in the kitchen waiting for you. She has some ideas she'd like to run by you before we get this over with."

"Great," I said, hoping that statement wasn't indicative of how the entire session was going to go.

Unfortunately, "getting it over with" seemed to be the theme of the Cavannagh family shoot. At least where Joe and the kids were concerned. Alyssa and I worked hard to get everyone to cooperate, but Joe's limited smiles and patience came across as wooden and forced in the pictures. The kids would barely sit still. If one was smiling, the other was sticking out her tongue or putting her hands in front of her face.

I begged. I bribed. I cajoled. I made stupid jokes and faces. By the end of the hour, I had tapped out every trick I'd read about prior to the session and every ounce of social interaction energy I had left. I felt like a bird trying to fly through a hurricane. A very small bird. A small, emotionally exhausted pigeon-type bird. I'm sure I looked a little like one too.

Eventually, I fell back on my documentary-style approach to end the disastrous session.

"Okay, kids," I said. "I think we're all done. Why don't you go play in the yard for a minute," I suggested.

They shouted in joy and took off out the sliding glass door. "Daddy, come push me on the swing!"

Alyssa looked defeated. "I'm so sorry, Alex. They're usually much more well behaved."

"I have one more trick up my sleeve," I said. "Go play with your kids. Pretend I'm not here."

"Really?" she asked. "But no one will be looking at the camera."

"Sometimes the candid shots are the best. If you don't like them, no worries. I think I got a few safety portrait shots earlier." At least I hoped I did. I may have to do some head swaps in post-production to get both kids looking and smiling in the same frame.

As the Cavannagh parents played with their kids on the swing set, the entire mood lifted. The pressure to get the perfect shot was off everyone. Even Joe seemed happier and less stressed. I know I was.

I sat on the ground to get some different angles of the kids on the swings. Their movement created some interesting sun flares as they swung in front of the sun. I managed to catch a sweet moment between Alyssa and Joe as they stood together watching their kids play.

As far as photography went, these were the best shots of the day. Interesting compositions, natural expressions, playing with the light. As far as client expectations, these were probably all throwaways. No perfect family sitting in perfectly matched outfits smiling perfectly at the camera. But I'd deliver them all anyway and let the Cavannaghs decide. If nothing else, maybe they'd be able to post these on social media or whatever.

After another half an hour or so of snapping away while the kids played in the backyard, I decided to call it a day. I'd already overstayed my welcome.

"Hey, kids, how about one last family hug before I go. Who do you think can squeeze Dad the hardest?"

Both kids squealed and ran to their father's outstretched hands. He lifted the two youngsters easily, and they smashed their arms around his neck, pressing their little faces against his. Alyssa came up beside them and joined the hug. I snapped away, even after the kids released to get the moment right after where they were all laughing and deciding the winner.

"That's a wrap. Thanks, Cavannagh family," I said. I packed up my camera as the kids went back to playing.

"Thank you, Alex. I can't wait to see what you captured," Alyssa said, shaking my hand. "Joe, can you walk her out?"

He nodded. As we walked through the house to the front door, he said, "So, you know Rodney Martingale?"

I huffed. "Sort of. We met while I was photographing his grandfather for the Aged Pines yearbook a few weeks ago."

"You seem like a nice girl, Alex. I'd be careful if I were you," he said.

"Careful? Of Rod?" I asked. He was a bit over the top, but I didn't get scary vibes from him. Of course, my idea of scary was being chased by a gorilla through the jungle. Although, after today, I might take the gorilla over trying to get two kids to smile for a camera any day.

"He's got a mean streak. I'd hate to see you get on the wrong end of it," Joe said cryptically.

"Okay," I said slowly. "How do you know him?"

"We do some business together. He seems to think he's got more power than he does."

"Well, thanks for the warning." I patted my camera bag. "I should have the proofs to you within a week. I hope you like them."

He let out a breath. "Yeah. Today wasn't as bad as I thought it was going to be."

"Really?" I said. It was much worse than I thought it was going to be.

"Really. Especially at the end. I almost forgot you were even still there," he said.

I smiled at that. Good. Goal number one of photojournalism—be invisible. "That is actually a really great compliment. Hopefully that translates into the pictures."

I left the Cavannaghs with mixed feelings about my first family portraiture session. The portrait part was not great. The playtime part felt more natural.

And the warning against Rod Martingale was interesting. I'd have to pass that along to Colleen as well.

All in all, it was a needed distraction from thinking about murder and death and demon cats.

CHAPTER 23

M Y GOOD MOOD LASTED until I uploaded the pictures from the Cavannagh shoot onto my computer. My favorite part of being a photographer was suddenly swept away on a tide of self-doubt and disappointment. I groaned as I looked at one boring and uninspired portrait after another after another. It was going to take a lot of post-production work—and trips to Scoops—to get a passable one of them all smiling and looking at the camera.

I started over at the beginning, marking the ones with open eyes and passable faces. A few when they were seated on the couch in their front room. A few from the front steps of their house. A few standing in the garden. Some seated. Some standing. My eyes started to swim after a while. Is this really what people wanted? The same basic pose in different settings? Is this really what I wanted my career to be?

I contemplated calling *Nature* magazine and begging for my old job back—pride and righteousness be damned. But I'd rather take on the demon cat than work anywhere in the vicinity of Rick again.

Speaking of the cat, I hadn't seen her today. I left my computer to find the flashlight. Duchess still cowered in the corner under my bed. I tried to coax her out again using sweet kissy sounds and kind words. She hissed at me from the darkness.

"Princess? You here?" My father's voice interrupted the lecture I was about to give the cat.

"Be right out!" I called. To the cat, I said, "Fine. Stay under there. But I'm willing to start over. I'd be happy to pet you and stuff."

I found my father in the kitchen, clicking through the photo-shoot photos.

"Ew," I groaned again. "Don't waste your time. You might need to burn the backs of your eyelids after looking at that mess."

"What are you talking about? These are great!" Dad said.

"Thanks," I said, wrapping my arms around his shoulders in a hug. He patted my arm and turned in his seat.

I asked, "What brings you by?"

"What, I need an excuse to visit my daughter?" he asked.

"Of course not. But you usually do. Is Mom trying to get you to join another club? Or help with some organization?" I teased.

"Not this time." He pointed to a covered dish on the counter. "She did send some pierogies and pork tenderloins we had left over from dinner. Have you eaten?"

I shook my head. "Not today." Maybe that was part of my bad mood—I was hangry not angry.

Dad laughed. "That's what she thought. Warm me up a plate too. She has me on a one-plate diet." His laugh turned to a grumble. "Something about my cholesterol. I don't know why she makes so much food, then."

"Well, I'm glad she did today. I didn't realize how hungry I was," I said, moving around the kitchen to get our plates ready. Dad continued to scroll through the photos.

"Wow, princess. These are really good," he said again.

I set the warmed plates on the table with an eye roll. "They're all the same. And no one is looking at the camera."

"Isn't that the point? They are playing and laughing and genuinely happy. This one of the little girl smiling up at her dad is priceless. I can feel their connection. You captured real love and joy."

I cocked my head at him. Were there tears in his eyes? I scooted my chair around to sit beside him. He'd scrolled past the posed shots to the end of the session when the kids were playing on the swings. The shot he stopped on did quirk my lips into a smile. The little girl's ear-to-ear grin was contagious. With the sunbeam behind the pair, this would look great converted into black and white. That would strip the colors competing for attention and draw the focus straight to the father-daughter connection. I couldn't resist the temptation to see it that way, so I nudged my dad out of the way to do a quick high-contrast monochrome edit.

"Brilliant," my father whispered beside me. "Taking out the color heightened the whole effect. I don't know how you see it so perfectly, Alex. You definitely have a gift."

"Thanks, Dad," I said. He was a little biased since I was his daughter, so I took that with a large helping of salt. "I wish this was the type of photo families wanted."

"Why wouldn't they?" he asked, taking a bite of pierogi.

I clicked back to the beginning of the shoot. "This is what they hired me for. Canned poses with everyone smiling. It was torture, and I completely failed."

He took a moment to look at the ones I flagged. "Are you sure this is what they want?"

"It's what Alyssa Cavannagh asked for. She even had Pinterest boards of outfits and poses ready for me to look at."

"I think she might change her mind once she sees the ones of the kids on the swing set. Sometimes people don't know what they want until they see it."

I sighed. "You weren't there. I had no control from the moment I stepped through the door. I'm not used to interacting with the people I shoot. I'm not used to dealing with young children. Besides babysitting for a few families when I was a teenager, I haven't really been around kids. The name of the game in photojournalism is invisibility. The name of the game with family photography is interaction and guidance. Apparently, I'm terrible at both of those things. I'll be lucky if I can piece together one salvageable family portrait to appease Alyssa."

My father put down his fork with a clatter and grabbed my hands in his. "Princess, you aren't giving Alyssa Cavannagh enough credit. I don't even know these kids, and this picture pulled at my heartstrings. There is no mother in the world that wouldn't see this picture and immediately fall in love with it."

"I'm not so sure. But thanks for the vote of confidence."

"Listen, Alex. I know we don't talk about... Harrison much," he said, clearing his throat. "If I had known what was going to happen, I'd have cherished every moment like this one"—he pointed to the picture on the laptop—"even more. And knowing now what did happen, that our moments together were short and limited, I wouldn't choose pictures like those stupid posed photos your mother made us get at the department store each year. I'd want physical reminders of Harrison's genuine smile or our connection or the two of you playing together. These pictures tell the story of this family. Not the perfectly posed shots that anyone with a camera could capture."

Now my eyes were watering. "You mean it?"

"A thousand percent. My favorite picture of you and your brother sits on my bedside table so I can see it every day when I wake up and every night before I go to sleep."

I smiled. "The one with us playing by the reservoir. I think that was right before Harrison shoved me in the water."

"Exactly," Dad said. "I look at that picture and remember not only the moment, but the joy and laughter surrounding that moment. The fake smiles in the posed portraits don't carry those same memories. All they remind me of is the pain of getting you kids into fancy clothes and all the whining while we were waiting in line at the store."

"Thanks, Dad. Now I need to convince the mothers of Piney Ridge this is what they really want."

He released my hands to pick up his fork again. "I think it's time to ask yourself; what do you *believe* in?" my dad asked with a smile. I smiled back, recognizing the quote from *Indiana Jones and the Last Crusade.*

"Should be easy if you keep taking pictures like this last set. Market yourself as a genuine-emotions photographer or something," he suggested.

I laughed. "Documentary photographer, Dad."

"Yeah, that has a better ring to it. A day in the life of a Piney Ridge family. I wish we had memories of an ordinary day of your brother. No fancy clothes or pressure to pose perfectly or fake smiles. Just an ordinary day full of ordinary moments so we could remember the real Harrison."

I patted his hand. "Me too, Dad. More than you know. I miss Harrison every day."

He smiled sadly and then cleared his throat. "Okay, enough of that. Tell me about Linc."

I pursed my lips. "What about Linc?"

"How are you two? Your mother seems to think there's something there. She said you guys were flirting at the book club."

I narrowed my eyes at him. "Did she send you with instructions to ask me about Linc?"

He shrugged his vest-covered shoulders and avoided my eyes. A small smile tugged the corner of his mouth.

"I'm not talking about Linc with you, Dad. Mainly because there is nothing to tell. We're just friends." I took a bite of my pork. "You don't know anything about cats, do you?"

"Cats?" he asked, confused by the change in conversation.

"I adopted Gladys Wickerson's cat. Now she won't come out from under the bed," I explained.

"You adopted a cat?"

"I felt bad. No one else wanted her."

"I'm no help on that front. We've never had a cat. Sorry to hear about Gladys. Your grandmother was kind of shook up about it," he said, taking his now empty plate to the counter.

I frowned at his back. "Nana K's upset? I didn't even think she liked Gladys."

"It's not about that. There have now been two unexplained deaths at Aged Pines. Everyone is a little on edge thinking about who might be next."

"Turns out Camilla's death might have been an accident after all." I explained about the rainstorm and underground well reserve.

"Have you told Andrea Martinez your theory?" he asked.

"Not yet. I'll see everyone at the dedication tomorrow." That made me think. "I wonder if they're going to have two dedications."

"Probably. Your mother and I will be there to support your grandmother."

I followed him to the door. He wrapped me in a warm hug.

"Thanks, Dad. This visit was exactly what I needed. I hope you're right about the documentary family photo shoots," I said. If it worked out, maybe I could name the business Document Your Days Photography. The alliteration appealed to me.

"I know I am," Dad said. "Watch Alyssa's reaction when she sees those swing-set pictures. You'll see I'm right."

"I will. See you tomorrow," I said, waving him down the steps.

CHAPTER 24

"**W**HAT THE HECK?" I looked through the windshield at the already over-full parking lot at Aged Pines. I was a good thirty minutes early for the dedication, but there was not a parking space to be found.

"Why are there so many people here?" I complained to my empty car.

I parked the Fiat illegally behind a dumpster, then followed the crowd to the activities area, where the new shuffleboard and tennis courts were installed. A little podium stood at the entrance to the fenced-in tennis courts. A large, decorative ribbon swept across the gate. Many familiar faces lined the crowd, both those from Aged Pines and guests from the town. Brody Wickerson, Shane Marjadi, Dennis Martingale, and a few others I didn't recognize, sat in a row of chairs in front of the standing crowd. It was the VIP section no one really wanted to be invited to in this case.

Andrea Martinez paced around the exterior of the crowd, scanning the faces for who knew what. Chief Duncan leaned against a tree in the shade, picking his teeth with a toothpick and sweating profusely despite the cooler weather after all the rain.

Thinking of the rain reminded me I hadn't told Andrea what Nana K and I found out about the well. In the guise of taking a crowd shot, I walked behind the podium to cross to the other side of the gathering. No sense pushing my way through the very peopley crowd when I could cut through up front. When I have my long lens on the camera, people tend to assume that I'm at events in an official capacity. Who am I to correct them? Especially if it works to my advantage.

Andrea nodded at me as I approached. "Alex, good to see you. Are you photographing the dedication?"

"Yup," I said, holding up my camera. "For the yearbook. Sure is crowded here today. I didn't expect so many people."

"Me neither. It isn't like this is a public park. Only residents and registered guests can use the facilities once they're open," she agreed.

"I guess Camilla had more community support than I thought. That's nice for Shane. To know he isn't alone in his grief."

She blinked at me. "You think these people are all here for Camilla?"

I snorted. "Well, I doubt Gladys had many friends. Not with her reputation for being kind of a pouty princess."

"I think a lot of these people are here because of the way Gladys died. It's the rubbernecking effect."

"Good point. Also the Piney Ridge gossip effect."

"Exactly," she said. "I'd also bet my badge that whoever killed Gladys is here as well." She gestured to my camera. "You know the drill. I'll want copies of all the pictures you take today."

"No problem." I looked at the crowd. She was probably right. Often perpetrators return to the scene of their crime or to an adjacent scene like a funeral or memorial service so they can revel in the aftermath of their actions. *Law and Order* taught me that one.

"Does Chief Duncan still think the nephew did it?" I asked.

Andrea scoffed. "He changes his mind by the minute. We can't rule Brody Wickerson out yet though. With the switch to electronic tolls, it takes a little longer to nail down his timeline. If he even took roads with tolls."

"I guess Gladys didn't kill Camilla after all," I said. "In fact, I think Camilla's death could have been an accident or a suicide like Chief Duncan originally thought."

Andrea lifted her eyebrows. "Really? What made you change your mind?"

I explained about the rainstorm and the well. She took out a notebook to jot down some notes.

When I finished, she said, "It's possible the two deaths are unrelated. But it seems unlikely that Aged Pines would have two sudden deaths within weeks of each other."

"I don't know if they are unrelated," I clarified. "Maybe one was a murder and one wasn't."

She tapped her pen on her notepad. "Could be. Wasn't it you who told me Gladys and Camilla had a contentious past?"

I nodded.

"Your rainstorm theory could point to accident or suicide. But it could also explain how her body got stuck in the opening after someone pushed her down there," she said.

I hadn't thought of that. "No one would have had to climb down there. They could have tossed her body down there, and the receding rain helped them hide it even further."

"Exactly." She swiped a hand down her face. The creases in her forehead were deeper than I'd seen them the other day: the bags under her eyes more prominent. She looked tired and worn out.

"You okay?" I asked.

"I'm swamped. Between Camilla's unexplained death, Gladys's murder, and the joint task force with the state police, I'm not able to give any one of those things the attention it deserves. I'm missing things, and it's making me crazy."

"This is why you should run for chief," I said. "Then you can hire people to help you. People that actually know what they're doing." I flicked my eyes toward Chief Duncan, who still leaned against the tree inspecting the back of his hand as though it held a treasure map to stardom.

Andrea sighed. "I'm beginning to think you're right. Of course, if I lose, the chief will give me grief about it for the next entire term."

"Trust me. You won't lose." Movement by the podium had us both looking in that direction. Tiffany Dawn was fiddling with the microphone in anticipation of the dedication starting.

"Tell Detective Spaulding I said hello if you run into him during your joint task force," I said to Andrea, referencing the state police detective who'd helped us in the past.

"He's homicide. Although, if nothing breaks soon, I might have to call him in on Gladys's murder."

"No shame in asking for help," I said, then gave a little wave as I moved into a better position to capture the ceremony.

I positioned myself at the edge of the group to take some crowd shots and check my settings again. Nana K waved a bedazzled arm at me from the middle of the group, where she stood next to my parents, creating a disco ball effect on the nearby spectators when the sun glinted off her sparkled sleeve. A few guests shielded their eyes until she put her arm back down at her side. I could barely see her rainbow hair over the rest of the throng. After waving back, I took some detail shots of the ribbon, podium, and dedication plaques. Sure enough, there was one for Camilla Marjadi and another for Gladys Wickerson. A beautifully carved sign detailing the "Memorial Activities Center" hung above the entrance to the tennis courts. I recognized Linc's work immediately and instinctively scanned the crowd for him. If he was here, I couldn't see him.

A high-pitched whine from the microphone had everyone covering their ears and groaning. When it dissipated, William Remora's voice boomed from the speakers.

"Sorry about that, folks. Who was in charge of testing this thing?" He forced a laugh. When no one joined in, he tugged on the collar of his mustard-yellow dress shirt. He'd paired that color disaster with another brown suit. This one was a little darker than the one I saw him in before. The pocket-square pattern matched the one I'd seen Dennis wearing the other day. Must have been a giveaway from one of the medical supply companies. I was seeing that pattern all over this place.

William Remora continued, "Uh, as you know, we are here today to open our newest state-of-the-art additions to the Aged Pines Retirement Community where aging doesn't mean quitting."

Only a handful of people clapped. William cleared his throat and shuffled his note cards. "I want to thank our generous benefactors and local businesses who donated time, money, and resources to make this happen." He went through the list. I clapped loudest for Scoops. In a way, I also contributed to the new shuffleboard lanes with every ice cream cone I ate. In fact, I'd have to eat more, so I did my part in continuing to help the community.

"Before we officially cut the ribbon on these amazing new activity areas, let's pause for a moment of silence as we remember two of our own who perished in sudden and inexplicable ways recently. Their memories will live on through the dedication of the Memorial Activities Center and the beautiful plaques I commissioned to carry their legacy. The shuffleboard lanes are dedicated to Naya Camilla Marjadi. Her spirit and work ethic will remain immortal every time someone shuffles the puck down these lanes," William said, brushing a nonexistent tear away from his eye as he finished. I took a picture of him with his head bowed at the podium and another of the crowd.

Instead of bowing his head to remember his wife, Shane Marjadi was staring daggers at the unaware William Remora. His eyes were dark and clouded with anger and pain. One leg bounced up and down as he wrung his hands in his lap. He reminded me of a cartoon character about to spew steam from his head.

Just as the crowd was beginning to shift uncomfortably, William Remora finally lifted his head and said a quiet, "Amen." I doubted anyone in the crowd thought he was praying. "Our tennis courts are dedicated to Ms.

Gladys Wickerson. She was a big personality here at Aged Pines, and her death will not go unpunished or unnoticed. To the person who took her life, hear this. Every bounce of a tennis ball on this court is like the seconds ticking away until you are brought to justice." He brought his fist down on the podium as a period, causing another crackle of the microphone. Was this guy for real? He was having a *Law and Order* moment up there. I wondered how long he sat in his office thinking of that line.

We held our collective breaths for another moment of silence, then in a rather chipper voice, William said, "Okay, let's open these facilities for our amazing residents. Where are those big scissors? Tiffany Dawn?" He snapped his fingers. Tiffany Dawn leisurely walked over dragging the largest pair of novelty scissors I'd ever seen.

William struggled to lift them toward the ribbon. He stumbled backward under the weight, and Tiffany Dawn had to push against his back to keep him upright. I caught it all on camera. When the ribbon was finally cut, another smattering of applause came from the crowd.

"Who wants to be the first on the Wickerson tennis courts?" William shouted.

Shane Marjadi stood so suddenly his chair fell over. "This is insane!" he shouted. "I don't understand why anyone would use a court named after that witch. She made everyone's life miserable. Just because she's dead doesn't change that fact."

He stomped toward the parking lot without a backward glance.

CHAPTER 25

M Y PARENTS WAVED ME over after the crowd, all atwitter with reactions to Shane's dramatic exit, started to disperse.

"Come walk Nana K back to her bungalow with us," my mother said, patting my arm. "You can take home a plate of chipped beef and popovers."

"That was quite an interesting ending with Shane Marjadi's outburst," I said, unable to help myself from joining in. "He didn't think too highly of Gladys at all, did he?"

"He's grieving. We shouldn't take anything he says seriously," Mom said in a rare moment of non-gossipy behavior.

"True. Anyone else wonder why there were so many people here?" I asked.

Nana K answered. "This happens whenever someone dies at the home. A notice goes out to all the families so they can talk to their aging loved one about it. Another side effect is the rate of visits goes up tenfold for about a month. People remember that time with the old fogies in their lives is not a given. It'll taper off in a few weeks."

"Makes sense," I mumbled. Since I was looking down at the sidewalk as we walked, mainly so I didn't trip on anything and wreck my camera, I didn't see the person coming toward us until his shiny, Oxford-clad feet appeared in my downcast eyeline mere seconds before my head collided with his chest.

Strong hands gripped my shoulders to steady me. I looked up, ignoring the pang of disappointment that it wasn't Linc. Instead, Rod the Bod smiled at me from under his greased-back hair.

"We have got to stop meeting like this," he said with a toothy smile and a wink. I'd never seen anyone wink as much as this guy.

"Hi, Rod," I said, extracting myself from his grip. "These are my parents, Connie and George. You know my grandmother, Regina."

He shook my parents' hands, placing a light kiss on the back of my mother's. Nana K gave him a fist bump.

"How is your grandfather holding up? Was today hard on him?" Nana K asked.

"He's fine. Gramps is pretty unflappable."

"Still, I would be upset if my bae just died. And so violently," Nana K said.

"Bae?" my father asked.

"Yeah, baby, significant other, boyfriend, lover," Nana K explained. "Tell them, Alex."

"I've never used that term before," I said.

Rod laughed. "Gramps and Gladys weren't in a romantic relationship. Can you imagine? They're way too much alike."

"But they went everywhere together," Nana K said, pouting. "He held the door for her and stuff."

Rod hooted, causing a few passersby to give us dirty looks. Being half bent over with laughter was hardly an appropriate reaction to the day's events.

When he calmed down enough to speak, he said, "They hung out because no one else could stand to hang out with them. Plus, their equal ruthlessness made them practically unstoppable at cards. They were together because of greed, not romance."

Nana K huffed. "Fine. But my version is much saucier. In any case, tell Dennis I'm thinking about him. Losing a bridge partner is still bad." She marched a little way ahead of us, her image of Gladennis shattered. My mother scurried after her. Dad followed leisurely behind.

Which left me alone with Rod. "I should—" I started to say as Rod said, "Still waiting on that call."

"I've been so busy. Lots of editing and organizing to do." I held up my camera. "And now I have even more."

"You know what they say. All work and no play is not a great combination." He winked at me. Again.

"True. But work equals food in the pantry, so I'm stuck."

He maneuvered so he corralled me down the sidewalk with him. Slick move. I didn't realize he'd done it until we were walking side by side. His forearm kept brushing mine on the narrow path.

"I can help with that. I have a little... let's say, side hustle. I can get you in on it if you're interested. Easy money and all tax free," he said, dropping his voice to a whisper.

I blinked at him a moment before answering. Easy money and tax free equaled illegal more often than not. And although I wasn't as moral as Mother Theresa, I did have some integrity left.

"I actually like my job. Thanks though," I said. I picked up the pace a little bit as we neared my nana's bungalow. I watched her move around her small kitchen through the large glass patio door. With the light on inside and the darkness setting in outside, she wouldn't be able to see us out here on the path. Anyone could be lurking around spying on the residents of Aged Pines. I made a mental note to remind her to close her curtains.

My worry must have shown on my face because Rod reached over and tilted my chin toward him with two fingers. "Hey, there. Why so serious?"

"I was just thinking about how vulnerable my nana is. Are you worried about Dennis? Someone could be stalking the residents of Aged Pines. They are easy targets," I said.

A fleeting look crossed Rod's face, then disappeared before I could pin it down. Upon torture, I would have said it was amusement. But that seemed like an inappropriate reaction to our conversation. Although not much about Rod seemed appropriate.

"I'm not worried about Dennis. He's stronger than he lets on. Besides, from what I know, there aren't a lot of people sobbing into their pancakes over Gladys's death. My gramps might be a curmudgeon, but he's not snakebite mean like Gladys. I think both our grandparents are fine," he said. He leaned over and brushed his lips against my cheek. "Don't worry."

I forced myself not to recoil. "Thanks for the reassurance. Dennis is lucky to have a grandson who likes to visit so much."

"I could say the same thing about your grandmother," he said. "You're here as often as I am."

"True. But my visits are mainly due to the yearbook. I should really visit Nana more just because." I looked into the wide-open patio door again.

"Good to see you, Alex. Don't make me hold my breath too long for that dinner date."

I gave him a little wave and went to meet my family.

About an hour later, and loaded up with reheatable leftovers stuffed into a cleaned-out Cool Whip container, I crossed my fingers on my way to my car. Hopefully no one towed it even though it was in a no-parking zone. It wasn't trash night, for goodness' sake, so they didn't need to keep the area in front of the dumpsters clear. That would be my argument in court if it came down to it.

There were still a large number of cars in the parking lot by the new facilities. Nana must be right. People do get guilted into visiting when death comes knocking. I looked around to see if anyone else was carrying leftovers in plastic containers as they left their elderly relatives' abodes.

Nope. Just me.

There was an odd flyer stapled to the lamppost near my car that wasn't there earlier. I would have missed it had I not been glancing around the parking lot anyway. The patterned square was about the size of an index card and contained no words, only a time listed in bold, black ink. If one of the residents was trying to organize a meeting, they forgot some pertinent details. Old people were certainly eccentric and a bit forgetful.

As I fumbled with the leftover container while trying to rummage through my purse for my keys and not drop my camera bag off my other shoulder, a fast-moving shadow passed across me. I swiveled, dropping my keys on the ground and holding the plastic food container over my head like a weapon.

Danny Tidwell stood behind me with arms crossed over his chest and deep frown lines adding years to his usually youthful face.

I let out the breath I was holding and let my guard down a little. But only a little. His threat that I'd "be sorry" if I didn't put the brakes on my new photography business echoed in my brain.

"Danny," I said on an exhale, "I didn't see you coming. You startled me."

"I see you didn't take my advice."

"I'm still finishing the yearbook," I said. "Same commission as the last time we spoke."

"Really? Well, I took a few photos myself to freelance for the *Piney Ridge Gazette,* and they informed me they were waiting for your submissions before making any final choices."

This was news to me. I'd given them a few shots for other various community events, usually ones my mother organized, but hadn't considered offering them any from today. I told Danny this, but he didn't believe me.

"It took me years to build my business in this town," he spat, pointing a finger at me. "I'm not going to have some city-girl hack, who doesn't know how to work a flash, come along and take it all away."

My hackles raised. I was *not* a hack. "For your information, I do know how to use a flash. I choose not to. And I doubt the International Documentary Photography Awards would give an award to a hack, let alone three, which is how many they gave me. If you want to keep your clients, I suggest you up your game, Tidwell. I'm not going anywhere, and I won't be intimidated."

He looked a little flustered. Up until then, I'd been nothing but nice to him. But my mama, and Nana, didn't raise me to suffer bullies.

He scowled again and said, "Fine. I asked nicely—"

"No, you didn't," I muttered.

"But if you won't back down gracefully, I have no problem rubbing your face in your defeat when your business crumbles."

"Nice to see you, Danny," I said, bending to retrieve my keys from where they landed by my feet. "I'll be sure to send you a flyer when my business officially opens."

By the time I straightened, he was stomping away like a toddler having a tantrum.

I got in the Fiat and was about to back out of my impromptu spot when I noticed something under the windshield. Immediately, I thought it was another one of Rod's business cards and rolled my eyes. I was half tempted to leave it there and let the weather or the wind take it. But with my luck, rain would stick it to my windshield, and I'd be forever reminded of Rod the Bod. I sighed, put the car in park, and got out to retrieve the card.

Not a business card. A playing card. In the same pattern as the flyer stapled to the lamppost. Weird. I knew I'd seen this pattern before; I just couldn't place it. Maybe the cards at the bridge game? Most generic playing cards had a similar pattern.

I flipped it over. The queen of hearts. Okay, maybe it was from Rod after all. Another not so subtle reminder that he wanted something romantic to happen between us. As I stood there, contemplating whether to put the card directly in the dumpster or hold on to it, the headlights of an approaching car blinded me. The driver parked and quickly got out without turning off the engine. He squinted at the flyer on the post, gave me a little nod, and got back in his car.

He was neither a resident of Aged Pines nor Piney Ridge if his age and West Virginia license plate were any indication. Another oddity to add to an already weird day. I threw the queen of hearts in my purse and drove out of the community. I was seeing conspiracies and perpetrators everywhere. A good night's sleep would help calm my nerves and put things into perspective.

Rod was probably right. Gladys's murder had more to do with her personality and less to do with anyone randomly targeting old ladies. I trusted Andrea Martinez even if she was spread a little thin lately. There was no reason for me to continue to get involved in Gladys's murder. I'd drop the pictures from the dedication to the police tomorrow afternoon and wash my hands of the whole thing. If my encounter with Danny Tidwell was any indication, I had my own business to focus on.

CHAPTER 26

BECAUSE I WAS A glutton for punishment, I grabbed a flashlight and looked under my bed before leaving for the police station the next day. Even though I knew from the empty cat food bowl and full litter box that Duchess was still alive, I hadn't seen the demon cat in a few days.

"Come on, Duchess," I cooed in my most welcoming kitty voice. "Come on out. I'll pet you. We can be friends."

I swept the light across the area under the bed. Nothing but dust bunnies and my memory box. Weird. There weren't many places for a cat to hide in the loft space. I checked under the couch next. No luck.

The bathroom was empty except for Lash and damp towels. The top of the cabinets were also devoid of hissing felines.

"Here, kitty, kitty," I said, shaking the dry-food bag. That always worked when Linc wanted to bring Fang running.

Faintly, I thought I heard a muffled meow. I tried again with the shaking and the cooing. Again, I heard the meow. Louder this time.

I followed the sound to the edge of the loft where the outer wall stopped before the barn below began. The wall was almost as tall as the space but ended shy of the ceiling beams, which were exposed across the entirety of the barn. I looked up and saw a white fluff sitting between two of the highest beams.

"There you are," I said. "Come on down. You're giving me vertigo just looking at you."

Duchess meowed from her spot and didn't budge. Her eyes were wide and almost black, they were so dilated. Her ears were pinned to her head, and her tail twitched rapidly. I didn't need to be a cat expert to know that she was freaked out.

Great. Some people's cats got stuck in trees. Mine got stuck in the ceiling of a barn. I did the only thing I could think of. I called Linc.

"Do firefighters still rescue cats?" I asked when he answered.

"Why?"

"My cat is stuck in the ceiling rafters of the barn. Can you come help get her down? Bring a ladder or a dart gun," I said.

"I'll bring the ladder truck. I may be able to pull that into the barn to grab her. Give me a few minutes to get over there," he said.

"Thanks. Wear long sleeves; she's a biter."

I sat on the purple velvet couch with my door propped open a crack while I waited. Every so often I'd shake the food bag in the hope that Duchess would find a way down on her own. No such luck. I did get a high score on my phone game though.

Ten minutes later, the unmistakable sound of a large truck crunched on the gravel outside. I peeked my head out the door and motioned for Linc to come up. A small crowd from the farmers' market gathered around the ladder truck. In his rich, deep voice, Linc told them it was nothing to worry about and to go about their days. The crowd, in true Piney Ridge fashion, did nothing of the sort. A few of the kids ran around the large shiny engine, while their parents stood in clusters speculating wildly about what could bring out the ladder truck.

Linc eventually gave up and ascended the stairs to my loft.

He smiled when he saw me waiting in the doorway. "You know you can call me when you don't have a crisis or a murder theory to discuss."

I smiled back. "The phone works both ways last I checked. You could call me too. I don't think you've done that since I've been back."

His smile faltered a little as he considered that fact. "Noted."

I pointed to the cat, with the flashlight beam, when we entered the kitchen.

"Man, she's really up there," he said, taking the flashlight from me. He ran it along the beam she most likely used to access her hiding spot. It ran right to the top of the wall by the kitchen counter.

"If I remember correctly, the barn door should be able to accommodate the rig. If not, I might be able to back in enough to get the ladder extended to reach her. Can you call Anita Bachman and let her know what's going on? I don't want her to think her barn is on fire or anything," Linc said, walking back toward the door.

"Good idea." I pulled out my phone and made the call to one of my landlords. A few minutes later, I heard two male voices in the barn below. I left my vigil of the cat—clearly, she wasn't going anywhere—to descend into the barn and watch Bobby Bachman, Anita's adult son and my other landlord, help Linc back the fire truck into the barn. The group of spectators from the Bachman Family Orchard and Farmers' Market gathered to watch as well. We clapped when the ladder cleared the top of the door.

"Alex!" Linc called. I ran over to the fire truck. "Go back to the loft and help guide the ladder to the cat."

"Sure thing." I scampered back up the steps.

By some miracle, we were able to position the ladder perfectly, and Linc, wearing long sleeves and gloves, extracted Duchess from her perch. Surprisingly, she didn't try to claw his eyes out, instead clinging to his shirt with all four claws. He gently ran a hand down her back as he deftly descended the ladder, his lips moving in soft assurances that she was fine. My heart hiccuped watching how patient and gentle he was with her. What was it about strong men with animals? I refused to admit that it might be this one specific man.

Linc carefully detached Duchess's death grip on him one paw at a time and handed her over to me. I cuddled her to my chest with a "You're safe now," then put her in the bedroom where she resumed her place under the bed. I flashed the light under there and saw her vigorously licking herself. Probably to rid her fur from my cooties.

"Maybe some anxiety pills or a thunder shirt would help her," Linc suggested as I closed the door to the bedroom. "I think she's still a little scared from the sudden move."

"Do they have anxiety pills for cats?" I asked.

He chuckled. "They have psychiatrists for cats, if you want to go that route."

"*I* don't even see a psychiatrist," I mumbled. "I guess I'll have to find a way to close off access to that beam so this doesn't keep happening. I can't keep her locked in the bedroom forever."

"Some chicken wire would do the trick and wouldn't look too garish," Linc suggested. "Come on. Let's ride over to the feed store and grab some supplies. I'll help you rig it up."

"Right now?" I asked.

"Sure. I have some time."

"Okay. I need to stop by the police station anyway. Can I hitch a ride in your rig?"

"Sure thing."

I felt like a four-year-old boy riding in the front of the large ladder truck. Linc let me bweep the siren as we left the lot, to my delight and the amusement of the kids still standing in the parking lot. He was so patient as I asked him what all the levers and dials and buttons were for.

"Since when are you so interested in fire trucks?" he asked.

I shrugged. "I just realized I've never ridden in one. Ambulances, yes. Multiple times. But never a fire truck."

He was quiet for a moment. "I'm sorry I haven't been the one to reach out to you to hang out."

"You're a busy guy. I get it. Firefighting, EMT, your woodworking business." I ticked off his obligations on my fingers. Nana's words about some men needing a kick in the pants came to mind. He genuinely hadn't realized he'd never called me first.

"No excuse," he said. "I like hanging out with you, Alex." He gave me a quick, intense look before turning his attention back to the road and adding, "And Colleen, of course. Even if it is to discuss wild theories or chase down would-be killers."

"Thank you?" I said with a laugh. "We could do other things instead. Like read Jane Austen."

He groaned. "I think one Victorian fiction novel was enough for me. I'm liking Stephen King much better."

"Good. Maybe it will encourage you to actually read the book this time and not just watch the movie," I teased as we pulled into the joint parking lot for the fire and police stations.

"Hey! You admitted to watching the movie version of *Emma* too," Linc said.

I pointed a finger at him. "And if you ever tell my mother that, I'll curse you with fat ankles and horrible acne." I pulled the handle to get out, but it didn't budge. I tried again. "Do these things have child locks?" I asked, trying a different lever with no success.

Linc chuckled. "It sticks a little. I don't usually have a passenger, so I've been lazy in fixing it. Here, let me do it." He leaned across me to tug on the handle, his masculine woodsy scent immediately pervading my senses and making me a bit light-headed. I clasped my hands in my lap to keep from burying them in his hair. When he leaned back, I saw him let out a breath just as I did. He'd been holding his breath too. I discreetly gave my armpits a sniff to make sure it wasn't because I had bad BO.

"That should do it," he said, avoiding my eyes. I pushed the door open and jumped down.

After dropping the zip drive of pictures from the dedication to Andrea, Linc and I took his pickup truck to the feed store in town. Sure enough, they did have anxiety pills for cats. I also got a small bag of chicken treats for Nugget and the fencing Linc suggested. He picked up a deer antler for Fang to chew.

We pulled around to the loading dock to pick up the roll of fence.

"Got your ticket?" Gary, the loading-dock worker, asked when we backed into the spot.

I rummaged through my purse to find the loading ticket they provided at the register. With it I pulled out the playing card that was under my windshield the other day.

"Whoa!" Gary exclaimed when he saw the card. "You don't want to go flashing that around willy-nilly."

"Flashing what around?" I asked.

He jumped down from the loading area to stand close to me and whisper, "That card." He flicked the playing card in my hand. He lowered his voice and hitched a thumb at Linc, who was tapping his fingers to a country song in the driver's seat of the truck. "I'm pretty sure the goody-two-shoes fire captain isn't in the know."

I had a split second to decide whether to play along or tell him I had absolutely no idea what he was talking about. I played along.

"Come to think of it, he never mentioned anything to me about it," I whispered back.

"Listen, I won't say anything to *them*, but don't bring that card if you come tomorrow night. If they think you're cheating, they'll kill you," he warned. "They've done it before."

A shiver went up my spine. "I would never cheat. Same time tomorrow night?"

He nodded. "Anytime after eight o'clock. We're using the basement entrance under Remora's office this time."

I blinked a few times. Remora? What had I gotten myself into this time?

I swallowed and tried to make my voice calm. "Good idea. Thanks for the heads-up about the card. I'll be more careful."

"See that you do," he said and took the loading ticket from me. I slipped the card back into my purse while we went to get the fencing.

When I got back into the truck, Linc asked, "What were you two conspiring about? That was a rather lengthy conversation about chicken wire."

"I'll tell you when we get on the road. I don't want anyone overhearing."

He raised an eyebrow. "From the way you're bouncing your leg around, I can tell I'm either going to love this or hate it."

I gave a little wave to Gary as he threw the chicken wire in the back of Linc's truck. "Drive," I said to Linc.

He did. When we were out of the parking lot, I said, "I think William Remora has something to do with Camilla's and Gladys's deaths."

"Remora? I thought we decided Camilla's death was an accident after all."

"Now I'm not so sure. Listen to this." I told him about my conversation with Gary. "How would people be able to use an entrance under Remora's office without his knowledge of it? He has to know what's going on!"

"And what is going on, precisely?" Linc asked. "What does this clandestine entrance lead to?"

I scrunched up my nose. "I'm not exactly sure yet. But it has something to do with playing cards. Something others don't want anyone to know about. Or maybe the cards are a way to communicate." I gasped as I remembered what Rodney said to me after the dedication. "It could be an underground drug ring." When I noticed Linc's expression, I amended. "In any case, it's definitely illegal, or why all the secrecy?"

"Alex, you know I care about you, but you sound a little crazy right now," he said, pulling the truck into the parking lot beside my loft.

"No. This feels right. This feels like I'm on the verge of breaking the case wide open." I jumped out of the truck. Linc grabbed the chicken wire from the back.

"Okay, Nancy Drew," he teased, "but we still don't know what is going on in the basement of Aged Pines that's worth killing over."

"You know what? Nana K mentioned something the other day. I made a comment about how many playing cards were around. She said there was a legend that the retirement community's basement was made from discarded playing cards," I said. The memory tugged something in my brain.

Linc scoffed as I unlocked the door. "So, you think it's true? Why would someone kill to keep that a secret?"

"Not exactly true. But Gary totally freaked out when he saw that particular card in my purse. And I've been seeing the same pattern all over Aged Pines," I said. I retrieved my laptop from my bedroom while Linc pulled a chair over to the corner of the kitchen to adhere the chicken wire above the counter.

I booted up the pictures from the yearbook shoots, looking specifically for William Remora. I almost shouted in triumph when I saw his pocket square at the dedication. It was the same pattern as the playing card.

"There!" I shouted, enlarging the picture. "See?"

I held up the playing card beside the laptop screen. Linc put the last staple in the chicken wire and came over to see what had me giddy.

He leaned over the back of my chair, his face inches from mine as we looked at the screen. I refrained from turning my head to look at him. But just barely.

I may have leaned slightly in his direction to feel his arm pressed against mine though. But just slightly.

"The patterns are the same," he confirmed. "But what does that prove, Alex? That Aged Pines has a signature pattern? So what?"

I felt the heat rising in my face with my frustration. "I don't have all the answers, Linc. I just can't help feeling like there's something here. Something I'm missing. And there's one way to find out."

"Oh no. No, Alex. You are not going to Aged Pines tomorrow at eight," he said, reading my mind. He stood to his full height, but I wasn't intimidated.

"Why not? I was invited. Aren't you curious about what's going on?" I asked.

"I am. But I don't have a death wish. Tell Andrea about it. Let her go investigate," he suggested.

"Yeah, right. They know she's a cop. She won't get within ten feet of the place before someone spots her."

"How do you know what they're doing is even illegal? It could be a meeting for tea and lemon cakes for all you know," he said, pacing around my kitchen.

"Okay. That's why Gary was all 'If they think you're cheating, they'll kill you.' Because they don't want to share their lemon cakes," I said sarcastically.

He ran a hand through his hair. "Let me come with you."

"No way. You're almost as noticeable as Andrea. I'll take Colleen. We are average citizens looking for an easy score of dope to pass the time," I said.

"Score of dope? Yeah, you'll blend right in," he said. He looked at me a long time, a myriad of emotions passing across his face, then sighed. "I'm not talking you out of this, am I?"

I shook my head. "I'm going."

"Fine. Take Colleen. But don't stay long, and call me as soon as you leave."

"Yes, Dad," I teased. His face hardened. I added, "Thanks for the cat rescue and chicken wire."

"No problem. Although as a rule, firefighters don't really get cats out of trees."

"Technically, it wasn't a tree. It was a barn loft."

"A barn loft I helped make with trees," Linc countered. "Listen, hopefully Fluffy learned her lesson. If not, there is a bit of chicken wire left. We can put it up elsewhere too," he said, moving toward the door.

Before stepping out, he pulled me into a one-arm hug. "Be careful, Alex."

I wrapped my arms around his waist, surprising both of us. He turned to embrace me completely. Even with our height difference, we somehow fit.

I said, "I always am. This reminds me of when I was on location in Gāz Khun, Afghanistan. Most people think of the Taliban and war when they think of that country, but in the northern mountains, the people are peaceful and simple. I was photographing the Kyrgyz families when a little scuttlebutt about a few missing goats rumbled through the village. Everyone pointed fingers at everyone else. I'd been there a few weeks by then, and they mostly ignored me, so I was able to sneak into the suspected Kyrgyzes' yurt one night with ease."

"Did he have the missing goats?" Linc asked, releasing me so I could look up at him.

"Nope. Turns out there was a Himalayan lynx on the prowl. I got some beautiful pictures of it."

He smiled down at me. "I often forget you've lived an exciting life, while the rest of us stayed home."

"My point is that I can handle myself. I also understand that there could be nothing there except lemon squares and bingo. But I need to know."

"Please remember curiosity killed the cat. And I've already hit my quota of cat saving this month."

I patted his hard abs in reassurance. "Sure, sure. I'll be fine. I promise to call."

He surprised me by placing a quick kiss on my head. "Be sure that you do." Then he was gone.

CHAPTER 27

M Y MIND RACED WITH thoughts of playing cards and mountain goats and Linc. I couldn't sleep. Every time I thought my brain was going to make some sort of connection, Linc's quick kiss on my head sneaked in there and messed me up again. What did that mean? Was it like a big brother protector kind of kiss? Or an "I'm leading up to more" kiss? Or a "We're good friends" kiss?

Ugh! I kicked around under the covers in a mini temper tantrum. Why was dating so complicated? Why was not dating so complicated?

And why couldn't I concentrate enough to figure out what was going on at Aged Pines? I felt like I had all the puzzle pieces, but I couldn't fit them together correctly.

From my binging of *Law and Order* and true crime podcasts, I knew most investigations started with the victims. So, what did I know about Camilla and Gladys?

Camilla was married, up for a promotion at work, and having some financial trouble. She had that weird ledger in her possession with dates and dollar amounts. Not to mention the loan payable to Gladys Wickerson. If Shane were to be believed, she'd told none of that to her husband.

Gladys and Camilla didn't like each other, yet Camilla was paying her for something. Blackmail? A loan? But for what? Gladys had a reputation for being mean and greedy. She might have killed her first husband for his money. And there was the argument with William Remora I overheard. Gladys seemed to think her money was what kept Aged Pines in the black.

Were they just old-lady delusions? Gladys may have been eccentric, but she definitely had her wits about her when I spoke with her. Besides some narcissistic tendencies, she did have some influence around the retirement community.

And there did seem to be a lot of new amenities at Aged Pines lately. The new wing where Remora's office was located. The new shuffleboard lanes and tennis courts. The updated facilities in the kitchen. Remora said private donations and benefactors were to thank, but maybe Gladys was helping to fund some of the upgrades. Remora did seem to bend over backward to appease her.

It all came down to money. Camilla was rolling in debt, while Gladys was rolling in dough. But how did that equal them both dead?

Hopefully, tonight's rendezvous with the secret basement club would shed some light on the reason behind their deaths. If not, and Linc was right, I'd get some more of those yummy lemon bars, so the trip wouldn't be a complete waste.

I gave up trying to sleep around seven o'clock and texted Colleen to see if she was awake. She answered by calling me.

"I'm getting ready for work, so talking on speaker is easier than trying to text," she explained when I answered.

"What are you doing tonight?" I asked.

"Nothing that I can think of."

"Great. Want to come on a spy mission with me?"

"Um, yes," she said without hesitation, making me smile. I knew she'd be up for it. "Who are we spying on?"

I filled her in on the weird conversation I had with Gary at the feed store.

"You want to go to the secret meeting tonight?" she asked.

"Yup. But I don't want to go alone."

"Aww, and you thought of me before anyone else?" she cooed. "I'm flattered."

"Of course. Besides, Linc or Andrea would be too obvious since they are first responders," I said.

She scoffed. "So I wasn't the first one you thought about. Fine, I see how it is."

"Linc happened to be with me when I talked to Gary. That's all," I said, trying to soothe her ego.

"I'm teasing. I'm totally still going. Hold on while I put my shirt on," she said. I waited a moment to the sound of muffled cloth shifting around. "Okay, back. Should we invite anyone else?"

"Like whom?" I asked. "My mother? She'd love to get in on the gossip."

Colleen laughed. "Can you imagine? I love your mom, but she's about as subtle as a bowling ball at a marble race. No. I was thinking about someone who could protect us in case this is some sort of *Goodfellas* situation."

"I already told you Linc was out. No one would believe Mr. Golden Boy would do anything untoward," I reminded her. If only they knew about the time he let a bucket full of cicadas loose in the library. Of course, that was over a decade ago. I guess he probably matured since then. I know his physique did.

"Not Linc. I was thinking of Rodney Martingale," she mumbled.

"I'm sorry. I thought you said Rodney Martingale."

"I did. He's got some muscle and enough meanness to make him a bad boy," she said a little too wistfully for my taste.

"I thought you didn't want to go out with him again." I dragged myself out of bed to get ready for the day. Not that I had any real plans beyond editing pictures until we left for the spy mission. But I still wanted to at least brush my teeth.

"I was thinking about it, and everyone deserves a second chance. Maybe he was nervous on our first date? No one is their true self on a first date, right?" she said.

"Sounds like you're making excuses. I have a feeling that Rod the Bod is always his true self. Or his perception of his true self."

She tsked. "Sounds like you're jealous. Although you have no need to be if you and Linc would get over yourselves and go on a proper date. Meeting at Plum Crazy doesn't count," she added before I could say anything.

I sighed. "He's had plenty of chances to ask me out, and he hasn't. Besides, I'm enjoying my time being single. This is the year of Alex. I'm starting a new business. I'm trying to be a cat owner. I've got a lot going on. I don't have time to date anyway."

"Sure. Whatever you say. My money is on you two becoming a couple before Christmas."

"Don't hold your breath. He's better suited to someone exotic and morally sound like Andrea Martinez. Not me." I ran a brush through my hair.

"Well, he's had plenty of opportunities to ask her out, too, and he hasn't. Maybe he's a commitment phobe."

"Could be. Doesn't matter to me one way or another," I lied.

"You keep telling yourself that, sweetie. I'll meet you at your place around seven thirty tonight. That should give us plenty of time to get over to Aged Pines around eight. We want to be a little late, so we don't look too eager," she said.

"Good point. Thanks for coming with," I said. "I'll see you at seven thirty."

When I emerged from the bathroom a few moments later, Duchess was curled up on the end of my bed. I stopped in my tracks. Did she think I'd left? I didn't want to startle her and have her run back under the bed. At the same time, I didn't want to feel captive in my own bedroom. I decided to ignore her and go about getting ready.

She picked up her head slightly as I passed on my way to the dresser. Then lazily laid it back down on her paws to go back to snoozing. I relaxed my shoulders a little. Maybe we'd turned a corner since I rescued her from the beams.

After getting ready, I chanced a quick pet. Again, Duchess lifted her head and squinted her eyes at me. She really was a pretty cat—full white, long hair, perfectly pink nose, large golden eyes.

"You like that?" I asked softly. "Having your back pet? Can I pet your head?" I moved my hand slowly to between her ears. She leaned into my hand. I took that as a good sign. "Okay, Duchess. Now we're getting somewhere."

The cat actually made a gesture of peace. It gave me a good feeling about the rest of the day.

I spent the afternoon editing pictures. Editing the dedication photos was easy since there was an even light source. All I had to do was a little color correction and a slight contrast bump and fix the composition on a few shots. Dennis sat hunched and frowning in the front row beside an equally grumpy Shane Marjadi.

Shane Marjadi. He was still a viable suspect too. He was so angry with Gladys over her dealings with Camilla that he could have killed her over it. This whole playing-card pattern thing could be completely unrelated.

Except that Dennis's bow tie was the same pattern. Flipping back through the catalog of pictures, I found it in a few other places as well. Another card stapled to a post by the new tennis courts. Gladys's sash on bridge night. In William Remora's old office. The playing cards scattered on the floor in Gladys's bungalow on the night she died. I couldn't be sure because I hadn't photographed it, but I'd bet a week's worth of Scoops that the card by Camilla's body at the bottom of the well also held the same pattern.

As I was looking at the pictures of Gladys's murder scene, a figure in the background drew my attention. I had my f-stop rather wide open to really isolate the details in the center of the frame, so the figure was out of focus. He—I was almost certain it was a he—was reaching up as though grabbing something from the top shelf of the kitchen cabinet. I'd been so focused on capturing the details of the area around poor Gladys that I didn't notice anyone else in the area at the time. Andrea and Linc had moved into the bedroom to see if they could find anything. I couldn't remember anyone else being inside with us.

Regardless, all of that made me second-guess the importance of the pattern. Perhaps Linc was right, and it was as simple as a signature Aged Pines pattern. But then why wasn't it on the towels and linens and napkins? Why did Loading Dock Gary go all whispery when he saw the card with that particular pattern?

And round and round I went like Lash in her bowl. Does it matter? Doesn't it? Will there be lemon cakes? Won't there?

I was working myself up for nothing. I'd find out soon enough when Colleen and I went to Aged Pines tonight. If only the clock would freaking move.

CHAPTER 28

C OLLEEN ARRIVED, WEARING ALL black and an ear-to-ear grin, promptly at seven thirty.

"Let's go, let's go, let's go," she said, dancing from one foot to the other by the door.

I laughed at her excitement. "Not so fast. You were the one who said we needed to be fashionably late so we didn't look too eager. Besides, we need a plan."

"A plan? Our plan is to go see what this secret meeting is all about. You said yourself you were practically invited."

"So we simply waltz in like we belong?" I asked, grabbing a cardigan from my small closet.

"Exactly. Hidden in plain sight and all that," she said.

"Then why are you wearing all black?" I asked.

She giggled. "Seemed like the thing to do."

"You always say that. Come on. I'll drive slowly."

We parked in the back parking lot a few minutes past eight. The lot was already almost full. A card with a familiar pattern was taped to the doorframe.

"Like bread crumbs," Colleen remarked when I pointed it out.

We got out of the car and were about to start toward the door when a familiar figure emerged from the other side of the parking lot, moving with a single-minded focus down the sidewalk. I pushed Colleen into the bushes beside the sidewalk and jumped in after her.

"What the heck?" she said, pulling a branch from her hair.

"That was Shane Marjadi. What is the grieving widow doing here?" I asked.

"Better question. Why do we have to hide from him?"

I ignored her question. "New plan. You follow Shane. Make sure he isn't here to kill anyone else," I said. "I'll follow the trail of cards."

"You think Shane might have killed Gladys?" she asked.

"I don't know. He was really angry about the secret loan. And it seems weird that he's here." Shane disappeared around a corner. I shoved Colleen out of the bushes. "Go, go, go! You're going to lose him."

Colleen made a show of tiptoeing after him like a cartoon character cat burglar. She giggled and looked back at me. I shooed her on with a wave of my hands.

When she disappeared around the same corner as Shane, I made sure no one else was coming and then removed myself from our hiding spot. I followed the bread-crumb path of playing cards through the basement door, down a set of concrete steps, and along a dimly lit hallway. The muffled sound of voices got increasingly louder the closer I got to the end of the hall, where a door stood ajar.

I vacillated between approaching confidently like I was meant to be there and knew what it was all about or sneaking in like the cartoon character Colleen pretended to be. Since confidence wasn't my strongest suit on the best day, I opted for sneaking in. Pretending to tie my shoe, I waited for another pair to come down the corridor and then made myself the third of their party. Thank goodness there wasn't anyone checking IDs or tickets or secret passwords at the door.

I don't know exactly what I was expecting to find in the basement of Aged Pines Retirement Community, but it definitely wasn't what greeted me when I peeled away from the couple and pressed myself into the shadows against the wall.

Instead of an underground greenhouse full of marijuana or a more elaborate chemistry lab than Walter White in *Breaking Bad,* this room looked more like a Las Vegas casino. A huge electronic board hung against one wall, listing games next to dollar amounts. And by dollar amounts, I mean four-figure dollar amounts in most cases. The games varied from card games like poker and blackjack to betting statistics for every sporting event played that night or within the next week. There were also buy-ins for tournaments and electronic games. Whatever could be bet on seemed to be on that board. And based on the number of people in attendance already, the amount of money changing hands must have been astronomical.

I moved my eyes away from the board to scan the rest of the room. The area itself was the size of a large conference room, likely spanning the majority of the new wing of the retirement community, including William Remora's new office. The center section held dozens of tables, mostly full of people already engaged in card games or table versions of other betting games like roulette and craps. There were even some I didn't recognize.

Wait, was that table playing Yahtzee?

Along the back wall was a cashier station and concession stand where alcohol was clearly being served. It was a little mini-Vegas casino in the basement of the old folks' home. An *illegal* mini casino in the basement. A very lucrative illegal mini casino in the basement, if those numbers on the board were any indication.

"Color me flabbergasted," I whispered as things started clicking into place. Those figures could absolutely correspond to the values in Camilla's ledger. Was she in debt to the gambling ring? Was that her financial trouble? Was she unable to pay them back with money and so paid with her life? Or was she going to expose the ring, and someone killed her to keep her silent? And how the heck did Gladys fit into all this?

I refocused on the people's faces instead of the general ambiance. Some I recognized from town, but most I did not. I remembered the West Virginia license plate from the other night. How far did people drive to partake in this underground gambling?

I gasped when I noticed Betty from the book club. She knew about this? And kept it a secret? The latter was honestly the bigger surprise. I glanced from face to face to see if I recognized anyone else I knew. A few residents from the retirement community, but thank goodness Nana K was not among them. Actually, her not being here surprised me more than if she were.

Gary sat at a table with a few other men—one of whom I recognized as Joe Cavannagh. Was this the business he and Rodney discussed the day of the photo shoot? I quickly scanned the rest of the room to see if I could find Rod.

Instead of that Martingale, I found the other. Dennis stood stoically by the cashier stand, off alone to the side like he was in most social situations I'd seen him. Was Gladys also in the know about this place? If Dennis was, she must have been too. The bets going on here put their little wagers during the bridge games to shame.

William Remora stood off to one side as well, smiling smugly and watching the room like an overlord. He must be behind the whole thing.

When the reality of what I was seeing finally sank in, I realized I was right. Sort of. I was right to follow the money.

How far would William Remora go to protect his side hustle? Clearly, he was behind the whole thing. It all made sense. The argument about money between William and Gladys. All the new facilities and amenities at the retirement community. Camilla's financial troubles.

Could this also be part of what Andrea Martinez and the state police were investigating? There was definitely a lot of money changing hands without government approval. At least I assumed it was all done tax free under the table. Or under the retirement community, to be exact. Why else would they have to use secret patterns and secret entrances? And Rodney did mention a fast-cash, no-tax side hustle. If Dennis was here, I'd bet Andrea's badge Rodney knew about this place too.

I slowly removed my camera from my cross-body bag. I had to photograph this as evidence for Andrea. I adjusted the settings for what I thought the dim light would require and shot from the hip, hoping that at least some of them were in focus. Shooting from the hip was less reliable but also less noticeable. I moved the camera up to waist level and toward the large electronic board of games and dollar amounts.

A hand on my arm had me fumbling my camera. Good thing I had the short strap around my wrist, or it would have crashed to the ground.

"Jumping junipers," I cried, with a hand to my heart.

Colleen giggled beside me. "Sorry. I thought you saw me coming."

"What are you doing here? I told you to follow Shane," I said, slowing my breathing.

"I did." She pointed to the wall where Shane stood talking to William. They weren't exactly yelling, but even from across the room, I could tell they were animated. Shane's hands were moving a mile a minute as he spoke. William's smile was tight as he leaned against the wall with arms crossed.

"Where did he go first?" I asked Colleen, snapping a picture of the two men.

"To William's office. No one was there obviously. He banged on the door for a few minutes. When no one answered, he made his way directly here. He knew about this. I'm sure of it," Colleen said, looking around. "What exactly is this?"

"From what I can tell, an illegal gambling ring."

"Are those numbers dollar amounts?" Colleen said, focused on the electronic board. "That would be enough to fund the preschool for an entire year. And give me a raise."

A shout rose up from a table in the middle. Someone there rang a little bell. The board on the wall changed to indicate a multiple-thousand-dollar win from one of the patrons. I could feel the excitement and adrenaline, and I wasn't even playing. The chance to earn that much money in one night was certainly enticing.

"Can you imagine winning that much in a single night?" Colleen asked, echoing my thoughts. "I could buy so many shoes."

"Yeah," I said, "but can you imagine losing that much in one night? Not worth it for me."

"I can totally see how people get addicted though. It's definitely tempting."

"Don't even think about it," I said, putting a hand on her chest.

She pouted. "I don't think I'd actually do it. I can't even win at Keno." She turned to face me. "Do you think this place has something to do with Camilla's death?"

"Oh yes. It has to, right? Why else would Shane be here?" I took a chance and held the viewfinder to my eye. I wanted the picture of William and Shane still talking across the room in crystal-clear focus.

Colleen giggled beside me. "We should totally start a private eye business. This is definitely more fun than tying wet shoelaces all day. I feel like James Bond in *Casino Royale*. Do you think they have baccarat?"

Hiding my smile behind the camera, I took another picture of the electronic board to be extra sure I had one in focus.

Movement across the room arrested my attention. Shane had sat at one of the tables, his head in his hands, and row of cards in front of him. It looked like blackjack from where we were standing. It also looked like he didn't really want to be playing.

"Does Shane look distressed to you?" I asked Colleen.

"He's looked agitated all night. Wait, is he actually gambling?"

"I thought at first that Camilla was the gambler who got into financial trouble. But maybe Shane is the one racking up the debt, and Camilla was trying to fix it," I speculated.

Colleen nodded her head like a bobblehead. "Yeah. I could see that. What if he doesn't work night shift at all, but comes here to gamble instead?"

I considered for a moment, then remembered the expression on his ashen face after he learned about the loan to Gladys at the bank. No one in Piney

Ridge is that good an actor. "I don't think so. Besides, this gambling ring isn't open every single night."

I tracked the room for William Remora and saw him disappearing through a door in the opposite wall. If anyone knew the answers to our questions, it was the brown-wearing director.

With a small grimace, I switched my camera to auto mode—it hadn't been in that mode since I took it out of the box—and handed it to Colleen.

"Stay here. Take pictures of anything you think is relevant but try to be discreet. Shoot from the hip if necessary."

She held it like she was afraid it would blow up in her hands. "Why? Where are you going?"

"I'm going to follow William Remora. If I can get him one on one, maybe he'll answer some of my questions. If I'm not back in, like, twenty minutes, call Andrea, and tell her to bring backup," I said.

"For the record, you handed your precious baby to me. So I'm not liable if anything happens to it, right?" she asked.

"You'll be fine. Pretend it's one of the infants at work and don't drop it," I said, then lifted my chin and walked confidently through the center of the room like I belonged there. A few patrons looked up as I passed, but most were so focused on their games, I was barely a blip in their hyper-focused periphery.

When I opened the door William slinked through earlier, another set of concrete steps leading to the upper level greeted me. The sound of a door slamming shut echoed down the stairs.

I took a deep breath, said a little "Please don't let this be the biggest mistake of my life" prayer, and started up the steps.

CHAPTER 29

A NOTHER CLOSED DOOR WAS the only thing on the top landing of the staircase. I half expected it to be locked, but the knob turned easily in my hands. I eased it open slowly, unsure of what I would find on the other side. It opened into William Remora's old office. The dirty, dusty, dark one I went into by accident when I was delivering the portrait proofs. I stepped through the opening and realized the bookcase hid the door, which is why I didn't notice it the first time I was there.

I looked around the space again with my new knowledge in mind. The boxes of tablecloths and playing cards now made sense, extras for the casino downstairs. The boxes marked chips weren't full of sour cream and onion, but actually gambling chips. This was storage, like William Remora said, only storage for the illegal gambling ring and not for the retirement community.

The door leading to the hallway was also standing open. William must have used this as a quick way back to his new office. I pulled out my phone to grab a few evidence shots of this room as well. I considered trying to pick my way through all the boxes to see what information was in the file cabinets but didn't want to risk knocking things over or missing William if he was gathering his things to leave. Andrea could deal with that when she got here.

Hugging the wall, I moved out of the storage office and down the dark hallway. From across the foyer, I could see the light on in William's new office. He must still be in there. The rest of the place was as quiet as a cemetery.

That thought gave me the shivers. Bad choice of words.

On my way across the foyer, I decided a bold sneak attack would be best. I'd smash the door open with an "A-ha!" and demand answers. Should I pretend to have a gun in my pocket? The old finger and thumb under the clothes trick? When the mere thought of doing that had giggles bubbling in my chest, I discarded the idea. I fixed my face and swallowed my giddiness as I approached his office door.

Since the door was open a crack, I could hear him shuffling around and muttering to himself. I took another deep breath and pushed the door open so hard it smacked the wall, ricocheted, and slammed in my face. Stunned, I stood for a moment staring at it. Well, dangit, didn't see that coming.

Once recovered, I pushed open the door a little less forcefully and entered.

"What are you doing here?" an astonished Remora asked as I stomped toward his desk.

"I'm here for answers. I found Camilla's body, and I found your basement casino. Even if you don't want to talk to the police, I think I deserve the truth," I said, my voice sounding much more confident than I felt. My heart was rocking in my chest, threatening to burst through at any moment. I took deep breaths through my nose which I hoped he translated as anger and not panic.

"I don't owe you anything," he said. "Whatever you think you know, you have no idea." He began shoving more and more files into his briefcase.

I slammed a hand on the desk, making him jump. "Tell me what's going on, or I'll call the police."

He narrowed his eyes at me. "You are in way over your head."

"Did Camilla find out about your illegal operation? Did she threaten to expose you?" I went with the answer I hoped was true first.

He scoffed. "Yeah, right. More like she was a regular customer. She won big a few times and got a taste for it. Then her luck changed."

"So she was in debt to you," I finished.

"Oh yes. Until an unlikely benefactor helped pay some of it."

"Gladys?" I asked. He nodded. "Why would Gladys help Camilla? I thought they didn't like each other?"

"They didn't. But you've met Gladys. Anytime she could find a way to hold something over someone's head, she grabbed it. She would rub it in Camilla's nose every chance she got. Eventually, Camilla got tired of it, and worried that someone would overhear, and asked for the transfer."

"So, what happened? Camilla couldn't pay it all, so Gladys killed her? Why? As a warning?"

He laughed. "Do you really think a feeble, old woman could kill someone like Camilla?"

"You killed her," I whispered, realizing I made a terrible mistake coming here alone.

"I didn't kill her either," he said. I let out the breath I was holding. "I honestly have no idea what happened to her. Maybe she was so embarrassed about cleaning out her life savings, she offed herself," he suggested.

Now it was my turn to scoff. "You actually expect anyone to believe that?"

"I didn't kill her!" he repeated and sighed. "Look, I'm not even the one in charge of this whole thing. I get a kickback for providing the space and the supplies. And for my silence."

I crossed my arms, popped a hip. "The lies keep coming, huh? You can't help yourself. Why was Gladys killed? Was she in debt too?"

"I don't know. I don't kill people. I take the money and turn a blind eye. Look at all the good it's doing for the retirement community. Your grandmother is benefiting from these innocent little games." He started stuffing files into his briefcase again.

"Innocent? I don't think hardworking people like Camilla would think losing thousands of dollars was innocent," I pointed out. I moved so I stood between him and the door. If he wanted to make a break for it, he'd have to physically move me first.

He slammed the briefcase closed, anger flashing in his eyes. "All of those people are adults capable of making their own decisions. No one is holding them hostage. No one is forcing them to come week after week. They are doing it themselves. We don't rig any of the games. We run a fair establishment. So what if the government doesn't get a cut? The money we save on taxes directly benefits the residents of Piney Ridge and Aged Pines."

"Who is we?" I asked. "Who else is in on this with you?"

"You wouldn't believe me even if I told you." He picked up the case and walked around the desk. "Now, if you'll excuse me, I have to get back downstairs. My partners and I have some files to go through."

"I'm not moving until you tell me who these partners are."

"Why? So you can go running to the police? I don't think so."

I shifted my tactics from force to curiosity. If I got him to think I was okay with the operations downstairs, maybe he would open up to me more. I softened my features, uncrossed my arms and put my weight into my back foot. A very nonconfrontational stance. See, William? I'm your friend. I'm on your side.

Out loud, I said, "What do I care if the government gets a cut or not? When I was first starting as a freelance photographer, I worked for money under the table more often than not. And, like you said, the revenue helps my nana. I'm just curious. The whole thing is pretty fantastical. I mean, who would have thought an operation of this magnitude would go unnoticed in Piney Ridge. Not even my gossip-hungry mother knows about it, and I saw some of her friends down there. Whoever is running this must be really smart."

He narrowed his eyes, still skeptical, but listening. "It's a group effort," he said.

"There you go. I'm impressed a group was able to keep this whole thing under wraps. What's the old saying, 'Three can keep a secret if two of them are dead'?" As soon as the words left my mouth, another theory clicked into place. Were Gladys and Camilla his partners? Did he kill them to get full control?

He chuckled softly at my expression. "I know what you're thinking, but no. My partners and I don't partake in the gambling. So Camilla, with her vast debt, couldn't have been one of them. I wasn't lying earlier. Camilla was a patron in debt. She probably killed herself. I have absolutely no idea why Gladys was killed. She wasn't very likable, so I imagine there are any number of people that aren't crying at her graveside."

He made a move to go by me again, but I shifted my position, blocking his path. He sighed and ran a hand down his face.

"Tell me who your partners are. I'm impressed. I'd like to give kudos to those in charge. Maybe give gambling a try myself."

"If you want to play the games, you know where the entrance is this week. Go on down and give it a go. Buy-in on most games is a hundred dollars. The stakes go up from there," he said.

I whistled. "That's pretty steep. Do you have like a first-time-customer discount?"

"This is not like the penny bridge games we organize in the community room upstairs, Ms. Lightwood. This organization is tied to several others around the tristate area. It's bigger than you think. People come from all over—Maryland, Virginia, Delaware, Pennsylvania, West Virginia. Sometimes even as far as Ohio and New York. We aren't messing around."

I didn't have to fake my astonishment. "That's amazing. Congrats on your entrepreneurship. And the ingenuity of having it at the retirement community. I mean, I don't think anyone suspects anything like this," I said, hoping that stroking his ego would get him to drop more information even if it did make me throw up a little in my mouth.

"Hosting it here was my idea. The organizers and my partners were happy to fund the new addition as long as we put the conference room below." He smiled smugly, his eyes glazing over as he remembered. "It isn't the only one either. We move it around so no one suspects."

"Not the only place here at Aged Pines?" I asked. "Or here in Piney Ridge?"

"Here at Aged Pines. You said yourself we've had a bunch of new facilities and amenities put in over the last few months."

"All of them have an underground room?" The huge pile of dirt beside the shuffleboard lanes jumped to my mind. "Even under the shuffleboard and tennis courts?"

His smile broadened. "That was a particular stroke of genius. No one expects a basement under outdoor courts."

"But they're dedicated to Camilla who probably died as a direct result of the gambling," I whispered. Another shiver ran down my spine. My bones felt like ice.

"Couldn't be helped. Besides, with as much time as she spent with us, she might be honored." He laughed lightly, then shoved me aside so swiftly I barely had time to react. I bumped into the visitor chair as he swept by me toward the door.

He didn't get very far.

CHAPTER 30

I BREATHED A SIGH of relief when I saw the telltale red curls of my best friend. Colleen was here, hopefully with the police.

But my elation was short lived when I took in the horrified expression on her face. She stumbled into the office as though pushed from behind. A large, looming figure appeared behind her.

"Look who I found taking pictures in the casino," Rodney Martingale said, following Colleen into the office. "Although I'm pretty sure this camera belongs to Alex Lightwood."

He held up my camera, and I gave an involuntary little yelp. His head snapped toward me. "Well, well, well. Isn't this a cozy reunion."

"Can I have my camera, please?" I asked. The strap wasn't around his neck or wrist. I had a horrible vision of him smashing it onto the floor for spite. "I'll give you the memory card. Please don't break the camera."

"I already took the memory card. How good are you at catching?" he said a second before he tossed my beloved Canon at me. Luckily, instinct kicked in, and I was able to catch it without incident. Almost. I did bang my shin pretty hard against the small table between the visitors' chairs. If I survived this, I would have a nasty bruise to match the one on my knee from the last time I was in this office. Small price to pay to save my Canon though.

"Rodney, good to see you again. I was just telling William here how impressed I am with your establishment. Keeping it secret in a gossip-hungry place like Piney Ridge is no small feat," I said, looping the neck strap around myself cross-body style and slinging the Canon to my back to keep the camera out of harm's way.

"Really?" he asked, turning his eyes to Remora for confirmation.

He nodded. "Sure, but only after accusing me of killing Camilla and Gladys," William said.

Rod laughed. "You? Killing anyone?"

"What's so funny?" a new voice asked from the doorway.

Rodney turned to look at his grandfather. "Alex thought Remora killed Camilla and Gladys. Can you imagine? He wears brown suits for crying out loud." That made him dissolve into even more hysterics.

Dennis rolled his eyes. He looked from Colleen to me and back again. "What are you two doing here anyway?"

"We, uh, heard about the secret meeting and wanted to check it out. I think it might be what I need to help my fledgling photography business get off the ground," I said. I stomped on Colleen's foot.

"Ow," she said, scowling at me. I gave her a wide-eyed look. "Oh, right. And I really need new floors in my rancher. Being a preschool teacher isn't that lucrative. We're looking for some quick cash."

"And the camera?" Dennis asked. "We don't allow cameras in the gambling hall."

"Sorry about that," I said. "Old habit. I never go anywhere without it. I can put it back in the car before we try our hand at some of the games. What were you thinking, Colleen? Blackjack? Craps?"

She blinked at me, still a bit in shock about the whole situation. "Craps?"

"Craps, it is." I smiled at the three men, who were now looking at me like I had a few screws loose.

Dennis stepped farther into the office and shut the door behind him with his cane. He stood to his full height and placed the cane against the wall.

Every time I'd seen him, his hand had been so tightly wound around the handle, I never got a good look at it. I recognized it now.

"You have the same cane as Gladys," I said. And the same pattern of wound found on Camilla's head.

He glanced down at it. "Yes. We had very similar tastes."

"You two were very close," I said.

He smirked. "I suppose. But my father always said, 'Don't mix business and pleasure.' It is an adage I take very seriously." He walked easily around the desk and pulled a small lockbox from the top of the file cabinet. A strong sense of déjà vu washed through me. I'd seen that image before.

In Gladys's crime scene photos, the man in the back of the picture was reaching for something in the kitchen cabinet. It had to have been Dennis. He was the one to find her body. He was the only other one in the bungalow besides me and the first responders.

"You don't even need the cane," I said.

Dennis set the box on the desk and used a key from the ring at his waist to open it. "Nope. I'm fit as a fiddle. But it's amazing how invisible you become when you're old and decrepit. People glance right by you. Something to do with coming to terms with their own mortality, I think. Anyway, it's a great way to hide in plain sight."

Dennis was wearing the bow tie with the casino pattern. "You're one of William's partners," I whispered.

"Partners?" Rodney said from behind me. Too close behind me. I took a step forward to put some distance between us. He continued, "Is that what he told you? Remora isn't a partner. We pay him to provide the facility. That's all."

"Hey," Remora said, offended. "It was my idea to have it here. My idea for the signature-patterned cards."

Everyone pretty much ignored his whining. I was focused on what Dennis had removed from the lockbox. A shiny silver handgun. And he had it pointed directly at me.

"I try not to use this," Dennis said. "Much harder to make it look like an accident. But we're running out of time."

"An accident? Did you kill Camilla?" Colleen asked, finally catching on.

"Duh," Rodney said. "She threatened to expose the entire operation after she realized she was in too deep. She'd have to confess to her husband and didn't want to lose him. So she tried to blackmail us. She wanted us to erase her debt, or she'd go to the cops. We couldn't have that, could we, Gramps?"

"She thought because I was old, I was weak. She thought wrong. One quick whack to the head with my cane was all it took. I would have gotten away with it, too, if you hadn't fallen down that stupid well and found her body," Dennis said.

"Trust me, I wish that didn't happen either," I lied. Back to the plan of stroking their egos to buy time while I figured out a way out of this mess.

"What about Gladys?" Colleen asked. "Was she in debt too?"

Rodney and Dennis exchanged a glance. Rodney shrugged. "Can't hurt to tell them now. I don't think they'll be around long enough to tell anyone."

Dennis chuckled. "True. Gladys was our other partner. She funded the initial buy-in with the state guys. Unfortunately, she also thought that meant she was the more important partner. I got sick of her whining about her cut being the same as mine. And then when I brought Rodney in to help with enforcement and collection, she got all fussy about having to cut him in too."

"Greedy, greedy grinch. If she'd just accepted the way things were, she'd still be collecting her generous monthly check instead of being worm lunch," Rodney said. "Can't say I was sad when Gramps called and told me what he'd done. Now my cut is bigger."

I looked at Dennis in astonishment. "I thought you and Gladys were good friends?"

"Who could possibly be friends with Gladys? I tolerated her. Until I couldn't take it anymore. I figured I'd take advantage of Camilla's death and perhaps the stupid chief would think there was a serial killer or something on the loose," Dennis said coldly. He still had the pistol trained on me. "Which, of course, he did."

"Technically, you're one kill shy of being a serial killer," Colleen pointed out. I stared at her. What was she doing? "The FBI definition is three or more killings with a cooling-off period in between. You do have the cooling-off period. But only two kills." She gasped. "That we know of. Have you killed anyone else?"

"Not yet," he said, moving the gun to point at her instead. "But that's about to change."

"Wait!" I shouted. "Just wait a minute. You can't kill us. My cat is just starting to warm up to me. And you'd leave Lashatelle an orphan."

"Who's Lashatelle?" William asked.

I continued before anyone could ask any more questions. "I wasn't lying when I said we wanted in. I can use my photography business to expand your reach. I travel all over the place taking pictures."

Dennis considered for a moment. Then disregarded my suggestion. I had succeeded in turning his focus back to me and not Colleen. He said, "We're doing fine right now. You obviously saw those numbers on the board. That was just for tonight, sweetie."

I focused on Rodney. "Come on, Rod. It must get a little boring being around all these old people all the time. Colleen and I can add some youth, some fun." Taking a page from his book, I winked at him. "Don't you want someone to share all this with long term? Dennis isn't going to be around forever." I glanced at Dennis. "No offense."

Rodney pursed his lips. I touched his arm, laid it on thick. "You said it yourself. We'd be good together. Plus, with my international connections, we could take this operation global. There are some South American countries that would jump at the chance to earn even half of what you guys make. And the laws are much less strict outside the United States."

Only the part about me having international connections was a lie. Yes, I'd photographed villages and cities where corruption ran rampant. But I had no desire to ever contact those people again outside of an official assignment. Photographing unruly toddlers was a challenge but much less dangerous.

I batted my eyelashes and raised an eyebrow, hopefully sealing the deal with Rodney. I took a step toward him, holding my breath so I didn't pass out from the stench of too much bad cologne. Yikes, this guy was trying too hard to be some mesh of Al Capone meets aspiring rapper. I danced my fingers up the buttons of his shirt until they reached the open expanse of his hairy chest. Then, on a gulp, I ran my fingers through the hair and tried not to grimace.

It's for your life, Alex. Yours and Colleen's, I told myself. I'd have to take multiple showers if we got out of this mess.

"After seeing the amazing work you've done downstairs, I'm really impressed. I love a man who takes charge and gets what he wants, no matter what," I said, channeling my inner Jessica Rabbit.

Rodney caught my hand in his and brought it to his lips. "I would like nothing more than to trust you, Alex Lightwood." I smiled at him. My plan was working. I could hardly believe it.

I had all of three seconds to revel in my ingenuity before he shoved me backward and his face hardened. "But I don't trust you. You and your goody-two-shoes preschool teacher friend here are way too wholesome to want to be a part of this scheme. Though it is a waste." He clucked his tongue and shook his head. "I wish things could be different."

William spoke for the first time. "I can't believe you actually killed people. That wasn't part of the deal."

"Shut your mouth or you'll join them," Dennis shouted.

"Well, can you not kill them in my office. The carpet is new."

Rodney said, "We're not going to kill them here, idiot. That's too obvious." He shook his head again and looked at me and Colleen. "This is why he isn't a partner. He'd screw everything up."

"Enough!" Dennis shouted, banging his non-gun-holding fist on the desk. "Enough chitchat. Let's go." He waved the gun at us. "Remora, you first. Girls follow. Rod and I will exit last. If one of you tries to run, I'll shoot the other one. I don't care where or if anyone sees. Got it?"

Colleen and I nodded.

William started to protest. "Why don't I pop down to the casino to keep an eye on the place. What's the old adage, 'When the cat's away, the mice will play.' We don't want anyone trying to steal anything while we aren't there."

"And what are you going to do if they try?" Rod asked on a laugh. "Bore them to death with your stories?"

"No," Dennis said as he herded us out the door. "You're coming with us. It'll assure that you keep your mouth shut. Accessory after the fact and all that."

When we were both through the office door, Colleen pressed close to my side. "Rule number one in abductions is never let them take you to a second location," she whispered, her voice edged with panic.

"I know," I whispered back through tight lips.

"What are we going to do?" she asked.

"Hey, gossip girls. Knock it off," Dennis said from behind us. He gave me a little shove in the back, and like the clumsy fool I am, I stumbled to my knees. "Oh, come on. I didn't even shove you that hard. Get up."

"In a minute. My shoe is untied. Don't want any more stumbles." I took an extraordinarily long time pretending to tie my shoe while I tried to think of a way out of this. No viable options presented themselves. We were two petite women against three strong men. Well, two-and-a-half strong men. I could probably knock William over with a wet noodle.

A movement in the shadowy hallway pulled my attention. Was someone there? Or was my mind playing tricks on me so I didn't curl up into a ball and give up? I mouthed the word "police" to the darkness in case it was the former.

I squinted into the darkness but saw nothing else. My hands shook as I tied a third knot in my shoelace. We were on our own.

"Get up already," Rodney said, putting his hand under my armpit and hoisting me easily to my feet.

I put on my flirty voice again. At least I hoped it sounded flirty. "Oh, Rod. You're so strong. You deadlifted me with one hand. Do you work out?"

He puffed his chest a little. "I do work out. Being an enforcer means I need to keep fit."

"I can tell. You must have women falling all over themselves for you," I said, pressing against him and holding his eye contact. He still had a grip on my upper arm so tight I'd have bruises tomorrow.

"I get my fair share." He lowered his head. "Too bad it couldn't work out with us, sweetheart. I'd show you how a real man treats a lady."

"There's still time. I meant what I said about joining you. Being a family photographer is so boring compared to the life I used to lead. I'm a woman in need of adventure," I cooed.

Colleen hid her snort behind a cough. I discreetly kicked her in the shin.

I laid my head against Rod's broad chest to face Colleen. As soon as I felt Rod's grip on my arm relax, I mouthed, "Run."

Colleen slammed her eyebrows together in confusion. I mouthed it again as I took advantage of our positioning and kneed Rodney as hard as I could in his family jewels. Then shoved him backward into Dennis. Since they weren't expecting it, they both toppled into a heap on the ground. I grabbed Colleen's hand, and we ran out the front door into the darkness with feet pounding behind us.

CHAPTER 31

"FREEZE! NOBODY MOVE!" ANDREA'S voice had us skidding to a halt as soon as the glass doors slammed shut behind us.

"Inside," I gasped, trying to catch my breath. "Dennis and Rodney Martingale."

"Get behind the police cruiser," she commanded. We immediately did as she asked.

William Remora exited the foyer then. When he saw Andrea, he said, "Oh, thank goodness someone called the police. We were being abducted. I think Dennis has lost his marbles."

"Lies!" I called from behind the cruiser. "He's in on it."

William Remora shot eye daggers at me, then softened his expression to address Andrea. "I assure you I have no idea what that crazy woman is talking about. I found her snooping around my office after dark."

In one swift motion, Andrea slapped one end of a pair of handcuffs around his wrist. She expertly clamped the other end around the bike rack beside them.

"We'll sort this out in a minute," she said, moving her eyes back to the entrance.

"Dennis had a gun," Colleen shouted. "Be careful."

A state police cruiser zoomed into the lot and screeched to a halt beside us. Two plainclothes detectives got out and flanked Andrea. In hushed tones, they made a plan to enter the dark building.

Before they could enact whatever plan they concocted, a familiar voice shouted through the closed door. "I'm coming out with the perps. I've made a citizen's arrest. Whatever you do, don't shoot me by mistake."

Colleen and I looked at each other. "Nana K?" we said in unison.

Sure enough, Dennis and Rodney both exited the building with arms raised and looking a little worse for wear. Nana K's head popped out from behind them. She was barely visible behind their large frames. When she stepped to the side, I saw she carried Dennis's cane and his gun.

"Drop the weapon," one of the state guys commanded. All three police officers' guns were trained on the trio.

Nana K looked around. I waved from behind the cruiser. "Drop the gun, Nana. The police will take it from here," I called.

She tucked the cane under her armpit, expertly opened the chamber of the gun, and unloaded all the rounds onto the pavement, then tossed the gun to one of the state police. My jaw hit the pavement. I didn't even know Nana K knew how to use a gun.

Brushing her hands together as though wiping off dirt, she said, "I guess my work here is done. I'll go wait with Alex by the cruiser while you arrest these fools."

With a bounce in her step and twirling Dennis's cane like Charlie Chaplin, she trotted over to us. I gave her a huge hug. Then a well-deserved lecture. "What the heck were you thinking? You could have gotten killed!"

"Nah," she said. "As soon as you knocked Rodney on top of him, Dennis dropped the gun. It skidded right over to me."

"You were the one hiding in the hallway?" I asked. So, I had seen someone.

"Yup. I saw Director Remora's car still in the parking lot, so I thought I'd go see if he wanted to hear my theory about what happened to Gladys.

That's when I saw the five of you crammed into his office. I'd already called the police by the time you all made your grand exit," she said.

"And Rod and Dennis immediately fell under your petite command?" Colleen asked.

"I persuaded them with a few well-placed whacks with the cane first. And reminded them that I am an excellent marksman. I was president of my high school gun club back in the day," she said. "You know, before they didn't allow gun clubs in public schools any longer."

"I had no idea," I said, looking at my nana in a whole new light.

She laughed and hugged me again. "I've got a few tricks up my sleeve you don't know about."

We watched as Andrea led Remora to the back of her cruiser. He was still professing his innocence.

Dennis and Rodney were deposited into the back of the state car. Their anger was focused on each other.

"I should have known a pretty face would be your undoing," Dennis spat at his grandson. "You're even more worthless than Remora."

"Shut up, Gramps," Rodney said. "Everything in a police car is recorded."

The state guy shut the door on their argument.

"Andrea, er, Officer Martinez," I said. "This is all to do with an illegal gambling ring being run out of the basement of the retirement facility. If you search Rod, you'll probably find a camera memory card with pictures of the place on it."

She and the two state detectives exchanged glances. "Can you show us?"

"Sure," I said. As we were walking back into the building to show them the secret staircase, a third police car drove up. It jumped the curb and came to rest inches before hitting a tree.

Chief Duncan oozed out of the driver's side, arriving after all the action as usual. He wiped his hands on his shirt leaving streaks of something oily in their wake. Clearly, dinner had been more important than backing up his fellow officers in an armed kidnap situation.

"Good work, Officers," he said in what he thought was an authoritative voice. "I see you have the situation well under control."

"Thanks to these three ladies," one of the state guys said, pointing at me, Colleen, and Nana K.

Chief Duncan gave us a quick glance and a grunt. "Right. I'm sure. Don't go anywhere. We'll need your statements."

"Actually, Chief," Andrea interjected, "we need them to show us something. Apparently, there is an illegal gambling ring being run out of Aged Pines."

He laughed out loud. "That's a good one. Gambling? Here? No way."

"Yes, way," Colleen said, crossing her arms over her chest. "We saw it."

"Okay," he said. "You go on your wild-goose chase. I'll wait here to watch over the real criminals. See you in five when all you find is old ladies playing bingo and bridge."

Andrea motioned for us to lead the way. Nana K followed.

"You can wait here, too, Nana," I offered. "There's a lot of steps."

"I'd rather climb a thousand steps than be stuck in the same air pocket as that doofus," she said, hitching a thumb at Chief Duncan.

"I don't blame you," I mumbled.

"Hey, Andrea," Nana K said, turning to walk backward so she could look at her. "When are you going to run for sheriff? We could use a change around here."

"And some competency," I said.

"I've been thinking about it," Andrea answered.

"Think faster," Nana K said, turning back around to maneuver through the cluttered office and down the stairs.

When we reached the bottom of the stairs, Andrea peeked through the doorway without opening it all the way. She gasped when she saw what was there and quietly closed the door.

"This is it, guys," she said to the state guys. "The place we've been after." She took my hands in hers. "Thanks, Alex. I think you've just solved our money-laundering case as well."

"Happy to help," I said with a smile.

"Okay, boys, let's call in the cavalry. We're going to need a lot of feet on the ground to help cover the runners," she said.

A sinking feeling hit me. "Wait." I stopped her from radioing for their backup. "Will all those people in there be charged with something? Will they all go to jail?" I thought about poor Betty and Gary from the feed store. Images of Joe Cavannagh playing with his daughters morphed into visits behind plexiglass. Those were our neighbors and friends: all regular people just trying to get by.

Andrea patted my hand on her arm. "Some of them, yes, depending on their records. Most of them will get a fine and slap on the wrist. Especially if they agree to testify. You did the right thing, Alex. This is going to help more people than it will hurt." When I still frowned, she added, "Think of how many other Camillas are in there. How many other innocent people are being taken advantage of by this situation."

I sighed. "I guess you're right. This is gonna take a while, right? Can we wait in my nana's bungalow for you to finish?"

"I think that'd be fine. We'll come find you when we need your statements."

One detective waited by the door to make sure no one tried to exit this way. Andrea and the other detective followed us up the steps. I explained where the main entrance was. They trotted around the building. We exited the main foyer to see Chief Duncan leaning against Andrea's cruiser talking with William Remora, who was no longer handcuffed to the bike rack.

"Back so soon?" he asked when he saw us. "Just like I said."

"They're calling in backup to raid the casino," I explained, looking at William. "State guys should be here any minute."

William paled. "I-I don't know a-anything about that," he stammered. "Dennis and Rodney must have gone behind my back."

"A picture is worth a thousand protests," I said. "And I have plenty of them with you as the star."

"Rodney took your memory card, so it'll be my word against yours."

I tsked at him. "You forget modern technology, friend. Even if Rodney somehow manages to lose the card before police can find it, all of my photographs are immediately backed up to the cloud as soon as I take them. Isn't WiFi great? I'm so glad you had the funds for the high speed, highest quality connection here at Aged Pines."

He scowled at me as I walked away to join Colleen and Nana.

"Anyone up for some cheesecake?" Nana K asked as we walked arm in arm to her bungalow to wait for the police to take our official statements.

"You bet your Polish dupa, I am," Colleen said.

"We can play rummy while we wait," Nana suggested.

"Oh no," I said. "I don't want to see another card game for a long while."

CHAPTER 32

A *FEW WEEKS LATER*

Unlike my current mood, the weather was crap again. We'd moved from second summer past the cool breezes of fall and straight into icy rain. Everything was soggy and brown and cold. But I wasn't going to let that dampen my spirits. I'd just come back from my third family-holiday-card photo shoot since the Cavannaghs. Turns out, my father was right. Alyssa Cavannagh loved the documentary-style photos from the end of the session even more than the more traditionally posed photographs. After things settled with Joe and the casino—he, and most others, received a fine and probation—she sent me a proof of their Christmas card, which had a collage of her favorites from the swings surrounding the posed photo of all of them.

And then she showed her friends, who immediately blew up my phone to book me.

And then I needed to get off my dupa and formally register my business.

All good problems to have. Hence my good mood.

I stopped by the post office to check my PO box and squealed when I saw the little box from the local print shop. Business cards. I'd already registered the business name and opened a business account at the bank, but it didn't really feel official until I had this little box in my hands. The last step was to create a website.

I didn't even wait to leave the post office before tearing open the box to reveal the newly printed cards.

Just Clickin' It Photography
Capture the Beauty of your Everyday Life
Alex Lightwood, Photographer & Owner
www.justclickinit.com

They were gorgeous. One of my favorite photographs I ever shot was on the back in full color. I paid a pretty penny for that quality, but seeing them now, it was totally worth it.

I bumped into Danny Tidwell on my way out the door and cringed, waiting for another scathing berating.

I will not let him ruin my mood. I will not let him ruin my mood.

He surprised me by smiling. "Alex. I guess I should thank you."

"Thank me?" I asked. "For what?"

"For trying to stick to your photojournalism background with clients," he said. "It's a noble cause but one that will have you out of business before you even start. Normal people want smiling poses."

"Some people want that, sure," I said. "But some people like the more candid, real feel. Which is why, like I said, there are enough clients for both of us to be successful."

"Uh-huh. You keep telling yourself that while I keep booking all the clients," he said. "Have a nice day!"

"I will," I said to his retreating back. If the first two families I photographed were any indication, my more documentary style was going to do just fine.

I popped my umbrella open and would have skipped to my car if I were a skipper. But I was not.

Still, there was a bit of a bounce to my step, and I couldn't wipe the smile off my face if I tried.

"Hey, Alex!" a voice called from across the parking lot. Linc took shape through the falling rain. When he reached me, I handed him my umbrella so he could hold it over both of us.

"Linc!" I squealed. "Look what came today!" I shoved a business card into his free hand. "Look, look, look."

"I'm looking." His rich laughter surrounded me like a warm blanket. He looked at the photo on the back, then flipped it over to read the information. "Just Clickin' It. I like it. Congratulations, Alex. Looks like you are officially the new photographer in town."

"So far people seem to like my style. I just hope the novelty doesn't wear off," I said, my smile faltering a little as I looked at the ground.

He slipped the card into his back pocket and gripped my chin to make me look at him. "I've said it once; I'll say it a thousand times. You are an amazing photographer. Any one of these small-town nobodies should be honored to have you photograph them."

"Thanks, Linc. You're great for a girl's self-esteem."

"Does that mean you'll squeeze in time to hang out with me between all your photo sessions?" he teased with his signature smirk.

"Of course. Who else can I manipulate into buying my fries at Plum Crazy?"

We smiled at each other for a moment, but it devolved into awkwardness pretty quickly. I was having a hard time not looking at the way his wet shirt hugged his sculpted torso.

"Guess I was right about Rod, huh?" he said. "He wasn't a good guy after all."

I rolled my eyes. "Yes, you were right. Although I have to give him a little credit for agreeing to testify against the leaders of the gambling ring. That couldn't have been easy. They are some nasty fellows."

"True. William also sang like a canary as soon as they got him in the interrogation room. Do you give him credit too?"

"Sure." I smiled. "But not as much. There was no doubt he was going to spill his guts. Rod, on the other hand could have gone either way. Maybe I have a little soft spot for him since he did call me beautiful and ask me out. No one else seems to be doing that lately."

Linc was quiet. I blushed crimson. Okay, he didn't take the bait. Guess Colleen and Nana K and the entire book club were wrong: Linc wasn't into me after all. To my surprise, instead of ignoring it, I called him out on it.

"Fine. Don't take the hint. I'm done asking for a phone call from you. Apparently, I'm only interesting in embarrassing situations." I turned to open my car door. "See you around, Towncar."

"Alex," he said quietly, his voice gruff and raspy. I looked over my shoulder at him. His eyes were as dark as the stormy sky overhead, jaw clenched, and lips tight. I hadn't seen him this serious since the diner when he told Rod to take a hike.

I turned around fully, drawn to him by a force out of my control. His dark hair fell in wet tendrils over his forehead. I reached up to brush them aside. His Adam's apple bobbed in his throat as he swallowed, hard, and leaned into my touch.

"You're all wet," I said lamely.

He caught my hand in his, brought it to his chest where I could feel his heart beating under the wet cloth as fast and hard as mine. He leaned toward me.

"What are you doing?" I asked breathlessly.

He dropped the umbrella, but I barely felt the rain now pelting us both. His hand cupped my jaw as he stepped against me.

"Kissing you, Lexy. Finally kissing you."

And as his lips met mine—so perfect in their sweetness, so absolute in their conviction—I thought, *Well, this is going to change everything.*

THE END

215

Finally!! Linc and Alex kissed! To follow their story and see what other mysteries Alex can solve, be sure to check out the next book in the series coming Spring 2022. In the meantime, head on over to the blog to check out some new photography tips inspired by this story. And follow me on social media so you don't miss an update!

Also By Kari Ganske

<u>Alex Lightwood Series</u>

<u>Secrets in a Still Life</u>

<u>One Click in the Grave</u>

<u>Bait and Click</u>

(a Halloween short story available Fall 2021)

<u>Lenses Leather and Lies</u>

(a FREE novella for <u>subscribing to Kari's Cozy Newsletter</u>)

Author's Note

I 'D LOVE IT IF you could leave a review on Amazon. Good, bad, or in between, I genuinely care about what readers think. I'd love to say I write for myself, but really, I want to reach readers like so many authors have reached me. I read every single one of the reviews and take any feedback with me when writing and editing the next book. Reviews are one of the best ways to help support indie authors like me.

About the Author

Kari Ganske, pronounced Gan-ski, is a wife, mother, reader, writer, photographer, fountain soda addict, and true crime aficionado. She married her high school sweetheart and has been a hopeful romantic ever since. She lives with her husband, two daughters, and a menagerie of animals on a small farm in rural Maryland. When she isn't writing, you can find her binging true crime shows or stalking her kiddos with her camera.

She has a dual B.A. in English--Secondary Education and Psychology. Kari's Master's Degree in Liberal Arts included classes in ceramics, grammar/linguistics, the madness in genius, and juggling among other things. She still practices juggling with oranges in her kitchen much to the delight of her children and horror of her husband.

Check out Kari's official website for Giveaways, blog entries, and more. Follow her on the socials for updates. Or join her mailing list to help make decisions about future novels! She loves connecting with her readers about reading and photography.

Newsletter Sign-up (FREE novella for subscribing): https://dl.bookfunnel.com/ssn3i8nmeh

Email: kariganskeauthor@gmail.com

Instagram: @kariganskephotography

Amazon Author Page: https://www.amazon.com/Kari-Ganske/e/B093HHB4TL

Goodreads: https://www.goodreads.com/author/show/21452303.Kari_Ganske

Bookbub: https://www.bookbub.com/profile/kari-ganske

Website: https://kariganske.com

Made in the USA
Middletown, DE
01 October 2021